# HORIZON

## BY

## TABITHA LORD

ISBN 13: 978-1-940014-79-1
eISBN 13: 978-1-940014-78-4

Library of Congress Catalog Number: 2015953155
Printed in the United States of America
First Printing: 2016
20  19  18  17  16      5  4  3  2  1

Cover and interior design by Steven Meyer-Rassow

Wise Ink Creative Publishing
837 Glenwood Ave.
Minneapolis, MN 55405
www.wiseinkpub.com

To order, visit www.itascabooks.com or call 1-800-901-3480.
Reseller discounts available.

*For Ray, who believed I had stories to tell long before I did.*

# PART I - ALMAGEST

# CAELI

## CHAPTER 1

She felt them before she heard them. The sudden wave of panic gripped Caeli so fiercely that she fell to her knees. Sweat beaded on her forehead and her body shook with another person's cold fear. *We're losing altitude. I can't keep her nose up. Time is running out.* A voice echoed in her head, frantic. The words were strange and foreign, but she felt their intent.

A ship pierced the white clouds overhead. Frozen in place, Caeli tracked it streaking across the sky, her consciousness now fully merged with one of the desperate occupants onboard. Her breath came in short, gasping bursts. Seconds later a shattering pain exploded through her body and she screamed. The ground shook violently beneath her, and then nothing.

Caeli collapsed onto the ground, barely conscious, her body spent and her mind blank. For a few silent moments she lay empty and still.

Her sense of smell returned first. She inhaled the earthiness of decaying leaves and the tangy scent of seawater in the distance. Familiar things. She'd fallen face down with her pack on the ground next to her. Bursts of red berries scattered over gray-brown dirt. Her memory crept back in fragmented pieces. She'd been gathering fruit and exploring this section of the forest.

The ship. The crash. Her eyes flew open and she sat up trembling. Reaching her mind out, she searched for any trace of life. There it was nudging against her consciousness like a persistent but incoherent whisper. And it was fading quickly. Whoever was in that ship wasn't going to live much longer. She had to hurry. Her heart raced as she struggled to her feet.

Sprinting to her campsite, Caeli rummaged through her meager supplies. She felt her utility knife resting in her pocket, but looking around the space, she found little else of use. There hadn't been enough time to gather all the necessary basic provisions, never mind time to collect medical supplies. It hadn't occurred to her that she'd need them. Out here she had no patients, no clinic.

A hill just outside the campsite provided an unobstructed view of the ship's vapor trail. Southeast, toward the shoreline, a cloud of dark smoke billowed up from behind the brush. It wasn't far, but that part of the terrain went quickly from forest to thick, tangled brush. As she stumbled through it, her clothes caught on branches and hidden brambles carved stinging scrapes on her legs.

Then, quite suddenly, a scorched path led to a fractured, smoldering ship. The craft's fuselage was dark and sleek but sheared completely in half, and chunks of debris littered the surrounding area. The wildlife had scattered, and it was eerily quiet except for the hiss of rising steam. Heat emanating from the silent engines rippled the air.

Caeli took a step closer, her eyes drawn to the strange writing engraved over the aft section. This ship was not from her world.

Swallowing hard, she hesitated a moment before wrestling

the cockpit door open and stepping into the still compartment. Wires hung from the ceiling like cut vines, and instrument panels lay in shattered pieces. The nose of the craft had breached the cockpit, crushing inward and compromising the already tight cabin space. *How could anyone have survived this destruction?* she wondered. But someone had.

Two human bodies were strapped in their seats, both sprawled forward. Without touching them, she knew one was already dead and one was dying. The connection was through her mind, but she could feel the survivor's life force in her whole body, like a second heartbeat drumming a discordant rhythm. Fading but insistent, it pulsed beside her own.

Treat the living or try to resuscitate the dead? If she hadn't been alone, she might have been able to do both, but now there really wasn't a choice. Ignoring the sharp stab of regret that twisted in her gut, she approached the survivor.

Placing a gentle hand on his shoulder, she pushed her mind inside his damaged body. Immediately she could feel the blood coursing through his vessels, the air struggling to move in and out of his lungs, and the essence of his consciousness deeply embedded in his physical form. She had been intimately linked with this man moments before his ship fell out of the sky. She'd felt him fighting for his life, felt his pain as if it were her own. And now he would die if she didn't act quickly.

Her mind swept through his body, methodically probing his vital organs. It snagged on fractured bones and tracked a broken rib impaled in his lung. She felt warm blood pooling in his abdomen and leaking into his brain and followed the deadly streams back to ruptured organs and severed vessels. There was just so much damage. Urgency bordered on panic, but she took a deep breath and forced herself to move.

Supporting his body with hers, she unfastened the clasp of the seat harness and gently lowered him onto his back. He was not a small man, and Caeli's knees buckled under his weight. She caught his head before it ricocheted off the ground, and her hand came away slick with blood.

His lips were tinged blue and his breathing ragged. Placing her hand on his chest, she channeled her energy directly into his body, to the site of the injury, and moved the bone. Coaxing the jagged edge of the rib out of the soft tissue, she realigned it properly in its place, like fitting two pieces of a puzzle together. She felt the bones begin to knit and prodded them with her mind to weave and solidify.

She tore open his clothing and used her utility knife to make a small, quick incision between his fourth and fifth ribs. The trapped air from his leaking lungs hissed as it escaped from his body. Caeli breathed a small sigh of relief when his chest began to rise and fall in a regular rhythm and his lips flushed pink.

She worked similarly to repair his internal organs, visualizing the damage and then concentrating her energy to stop the bleeding, cauterize a shredded vessel, and knit together his torn spleen.

The work was taking its toll. Her body began to tremble with exhaustion, her limbs heavy and her movements sluggish. But she couldn't stop. Not yet.

She turned her attention to his head. Blood covered his face and congealed in his dark hair. Placing her shaking hand on his forehead, she searched along the vessels of his brain until she found the damage.

With her mind so intimately linked to his, she couldn't help but brush against his thoughts, experience his sharpest memories. *Why didn't we see that ship? They're firing on us! We need to get a message to* Horizon. His voice echoed in Caeli's mind just as it did before the crash, but this time, with physical contact, she perceived more. Disjointed words, names, and strange places flickered through her head and settled next to her own memories, distinctly foreign but now irrevocably embedded.

She did her best to ignore the noise of his thoughts and concentrate only on repairing the damage. Tiny, ruptured vessels leaked into soft tissue. It was exacting work to locate and seal them all off, and Caeli could feel her focus slipping. *Almost there. Stay awake,* she ordered herself.

Finally satisfied, she sat back on her heels and closed her eyes. Soon her body would simply stop and she would be as unconscious as her patient. Before that happened, she needed to get them both back to her camp, where at least there was shelter, water, and food.

Ignoring the heaviness in her limbs, Caeli gripped him under the shoulders. Then, standing on shaking legs, she began to pull. Grateful he was so deeply unconscious, she dragged him awkwardly out of the fuselage, wincing when his splintered leg jostled along the rough ground.

Outside the ship she wiped her forehead with the back of her hand and blew out a frustrated breath. There was no way she could wrestle him through the trees to camp. There had to be an easier way. She knelt by his side and leaned in close to feel him warmly exhale against her cheek. His lips were still pink and his chest rose and fell rhythmically. Satisfied that she could leave him for a moment, she got up and headed back to the craft.

Pausing in front of the second body, she blinked back stinging tears. Less than an hour ago this young man had been alive, but in an instant the universe had irrevocably shifted.

Now all she could do for him was promise to come back and perform the funeral rites that were customary for her people. Waves of carefully stored grief threatened to surface. *No,* she reprimanded, *there isn't time for that.*

Brushing a stray piece of hair out of her face, she detached the harness straps from both seats and gently lowered the body to the ground, placing him on his back with his arms folded across his chest. Then, gathering the pile of material and buckles, she returned to her living patient.

Nearby she found two large, straight boughs and wound them through with a length of vine to make a simple stretcher. Using the harness straps from the ship, she secured his body to it and began the slow, arduous trek back to her camp.

With every step, the last reserves of her energy drained away. Soon she was staggering, barely able to stay upright. *One breath at a time,* she coaxed herself. *One step at a time.* When the familiar rocky formation of her campsite was finally in view and she could hear the rushing water of the brook, Caeli nearly sobbed with relief.

Dragging him the final few feet into the small cave at the base of the hill, she stumbled onto her knees. Hopefully she'd done enough and he would survive the next few hours. With her hand on his chest, she collapsed into sleep.

# CHAPTER 2

His mind prodded her awake. Caeli's hand was still on his chest, and she could feel his thoughts moving, beginning to take form and surface. She sat up quickly, rubbing the sleep out of her eyes. She had hoped to deal with his broken bones before he fully regained consciousness.

Kneeling at his feet, she gently removed his boot, but immediately his eyes flew open, wide with panic and confusion. He struggled against the harness straps that still secured him to the stretcher and cried out in pain. His skin paled, and a sheen of sweat glistened on his forehead.

She crawled forward and softly touched the side of his face. Though she suspected he wouldn't understand her language, she hoped the tone of her voice and the thought of her intentions would reach him. "You're hurt. I am helping you." He stilled.

Speaking to him in a soft, even voice, she returned to work. His skin was warm, and as soon as she touched him, the displaced femur fracture was clear in her mind's eye.

"This will hurt," she said directly into his mind. Then, placing a hand beneath his knee and another atop his shin, she pulled with all her strength, realigning the bone in one quick movement. He gave a sharp cry and passed out.

She splinted the leg and then sorted out the other broken bones. Before she finished, his eyes opened again and she stopped to offer him water. Lifting his head, she tipped the bottle up for him to drink and really looked at him.

His face, crusted with dried blood, was already beginning to bruise. He was young, with strong features and thick, dark hair cropped short. Deep blue eyes stared back at her with a flicker of recognition beneath a glaze of pain.

Tearing her gaze away from his, she looked outside. The diminishing sunlight worried her. She needed more supplies, and it would be far more difficult to find them once it was fully dark. While she could visualize and heal structural damage with her mind, treating infection and fever required traditional means. There was a wealth of medicines she knew she could make—remedies to help knit bone, build blood volume, and ease pain—but she had none of the raw materials on hand.

Starting a mental list, she stood up. She gestured at her pack and water bottle and tried to explain, "I have to get supplies and refill our water." Reluctant to leave him but impatient to find what she needed, she hurried out.

When she returned an hour later with her pack stuffed full of medicinal plants, he was feverish. Caeli had to fight a rising sense of panic that she would not be able to move fast enough, that her medicines would not be strong enough, or that she would simply not have the skill to save him.

Shaking her head to clear it, she knelt by his side. He was not going to die. She was not going to let him. *Start the remedy and get him cooled down,* she instructed herself.

The cooking area was already stocked with wood and ready for a fire. She mentally thanked her childhood camp guide, who constantly preached about good habits and preparedness, as she lit the fire and poured water into the pot to boil. On a piece of flat, hard slate, she chopped and mashed the plants and tossed them all into the pot, then left it to steep and went back inside.

He was burning up. Peeling back the blanket, she carefully removed his torn clothes, wet a handful of absorbent moss she'd found during her search, and began to rub down his body. The evaporating water brought his temperature back down, and when he started to shiver, she covered him again with the blanket. Only semi-conscious now, his eyes were open but unfocused and he was restless and moaning softly. She touched his forehead to try and soothe him.

Caeli paced back and forth between him and the fire, briskly stirring the mixture. She needed this remedy in her cooking pot to fight the infection raging inside him. Her efforts to cool him down had only provided a temporary reprieve. When it was finally ready, she held the cup and coaxed him to drink.

\*\*\*

The first bit of color was brightening the dawn sky when his body temperature finally normalized. He blinked at her lucidly for a moment and spoke in a hoarse whisper. She didn't quite understand the words, but she smiled at him with relief.

When his breathing became deep and regular with sleep, she stretched and stood up. There was something else she had to do. As she left the cave, she dragged the makeshift stretcher behind her. No urgency propelled her forward now, and though the trip from the wreckage to the camp felt like a journey of hours yesterday, it hadn't been all that far.

Back at the ship, the second occupant was just as she had left him. As gently as possible, she pulled his body out of the ship, strapped him onto the stretcher, and stumbled toward the beach.

It took almost an hour to collect enough wood for the fire. Finally satisfied that the pyre would burn long enough, she maneuvered him onto it. A medallion around his neck glittered in the sunlight and caught her eye. Removing it, she placed it carefully over her own head.

At home there had been people who could follow the spirit of the dead as it left the body. They could feel the life essence of a soul lingering close by, often for a few days, and they could share the journey with that soul for a little while to ease the transition from this state of being to the next.

Although Caeli did not have the gift of following, she knew the funeral rituals well, and so began to sing to him as she lit the fire. Tendrils of flame became a scorching blaze. She sat a few yards away with her arms wrapped around her knees. Her eyes stung from the smoke, and sweat mingled with the tears trickling down her face. When her voice broke, she forced herself to keep singing. She hoped her songs might help him find his way.

Soon only smoking embers, a blackened pile of ash, and bits of bone remained. The wind and rain would scatter these, and there would be very little left to mark what was now a sacred place. Unnerved by that thought, she scoured the beach for stones to create a small cairn.

As she finished the monument, tears threatened again. In the last year, her world had been transformed by death and ruin. And here was more. Collapsing to her knees by the stones, she put her head in her hands and finally allowed the tears to flow.

\*\*\*

Nagging hunger finally stirred her out of despair and into motion again. It was time to go back. When Caeli returned to the cave, her patient was still sleeping lightly.

Careful not to touch anything else, she tossed some soap into the cooking pot, gathered the dirty dishes, and headed to the river to wash. The morning air was cool, but held the promise of warmth, and the sun's rays reflected off the blue water.

As she knelt by the stream, a familiar loneliness crept into her bones. But the sound of water against the rocks soothed her, and as she let the liquid run through her fingers, the tension began to seep out of her body. She'd been coming here every morning to wash and collect water, and also to remind herself that she was alive, that she was connected to this planet, and that she could go on, *would* go on, for at least another day.

When she finished with the dishes, she stripped off her clothes and slid into the water. Blood and ash were still crusted on her hands and arms. As the dirt, sweat, and grime washed down the river, more of her anxiety and sorrow went with it. She emerged feeling weary but peaceful.

The air was warming as the sun rose higher, and Caeli's eyes felt heavy. She allowed herself a few precious moments of rest while waiting for her things to dry.

While her mind drifted, it played over his memories. Those terrifying moments from just before the crash, conversations between him and a dark-haired young woman, and images of a decimated city all filled her head. There were more, and strong emotions accompanied all these pictures, but she did not try to sift through them. It was an intimate experience to share one's thoughts with another, and she felt intrusive and slightly embarrassed.

She *knew* him without really knowing anything at all.

# DEREK

## CHAPTER 3

She was gone when he woke up. From the amount of light filtering into the cave, Derek assumed it was late afternoon. More clearheaded than he had been since the crash, he actually felt considerably better than the last time he was conscious. The excruciating pain that accompanied his every movement had dulled. His entire body still ached, but it was nothing compared to the blinding agony he experienced the last time he opened his eyes.

This seemed impossible. Maybe he'd actually been asleep for days? That was the only explanation he could think of for how quickly he seemed to be healing. Whatever the case, he *was* better, but he was starving, and annoyingly, he had to pee.

The contraption on his left leg would make standing up on his own challenging. He understood that he most likely had a femur fracture, that this was very bad, and that it had hurt like hell. The sharp, searing pain in this leg was what first jolted him back to consciousness after the crash.

Derek remembered his own confusion and disorientation in those first moments. He knew he was in bad shape as soon as he opened his eyes, but his head had been cloudy and he didn't know where he was or how he got there.

And there was the girl. She had touched him and he instantly felt calmer. He remembered thinking maybe he was dead, and maybe it wasn't so bad. But his version of the afterlife did not include a broken leg, a splitting headache, and chest pain.

He sat up and shrugged off the blanket that covered him. Then, leaning toward what he now thought of as his *good* side, he tried to put weight on his uninjured leg and use his right arm to push himself up. He managed to get to his feet, holding on to the cave wall for support. With an uncomfortable hopping, shuffling motion, he staggered out of the cave and around the corner to relieve himself.

The effort left him sweating, exhausted, and lightheaded. *Shit,* he swore. He was probably going to fall and break his other leg on the way back inside. As he lurched around the corner, the young woman walked back into the camp clearing. Her eyes widened in surprise when she saw him standing, and she hurried over to help him. Instead of guiding him back into the cave, though, she led him to an outdoor hammock near the fire pit. She helped him onto it and then went back inside to retrieve his blanket.

He watched her efficiently start a fire, fill the pot with water, and begin to chop vegetables. *Is she living out here alone?* he wondered, looking around the site. If so, she was doing a good job of it.

He was more than curious about her. Her knowledge of healing had saved his life, and he had some odd sense that he knew her better than should be possible. Despite how awful he felt, he found himself staring at her.

She looked up from her tasks and saw that he was watching her. She gave him a small smile, and he grinned back, pointing at the cooking pot. She nodded her head, tossed all the roots and vegetables in, and gave it a stir.

Her quiet attention to these domestic activities comforted him in a way he couldn't easily explain. He knew he needed her to take care of him, and he was surprisingly at ease with this. Maybe it was because the effort to stay alive after the crash had been so exhausting, and he was just spent. But there was something about her that allowed him to be vulnerable. He dozed in the swaying hammock.

Traces of memory from the crash jolted him out of his short nap. She was already next to him, touching his shoulder and soothing him with her soft voice. He took a deep breath and felt his body relax. When his stomach growled a few seconds later, she raised her eyebrows at him, looking amused. Collecting two bowls, she scooped out a large portion of the hot soup into each and set them on a flattened log to cool. His mouth watered.

Positioning herself on his right side, she placed his arm over her shoulders and helped him first to sit, then to step onto the ground. She guided him over to a tree and sat him down with his back supported by the trunk.

His splinted leg was straight out in front of him, and his left arm was stuck in a sling. His head hurt, but not as much as before, and his chest ached, but he could breathe comfortably. *All in all it isn't so bad*, he thought. But the dark purple bruises all over his body told a very different story.

As he looked down at his impressively colorful skin, it occurred to him that he was in his underwear. He had a sudden image of her undressing him, and *that* thought needed to stop. When he looked up, as if reading his mind, she blushed and went to get his blanket from the hammock.

With only one hand, he couldn't maneuver the bowl very well and he couldn't use the crudely sharpened sticks to jab at the chunks of vegetables. She must have been hungry, but she sat next to him and helped him eat first. The meal was warm and filling, and he was sorry to see his bowl emptied. She got up, scooped another helping, set it aside to cool again, and then started on hers.

When they were both finished, she piled the bowls and sticks together near the cooking pot and sat on her knees facing him. Her expression was somber as she looked into his eyes. She said something that he couldn't understand, then pulled a medallion on a chain out from underneath her shirt and placed it in his hand.

Derek grasped the medallion, leaned his head back against the tree, and squeezed his eyes shut, trying and failing to keep the sudden, devastating pain at bay. His chest tightened, and he felt the sting of hot tears threaten. She touched his arm then discreetly gathered the dishes and disappeared into the woods.

Of course Tommy was dead. He had known this all along, but now the proof in his hand made the reality of it sharp and terrible. This was not how it was supposed to be. A hint of anger surfaced next to his grief. He did not lose people under his command on routine missions.

As he replayed the crash in his mind, he couldn't think of a way to change the outcome, but that didn't matter. He was responsible, and he would carry the weight of that with him for a long time.

*** 

When the unidentified ship came out of nowhere and fired on them, they were caught completely off guard. Derek's ship, *Equinox*, shuddered violently and pitched hard to port.

"Where the hell did that come from?" Tommy shouted, and a string of curses followed as he tried to correct their course.

"Get the weapons online," Derek ordered, taking the helm. The little ship carried a powerful complement of weapons, and Derek was eager to put them to good use.

"We're set!" Tommy yelled over the blaring alarms.

"I've got a lock!" Derek shouted back and fired. He squinted as a bright flash of light filled the cockpit and the other ship exploded into large metal chunks.

"Nice shot," Tommy offered.

Derek grinned at him and wiped the sweat from his forehead, relieved.

But his satisfaction was short-lived. The port side engine was failing, and the life support alarms were among the chorus of those wailing through the cockpit. They were never going make it back to *Horizon*, their command ship, in this shape.

Derek knew one of the planets in the nearby system was habitable from the spectrum data they'd taken earlier in the day, and he thought they might have a better chance of making it there.

They'd been on a three-day trip to this relatively unmapped sector of space. Their job was to grab a little data about the system and then drop small, nearly undetectable sensor markers at strategic points in the region.

"I'm heading back to the planet," he said to Tommy and made the necessary course corrections. "And shut down the damn alarms."

Their earlier lighthearted mood quickly turned into one of brisk efficiency. Derek focused on flying while Tommy tried to repair as much of the ship as he could before they would have to try and land it.

Derek's first order of business was to get the ship on course to the planet, but the second was to send out a communication to *Horizon*. No other ships should have been in this region, and *Equinox* had not registered the ship on any of its sensors until it was right on top of them.

This second fact concerned Derek the most. *Horizon* utilized the best stealth tech in the galaxy, and *she* wouldn't have been able to come within firing distance of another ship completely undetected.

This was information *Horizon* needed to know—that and the fact that two of her pilots might soon be stranded on a strange, remote planet. He sent the transmissions while Tommy's colorful language filled the cockpit.

"Status report?" Derek asked Tommy.

"Life support will hold," Tommy answered. He paused then continued, "The engine's fried, though, and the stabilizers are shot. I did my best, but . . ." His voice trailed off.

Derek knew from Tommy's tone that the ship was just too badly damaged. It would be a near-impossible landing with almost no control.

As the planet went from a small speck in the distance to a large blue-and-green ball, they both became quiet.

"It's been an honor, Commander," Tommy said. The words were formal and traditional, but no less heartfelt. It's what they knew.

Derek swallowed hard and nodded at the younger man. "Engage the heat shields. Let's do this."

The ship shook violently when it entered the planet's atmosphere. Derek struggled to maintain control. They were losing altitude way too fast. His heart pounded as he fought to hold *Equinox* on course.

"I can't keep her nose up!"

Derek wasn't sure if he said the words out loud. It didn't matter anyway. Time slowed as they plunged through the clouds. *Tommy has a daughter. Where did that fucking ship come from? I can't fix this. I don't want to die.*

There were only seconds left. His stomach clenched as the planet rushed up to meet them. With a deafening blast, *Equinox* impacted the ground, and for a split second Derek could feel his body shattering along with his ship. Blinding pain was followed by merciful darkness.

# CHAPTER 4

Derek was still holding the medallion when the young woman came back into the camp, moving quietly around him while he was lost in his thoughts. Eventually she knelt at his side and put her hand on his arm. He held the medallion out and said simply, "Tommy."

She repeated the name, took the medallion from him and placed it around his neck. Then she motioned that it was time to move. As before, she went to his right side and helped him up, this time leading him back into the cave to the sleeping pallet. She lit a fire in the stone pit, and its orange glow filled the small space.

He watched, a little nervously, as she carefully began to untie the bindings around his leg and then removed the splint entirely. Placing both of her hands over what he assumed was the site of the fracture, she closed her eyes. Immediately he felt a warm tingling in his leg. It was a strange sensation but not altogether unpleasant. When she was finished with his leg, she moved first to his chest and then to his arm and shoulder, repeating the same gesture and producing the same sensations in his body.

Finally she sat back on her heels and sighed deeply. She looked exhausted, and he had a moment of fleeting guilt, but then she opened her eyes and smiled, motioning for him to try and lift the arm.

He did so and the movement only caused a dull ache, not the sharp pain he was expecting. Derek looked up in disbelief. Gingerly he bent his knee to move his left leg and this produced a similar soreness, but nothing compared to earlier. She had just accelerated the healing of his bones *with her touch*. How was that possible? He really didn't understand what had happened, but he was more than pleased with the result and he gave her a grateful smile.

She sat down next to him against the cave wall, leaned back, and closed her eyes. It did not look at all comfortable to him, but he realized with some embarrassment that *he* was in her bed. This might have been okay when he was a total invalid less than a day ago, but now there was really no excuse.

"Hey," he said to her.

Startled, she opened her eyes to find him sitting up.

"Come on, there's room." He motioned for her to lie down next to him. The pallet cushion wasn't thick, but it was much better than the bare ground or the cave wall, and there was enough room for both of them.

She sat very still.

"I won't bite." He motioned again, knowing she didn't understand his words, but hoping she got the sentiment. "Please, you're tired."

Reluctantly, he thought, she crawled over next to him, and he could tell she was asleep within moments.

He had been sleeping on and off for a few days and wasn't really all that tired, but he didn't want to move and disturb her. Staring at the cave wall, he thought about the strange turn his life had taken. He wondered if *Horizon* had gotten his last message, but stranded on this remote planet and lying next to this mysterious young woman, his mission seemed a distant memory and his entire world felt far away. Disparate emotions sparred in his mind.

Tommy's death hit him again like a blow to the gut. He silently wondered in what universe it was okay for him to be alive, almost completely healed even, and Tommy to be gone.

Then, looking at the sleeping girl beside him, he felt strangely protective. There were some memories in his head that didn't seem to be his own. Vague and disjointed, they were filled with people he didn't know, places he had never been, and some considerable violence that he couldn't make sense of. Confused and worried, he finally drifted off to sleep.

*** 

When he woke, it was barely dawn. She was already up and clearly had been for a while. There was a small fire in the cave and another outside in the cooking area. An appetizing smell wafted over from the pot, making his mouth water, and everything in the cave seemed neat and in good order. *Does she ever sleep for more than a few hours at a time?* he wondered.

Wrapping himself in the blanket, he went out to join her by the fire. She said something pleasant, probably "good morning," and handed him a steaming bowl.

When they were both done eating, she knelt in front of him as she had the day before and clearly wanted to communicate something. She gestured at his leg, arm, and chest and then pointed at herself. Then she tapped her head and his head and looked at him questioningly.

Whatever she wanted to do, he certainly wasn't going to refuse. He didn't know why she was even trying to ask, but she wanted his permission for something, so he nodded. She moved closer to him and put one hand on his forehead and another on the back of his skull. The same warm, tingling feeling he'd felt when she had touched his leg began to course through his head.

She stayed in that position for some time while he tried to remain as still as possible. When she moved away from him, she seemed satisfied and was even smiling a little. "How are you feeling?" she asked in his language.

He was certain that his jaw dropped. "What did you do?" Of all the questions he could have asked, this was what he came up with?

But she answered him seriously, "I understand how a brain works. Your language is really not so different from mine, but it would have taken us a while to learn, so I . . ." she searched for the right word, "cheated a bit, maybe?"

Her accent had a lilting, musical quality to it, and she was awkward with her pronunciation, but he could understand her perfectly. "Well, shit, that's impressive."

She laughed and nodded. "I guess it is."

"You're a doctor," he said, more a statement of confirmation than a question.

"I would call it something a little different, but essentially, yes," she answered.

He wanted to ask her how he could possibly still be alive, how she was able to mend his broken bones and heal his bleeding brain with only her touch. He wanted to ask what she was doing in the middle of the forest alone. But his instinct told him to tread lightly, that he might overwhelm her if he pried too much, so what he said was, "Lucky for me."

He paused for a moment and then touched the medallion hanging around his neck. "What happened to Tommy?"

"He died on impact. His neck was broken. I might have

been able to fix the damage, but his life force was gone and sometimes the body won't have it back. I had to make a choice. You were still alive and he wasn't." She held his gaze and said in a soft voice, "I'm sorry."

She was probably feeling the weight of responsibility for Tommy's death too. Although there was nothing either of them could have done to change the outcome of that day, it didn't matter. He had no words to offer, but he took her hand. "I'm Derek. Thank you."

She looked up at him and repeated his name. "I'm Caeli," she said back.

They sat quietly for a few minutes, and then she got up and began to gather the dishes. "Would you like to wash? We can go to the river and clean up, and I'll try and fix your clothes the best I can." She went into the cave to gather some items, his clothes included. "Do you feel like you can take a short walk?" she asked, scooping up the dishes and the cooking pot.

"Definitely," he replied, eager to move around a little bit and maybe even to be useful. Carefully, he got to his feet. He was still sore and felt a little unsteady, but he could put weight on the left leg and he was happy to follow her. They walked a short distance to a wide brook. The clearing where she stopped had soft dirt on the shore and several large, flat rocks. She set down the cooking pot and his clothes and began to take a few things out of the bag she carried.

"Soap," she said placing a handful of hard-shelled nuts in his hand.

He looked at them, puzzled.

"They'll lather in the water," she explained. "I'll wash your clothes, and you can use the blanket like a towel while everything dries."

She was definitely a planner. He could appreciate that.

"It's not too cold once you get in," she added.

He sat down on the edge of the rock and dipped his toes in the water. *Pleasant actually*, he thought and slid into the stream. Turning back to the rock, he gathered up the soap while she first began to wash the dishes and then moved on to scrubbing his clothes.

Soon a pile of bubbles surrounded him, and he groaned out loud with happiness as he scrubbed himself clean. When he finished washing, he reached for the blanket, wrapped himself at the waist, and climbed out of the water onto the rock beside her.

He enjoyed watching her work. Damp curls framed her face as she leaned over the riverbank washing the dishes. Her eyes were light blue, and the sun had darkened her smooth, fair skin a little. She was small-boned but strong, fit, and on the thin side, though her body looked like it would be curvier if she ate more. Her hair was thick and dark blonde with lighter streaks running through, and it was tied back in a disheveled manner. Her movements were economical and graceful, and her demeanor was quietly competent. She was beautiful in a simple, satisfying way.

She seemed comfortable in the silence while he lounged in the sunshine and she industriously attended to one task after another. Finally finished, she laid his clothes out on a rock to dry and put her own feet in the water.

He was not as comfortable with silence and never had been. *And*, he thought, *maybe now would be a good time to get a few answers.*

"I have some images in my head that I don't think belong to me. Are they yours?" he asked in a gentle tone.

"Yes," she answered looking at him. "You had a pretty severe brain injury. I have some of your memories now too." She pulled her knees up, wrapped her arms around them, and looked down. "I couldn't ask your permission. I'm sorry."

"I'm glad to be alive, with a fully functional brain, so please don't worry about it," he said with intentional levity.

"But it's a . . ." She searched for the right word. "A violation. I just couldn't heal you any other way." Her expression was pained.

"It didn't feel like that. It was like meeting you. More than meeting you," he tried to explain. "I feel like I *know* you."

"It's like that," she said quietly.

"Some of the actual memories, though—they're intense." He hoped she'd be willing to give him a little context for the disturbing impressions now seared into his brain.

"They're probably some of my strongest memories and experiences, good and bad," she explained. "I couldn't control it." Her discomfort with the conversation was now palpable.

Derek understood that something terrible had happened, and afraid she might shut down completely, he changed the subject.

"How are you so good at this?" he asked, gesturing to the cooking pots and clothes. "So capable of living out here all by yourself?"

He knew this was safer territory by her smile. "Well, I had a very good camp guide growing up." She stretched out on her back in the morning sun, and he did the same. "Every child learned survival basics. It was part of our education. The process was designed, at least in part, so that we could really understand our planet and our relationship to it."

They fell into a companionable silence, one more comfortable than before. He closed his eyes and sighed audibly, tired from just the short walk to the river. She turned on her side and faced him.

"Your body still needs rest. It's healing at an accelerated rate, and it's depleted. I need to get some more food. Stay here, and I'll come back in a little while. Your things should be dry by then anyway."

Irrationally, he didn't want her to leave, but he wasn't going to admit that. Still shaken by Tommy's death and the nearness of his own, he felt unsteady. She was warm and alive, and her presence was becoming comfortingly familiar.

With a forced grin he said, "I'm usually more helpful than this."

"And I'm sure you will be soon," she answered standing up and picking up her bag, "but right now I've got this. Sleep. I'll be back."

# CHAPTER 5

Caeli gently tapped his shoulder. "Derek. It's getting too hot. We have to move." He blinked at the bright midday sun and yawned. Handing him his clothes she said, "They're dry and mostly repaired."

"Thank you," he said rubbing his eyes and sitting up. She waited on the rock facing the river while he pulled on his pants and shirt. "All good," he said to her, and she turned around, getting to her feet.

"Come on, and I'll make us some lunch." At the mention of lunch, his stomach growled again. He was continuously hungry, it seemed, and the thought of her cooking made his mouth water.

They were back at the camp within a few minutes, and she began to empty a collection of fruits, vegetables, and nuts out of her bag. "Can I do anything?" he asked.

She handed him a green fruit and said, "You could peel this." While he peeled, she chopped and shredded the other ingredients into one of her bowls and then pulled apart a large, leafy vegetable.

"Hold this." She took the fruit out of his hand and replaced it with a leaf. She filled the leaf with the ingredients from the bowl and, cutting the fruit into quarters, she put two pieces on top. "Try it," she instructed.

He took a bite, and the fruit burst in his mouth, tangy and sweet. She smiled, apparently pleased with the results. "My meals have been rather boring. It's kind of a chore to cook only for yourself, but now I'm inspired to be a little more creative." She had one leaf. He ate the rest.

When they were finished, she resumed her chores. "You're very industrious," he commented, then joked, "Do you ever stop?"

"When I'm asleep," she answered with more seriousness than he expected. He noticed that it was nearly impossible for her to sit still, and he recognized this need to keep moving for the survival technique it was. He stored this piece of information away for later consideration.

"I need to see my ship," he said, interrupting her work.

She looked at him, curious. "Right now?"

"I've had a good rest, and I've been well fed. I think I can make the trip," he reasoned. "I'd like to go, if you don't mind."

"Okay. We can do that." She went into the cave to retrieve the water bottle and then they left the camp, walking in companionable silence. It was a beautiful day, and the air smelled fresh and pure. Caeli kept the pace intentionally slow, slow enough for Derek to enjoy the walk, even though he knew that what he was going to find at the end wouldn't be pleasant.

As they got closer to the crash site, a pit formed in his stomach, and when they arrived at his ruined ship, he stared in silence. The port engine was nothing more than a scorched shell, and there were weapon burns all along the side. No wonder they'd had so little control for landing. The heat shielding had held, but the ship had broken apart on impact.

Slowly he approached the flight deck.

"Are you sure you want to do that?" Caeli asked.

He nodded. She stepped away, and he cautiously walked into the cockpit. The integrity of the compartment had been breached and the instrument panels were smashed. Wires hung from the ceiling. The floor was smeared with a trail of dried blood from beneath one seat to the exit, and he realized, with discomfort, that it was his own.

Taking a deep breath, he grabbed his sidearm from beneath the seat, shoved it into the back of his pants, and moved out of the fuselage toward the tail section of the ship. He wouldn't be able to remove the flight data recorder, but he knew it was there and it was intact. Hopefully it contained information about the ship that attacked them. *Horizon* would have use for it — *if* they received his transmission and *if* they came looking.

He stood for a long while staring at the wreckage, reliving the last few seconds of the crash in his mind.

"Don't do that," she said gently. Back by his side she touched his arm. "Come with me." She took his hand and led him out of the brush and to the beach.

At first he didn't realize what he was looking at, but when she knelt by the modest stone monument and pulled him down next to her, he knew. He reached for her. Her hand was a lifeline, and he desperately needed the human contact. She put her arms around his waist, resting her head on his shoulder. It was a comforting gesture, both intimate and innocent. He leaned into her gratefully and grieved for his friend.

Eventually he looked up toward the ocean and breathed in the salty air.

Caeli broke the silence. "I don't know what your customs are. This is our practice," she gestured to the pyre. "I hope it was the right thing to do." Her voice held a question.

"Tommy would have appreciated it, and it will mean a lot to his family that he was taken care of, if I ever get to tell them," Derek answered, uncertainty in his voice. "My ship will try to find me, but there are a million reasons why they might not," he added, to himself as much as to her.

"Sometimes it doesn't help to think beyond today," she offered.

He felt her truth in those words and nodded. "How long have you been here?" he asked, thinking she might be willing to share a little more with him now.

"Almost a month. Before that, I was traveling for a few weeks. I needed to get further south. I didn't think I could survive a winter, and I had to get far enough away."

*From what?* he wondered, but before he could get the words out, she said, "I can feel your thoughts."

It was an abrupt subject change, but interesting enough that he was compelled to ask, "What?"

"I can sense your strongest emotions. The stronger they are, the more clearly I can interpret them. I would never try to purposely read your mind or invade your privacy," she hurried to explain. "My people understand this about each other, but for someone else, it might feel strange or intrusive. I just thought you should know." She looked down, as if she'd done something wrong.

"Caeli," he said gently. "I want to understand."

She hesitated, so he turned to face her. "Please," he said.

She took a deep breath, "Before the crash, when your ship got close enough, I could feel you. I can feel you now."

"So you're empathic?" She seemed to consider the word and then nodded.

"And the healing part, tell me more about that," he prodded, now that she was opening up.

Her shoulders relaxed, and she even smiled a little. "Much of my education is in human anatomy, physiology, and natural pharmacology, but I can also diagnose illness and injury with my mind. It's like I can see inside the body with a different part of my brain," she explained, her voice animated. "I can effect change too, but it costs me a lot of energy to do it, so that's really a last resort."

"It's how you saved me," he said, and she nodded.

"Can all your people do this?" he asked, interested.

She shook her head no and explained, "In our very distant past, our best estimate is about a millennium ago, there was a global conflict. So much of our history was lost in the war that we don't even remember what we were fighting about." She shrugged. "What I do know is that afterward some of us had this *ability*. There are all kinds of theories as to why. It could have been the side effect of a biological weapon; we could have been experimenting with genetic engineering. No one really knows. But the change didn't affect the whole population. The Novali have it. The Amathi don't. And even among the Novali, it's expressed in different ways." She paused and then added quietly, "My gift is particularly strong."

Derek sat, processing this information, and Caeli got up to walk along the water's edge. Eventually he went to walk with her. With a gentle hand to her arm, he stopped her.

"Why are you out here alone?" he asked.

She looked at him like a frightened child.

"Your running," he continued. The story of this world's distant past interested him, but the memories lodged in his brain were not of the distant past. They were of Caeli's past.

"Tell me," he coaxed.

"I want to tell you. But I don't know if I can do it." She sat down on the ground and wrapped her arms protectively around her knees. "I am surviving because I try every day *not* to think and to just move from one moment to the next," she said, her voice a whisper.

He knelt down in front of her and, with his thumb, wiped the tear that had escaped from the corner of her eye. It was unfamiliar territory, watching this competent and self-possessed woman break down in front of him, and he was suddenly very sorry he had pushed her to this.

"Hey, it's okay. We don't have to talk about it."

She shook her head and looked up at him, determined. "Someone else should know."

He sat back on his heels and waited.

Taking a deep breath, she began, "The Amathi and Novali haven't lived together for generations now. Our vision for rebuilding civilization was just too different from theirs."

Derek nodded, urging her to continue.

"One of the biggest conflicts between us was our decision to keep Almagest, this planet, isolated. There's evidence that while we were recovering from the war, outsiders tried to exploit us. At first, everyone agreed it was necessary to stay hidden, so the most powerfully gifted Novali created a kind of shielding around our world. And it worked."

"But Almagest isn't hidden anymore," Derek said.

"There aren't enough Novali left to do it," Caeli answered in a whisper, and Derek's stomach churned.

She looked directly at him. "It might be easier if I show you what happened." The question was in her eyes. Did he really want to go there with her?

"Yes," he answered.

She sat back, took his hands, and closed her eyes. He could feel her consciousness gently nudging against his. His mind relaxed and opened up. Suddenly she was there with him in such an intimate and complete way that he could no longer imagine what it was like to be alone in his own mind, and he couldn't tell where his thoughts ended and hers began.

# BEFORE

## CHAPTER 6

Caeli was six when she saw Marcus for the first time. He was a young, charismatic man, but even in her child's mind she recognized something was off. She could feel a deep anger within him and a coldness that scared her. She knew she wasn't allowed to look any deeper, but sensing someone's mood or intentions, that was all right. It helped you know how to behave.

Marcus was in Novalis, Caeli's town, with his brother Dimitri, a slightly older man with more reserve and less fire in his demeanor. They had come to the meeting held twice yearly between Caeli's settlement and theirs. Well, really it was between her kind of people and theirs. Many generations ago, the two had split. She knew that some people thought it was a good idea because they were so different from one another. But she often overheard her parents discussing how bad this was, maybe even dangerous.

What Caeli knew for certain was this young man made her uneasy and she was glad when he left. She wondered if anyone else sensed what she did, but there wasn't an opportunity to ask, and then they were gone and the incident was relegated to a place in the back of her mind.

A few years later however, the memory resurfaced. She and a few friends had been outside the meeting hall, pretending to play but eagerly awaiting a glimpse of the strange foreigners from Alamath. They were not disappointed when Dimitri, the leader, emerged first, followed by his brother Marcus and a small group of other men. Dimitri's expression was blank, but Marcus was seething.

His face flushed with anger, Marcus grabbed his brother's arm and hissed, "I'm going back inside. We are *not* finished here!"

But Dimitri replied sharply, "We are finished for today. And you will walk away, right now."

Caeli saw the rage on Marcus's face and immediately remembered her discomfort the last time she was in his presence. She wished she could dig just a little deeper into his mind to see if her perception was justified.

"Caeli, come on!" her best friend Lia prompted excitedly. "Let's follow them."

Caeli hesitated. Lia was always the more adventurous one, and while most of the time her ideas were fun and innocent, sometimes she got them both into trouble.

Caeli had to admit, though, she was curious about these men, who dressed so differently and spoke with a strange accent, and about the distinctly separate culture that existed nearby, so close and yet so mysterious. The adults didn't give out much information about the Amathi, a fact Caeli found particularly frustrating, and she had an opportunity right before her that was too perfect to ignore.

After a moment she nodded with resolve. "Okay, let's go."

Lia grinned and they took off. Caeli and the other children of Novalis were excellent at tracking and could remain nearly invisible if they put their mind to it. They had to be especially careful while still within sight of the houses and buildings in their village, but once they entered the wooded paths heading to the northern hills, they became more confident in their ability to stay close and hidden.

The Amathi were quiet, barely speaking with each other until they were certain they were out of range of the town. Suddenly Marcus turned abruptly and stopped his brother with a rough hand to his arm. Caeli and Lia froze.

"They are a danger to us," he said between clenched teeth.

"They have not shown themselves to be," Dimitri answered, his voice even.

"It's only a matter of time," Marcus warned.

"Your paranoia is based on old legends and scattered bits of ancient history," Dimitri scolded, shaking his head.

"You allow them to make decisions for us, unchecked," Marcus accused.

"One decision," Dimitri answered in a placating tone. "And our people agreed that this was for the best."

"That was generations ago. We are stronger now, ready to make our presence known," Marcus argued.

"You, brother, are arrogant," Dimitri said.

"And you, *brother*, are weak," Marcus spat and stalked ahead.

Caeli looked at Lia in wide-eyed silence. She didn't understand why Marcus was so angry, but she felt a chill of fear creep up her spine. Quietly they waited until the visiting strangers were long out of sight, and out of earshot, before they began the trek home.

That night during dinner with her parents, Caeli cautiously asked her father, "Did we do something to make the Amathi angry?"

"Why do you ask?" He raised his eyebrows and looked at her in surprise.

"Well, they were here and they didn't look happy when they left. What happened?"

Caeli's father responded simply, "The Leadership Council keeps this planet safe by making it nearly invisible to anyone not from our world. It's the only decision that we've made, and won't change, regardless of what the Amathi think."

"And that makes the Amathi angry?" she asked.

"Yes," he affirmed.

"So why do we do it?" she pressed.

"In school you've learned about the last Great War that nearly destroyed everyone on the planet?" he asked.

Caeli nodded.

"After that war, we were very vulnerable. And although we've been rebuilding for generations, the Council thinks that we still can't protect ourselves from anyone who wished to do us harm," her father answered.

By his enthusiastic tone, Caeli knew her father wanted to talk more about the war and the reconstruction. She resisted the urge to roll her eyes and sigh. Her parents were historians and archeologists, and studying the past was their life's work. Caeli tried to get excited about it for their benefit, but it bored her to distraction.

She wanted to know more about why Marcus was so angry, why the Amathi lived somewhere else, and why they only visited Novalis twice a year. Maybe she needed to be more direct.

"Why don't the Amathi live here anymore?" she interjected before her dad could ramble on about the war.

Her father sighed, "We were all called Amathi once."

Caeli stared at him wide-eyed. She hadn't learned that in school.

"But we can do things with our minds that the Amathi can't," he said.

"Like how I can hear other people's feelings in my head?"

"Exactly," he confirmed. Caeli assumed everyone could do this, including the Amathi. No one had ever hinted otherwise.

Her father continued, "And because of our different gifts, we began to see possibilities for a way of life that the Amathi couldn't. Maybe this made them uncomfortable or afraid. Eventually they decided to separate from us and create their own society. We have meetings with them so we can continue to communicate and stay on good terms."

This was more information than she had ever gotten on the subject, so she persisted, "But we aren't really on good terms, are we?"

"Not right now, no," her father answered. Caeli wanted to ask if he thought things could be fixed, but without knowing why, she was afraid of the answer.

***

The next day she went to stay at Lia's house because her parents were leaving for several weeks. *They spend a lot of time sifting through old ruins*, Caeli thought as she bounced on Lia's bed. It was okay though. She liked it at Lia's. She had a dresser drawer reserved just for her things, and Lia's dad always made her favorite dessert the first night.

Lia's parents were botanists. They studied plants that were good for food, plants that were used for fabrics, and most importantly, plants that could be made into medicine. Lia thought it was tiring, but Caeli loved to follow them around outdoors while they collected specimens, and she paid careful attention to how they identified the different species.

One morning they delivered a particularly promising plant to the infirmary and she tagged along. She'd been to this clinic before, but only for a physical exam or when she wasn't feeling well. No one was paying attention to her now, so Caeli wandered uninterrupted around the neatly organized spaces. Jars and bottles of medicinal herbs were labeled and categorized on shelves. Bandages, suture kits, and other emergency supplies were neatly tucked away in closets. The sense of order and purpose to everything appealed to her. It even smelled good, clean and soapy.

Caeli stopped at the open door of an exam room and noticed a pregnant woman seated on a comfortable chair. She peeked in, interested in the woman's belly.

The woman looked up and smiled at her. "You're Caeli," she said. "Your mom and I work together. You were much smaller the last time I saw you."

Caeli smiled back and said hello shyly.

"Come on in. Would you like to feel the baby move?" Caeli entered the room and knelt on the floor to place her hand on the woman's stomach. Immediately she could see the baby. Not with her eyes, but with that different part of her mind that allowed her to sense other people's feelings. "I can hear her heartbeat too!" she exclaimed with wonder.

The woman raised her eyebrows and looked to the door. The physician was standing there and his eyes were wide with surprise as well. "Hello there," he said. "I see you've met Mari and her baby, but I don't think we've met. I'm Sam Gabriel. "

Caeli stood up, feeling awkward and even a little embarrassed. She'd never shown this side of her gift to anyone. None of her friends could do anything like it, and she felt self-conscious. But she knew her parents would expect her to mind her manners and introduce herself, so she said, "Pleased to meet you. I'm Caeli Crys."

Sam was a tall, slender man with a kind face and a warm, soothing voice. She began to feel at ease. "How do you know the baby is a girl?" he asked with interest.

"I can see her. I know where her hands and feet are, and I can see she's sucking her thumb. I can hear her too. When will she be born?" she asked.

"Remarkable," he said smiling, and then, "She should be here in a few weeks. And as for you, when you're a little older, come and see me. We'll have a lot to talk about."

# CHAPTER 7

At seventeen Caeli began to spend weeks at a time in the forest with a camp guide and a small group of students her age.

She met Daniel during one of these excursions. She noticed him on the first day and was secretly thrilled to be partnered with him on a fishing expedition. His hair was very blond and his eyes very blue, and she was attracted to his quiet intensity.

They spent a whole day out on the boat. Caeli caught him grinning as she wrestled with a particularly large fish.

"I've got this," she warned, her arm muscles straining.

"Absolutely," he agreed.

When she slipped backwards, he was behind her to catch her before she fell overboard, and they both dissolved into fits of laughter.

They caught plenty of fish in the first hour but spent the rest of the afternoon swimming and basking in the midday sun, reluctant to return to the group. Lying on the sandy shore of the lake, with the boat tethered to a tree and the fish secured in a net over the side, they held hands and dreamed of the future.

"I can heal with my mind," Caeli shared with him quietly.

"Wow. That's pretty rare." Daniel turned to smile at her. "Well, it will be a useful skill if I ever fall off a ladder or cut myself with the hand saw."

"You want to build things?" she asked.

"I do," he answered. "When I look at a piece of wood or stone, it's like I can see what it wants to become."

"You'll make beautiful things," she predicted, and she could feel him smile next to her.

During the following weeks, they'd sit together by the fire in the early mornings, hike together side by side through the wooded paths, and kiss by the river under the starry sky. Neither wanted their time together to end.

\*\*\*

When their group returned home, the Amathi delegation was leaving. They'd been away for the entirety of the meeting, but Caeli knew as soon as they approached that something had gone very wrong. There was a thick tension coming from the Council members, and the foreign delegation briskly and wordlessly departed.

Caeli's father looked worn out when he returned from the meeting, but he greeted her enthusiastically and then sent her off to bathe and sort out her pack. The hot water in the tub felt luxurious after so many weeks washing in a cold stream. She sank in and closed her eyes, wondering where Daniel was and what he was doing.

She emerged about an hour later, shriveled and scrubbed clean, with dinner waiting for her on the table. Her parents wanted to hear all about the trip. After all, much of their time was still spent trekking through the countryside to reach dig sites. Eventually, though, they got to the topic of the delegates meeting, and her father said, with more concern in his voice than she'd ever heard, "They've broken off all contact."

"Why would they do that?" Caeli asked, dread creeping up her spine.

He sighed. "Their opinion is we have nothing left to say to one another. We still won't budge on the shielding around the planet. They've become more and more secretive about their way of life . . ." His voice trailed off.

"What do we do?" Caeli asked and waited for him to collect his thoughts.

"I don't know. But what we shouldn't do is ignore the issue, and I am afraid that's exactly what the Council is going to do. They acquiesced when our delegation was refused entry into Alamath five years ago. They made no significant protest when meetings were reduced to once a year. And now, they've just allowed the Amathi to walk away indefinitely."

He sat heavily at the table and shook his head. Exhaling in frustration, he continued, "I suspect this outright break is Marcus's doing. He's always been more suspicious and radical than his brother."

Caeli remembered Marcus's words from years ago. "He's afraid we'll use our gift in some corrupt way."

Her father looked up, surprised.

Caeli gave him a small, guilty smile. "I overheard him speaking to his brother once after a delegates meeting. I never told you."

He smiled back and shook his head.

"Why would he think that?" she asked.

Her father looked like he wanted to say something else but then shrugged. "I don't know."

"If we don't communicate with the Amathi anymore, how will they know we don't mean them harm?" Caeli asked. "Marcus's perception of us will be all they have."

"This is one of my arguments with the Council. But they're more concerned with completing the irrigation project and opening an expansion settlement. All important things, don't misunderstand me," he acknowledged.

Caeli interrupted him. "But how can we make any long-term plan for the future that doesn't include the Amathi? We live on the same planet."

"You should run for Council when you're old enough," her dad said grinning. Then he added more soberly, "If we believe we're so fundamentally different that we can't even communicate, I worry it will be a quick path from resentment to hatred and from hatred to war."

She swallowed and felt a chill at the truth in his words. Why would people go to war and destroy each other? In her beautiful world, Caeli just couldn't imagine it. What could be worth that? Possibly she was being naïve. In fact she thought she probably was, because thinking about the Amathi caused her stomach to turn over, and for the next several nights her dreams were filled with a hollow darkness.

\*\*\*

On a lovely, blue-skied morning about a month before she was due to graduate from her general studies program and move into her specialty, she awoke with a start. She thought she heard her parents calling her name, but when she opened her eyes and her unconscious mind receded, she realized she was at Lia's.

Her parents were away. They were due to arrive back in a little more than a week, in plenty time for the elaborate ceremony that was planned for the graduating class. All day

Caeli wasn't able to shake the sense of dread that washed over her.

After school, Mari, the woman Caeli had met in the clinic years ago, was waiting for her at Lia's house.

"There's been an accident," Mari said, her face pale and eyes reddened from tears.

Caeli's knees gave out. If Lia's father hadn't been beside her, she would have collapsed.

"They're gone, Caeli." Mari's voice broke as she said the words. "The structure was unstable. It came down on top of them. There was nothing we could do. I'm so sorry."

All Caeli could do was shake her head in denial. In that moment, her world shifted. One part of her thought it was simply not possible, but on a visceral level she knew it was true. She had known it since that morning.

The days and weeks that followed had a surreal quality about them. Lia and her family were ever-present, making sure she had food, helping to organize the memorial services, and eventually helping to sort and pack up some of her parents' things. But for a while she would wake up in the morning, dress, eat something, go to class, and then arrive back home in the evening and remember absolutely nothing about her day.

Daniel would walk with her to class in the morning and bring her home in the afternoon, always a silent presence, but she could not find the energy or interest to engage with him. She had no room for anything but her own grief, and she barely noticed when eventually he stopped coming by.

She skipped her graduation ceremony altogether and instead went for a walk by the river. She sat by the bank and sobbed until she had no tears left and was utterly exhausted. It was evening when she finally started back to her empty house.

Lia's family had invited her to stay with them for as long as she liked, but she refused. There was comfort in her own home, and there were memories she needed close by to help get her through each day. When she arrived back, Sam Gabriel was seated at her front door. He stood up as she approached.

"Rough day today?" he asked gently.

"I just didn't want to be there without them," she answered.

"I imagine the ceremony would have been very difficult. But you *have* graduated, and I'm hoping you still plan to study with me. I know that it probably feels like a challenge just to get out of bed every morning, but I think getting started on your training might actually help you heal. You are going to be one of the best physicians we've ever had. Will you consider coming by the clinic tomorrow for a little while?" he finished.

She felt a spark of interest. It was small and it disappeared quickly back into despair, but for the first time in a while, she recognized herself again. "Yes, I'll come," she said with gratitude.

"Wonderful. I'm there at the crack of dawn until the next day at the crack of dawn, so anytime is fine," he joked.

"Thank you, Sam. I needed this."

First thing the next morning, Caeli was at the clinic door, and she grinned at the startled expression on his face when he arrived to find her seated on the front step.

"You took the crack of dawn comment literally, I see," he said, but she could tell by his smile he was pleased.

She followed him around the clinic all day and didn't leave until long after the sun had set. Sam sent her home with an armful of textbooks and reading assignments that would keep her up late into the night. She was grateful to lose herself in them and then to discover that she was truly fascinated and excited by the material.

Caeli loved the work, and she grew to love Sam. In the years she studied with him, he reminded her more and more of her father. He was thoughtful, intelligent, and passionate about his vocation. Happy in this role, he was as proud of her as if he *had* been her father.

***

One afternoon, a particularly busy one, she was needed to repair a deep leg laceration on a patient in the emergency area of the clinic. When she entered the room, it took her a moment to realize who her patient was. He had grown a few inches, his hair had darkened a shade, and his face had lost all its boyish softness. But it was still Daniel, and he grinned at the look of complete surprise on her face.

"What happened? This is impressive." She was only half joking. The cut was deep and jagged and was going to need some careful stitching in order to minimize the scarring.

"Lost my footing and slipped down the side of a pitched roof," he answered. "The building is unfinished, so there were still some exposed nails."

"Ouch," she said sympathetically, and then, "I'm going to clean it, which won't feel too pleasant. Then I need to stitch it up."

She worked carefully and in silence, absorbed by her task, and she was pleased with the result when she finally finished. When she stood and stretched, she noticed Daniel was watching her intently. Uncomfortable, she busied herself cleaning up the mess and giving him instructions on how to care for the wound.

"Stay a few more minutes," she said over her shoulder as she carried out the dirty linens and instruments. "I'm going to mix up a topical medicine that will speed along the healing." She hurried out of the room and ran straight into Sam.

"An old friend of yours I think," he commented with a sparkle in his eye.

She blushed and kept going. Sam's gentle laughter followed her down the hall.

***

About a week later, Daniel appeared at the clinic again, this time with nothing more than a bruised thumb. "Hit it with a hammer." He had the good grace to look a little embarrassed.

"Um okay, I can get you something to reduce the bruising." She left the room and headed toward the pharmacy to mix up another salve.

Sam caught her eye and followed her. "Are you checking on his leg?" She knew he was referring to Daniel.

"No, he seems to have hit his thumb with a hammer," she said skeptically.

"Caeli, go out with the boy before he really injures himself trying to pretend to injure himself," Sam said laughing. "It's time for you to move on with your life."

"I have moved on," she said defensively. "I love my work. I love everything about it: the science, the patients, and the research. I'm totally satisfied with my life right now." This had seemed true just a few days ago, but now she was willing to consider that maybe there could be more.

"You keep yourself so busy that you have no time for fun, and you go home alone at night, and you don't let anyone get really close. Shall I go on?" he paused.

"No. I just cut him off, though," she sighed, referring to Daniel.

"He was there for me, doing all the right things, and I could barely even look at him."

"That was years ago, Caeli, and you were grieving. There is no right or wrong way to do that. In any case, he's here now, and I'm pretty sure it's not for that concoction you're mixing up." He nodded at the bowl she was holding.

She entered the exam room again and sat down to apply the salve. In the narrow world of her own grief, she had shut Daniel out so completely that she'd forgotten his dream of building things. She took a breath and asked, "What are you working on?"

"A new library," he answered.

She looked up at him and her eyes widened. "Really? That's wonderful!"

"The Council finally approved the structure, and I pushed hard to get them to look at my designs. They did, and now it's my vision that's going up," he said with a tinge of pride in his voice. "And there's something I want to show you. Maybe you could stop by after you're done today?"

She finished rubbing salve onto his barely bruised thumb and nodded, "I'd love to see it."

When she arrived at the construction site that afternoon, Daniel was on the roof, hammering something into place. His shirt was off, he was sweating, and she found herself staring. His seventeen-year-old, boyish body had been replaced by a man's broad chest, muscular arms, and trim waist. A piece of her that had been dormant during the fog of grief, and that she had largely ignored in the years following, suddenly leaped to life. He was beautiful in all the ways a man could be. And she wanted him.

At that moment he looked up and saw her there. He grinned, waved, and made his way carefully down the ladder and onto the ground. "Hi," he said shyly.

He self-consciously ran his hand through his hair, and she could only smile back.

"Come on. I want to show you." He moved toward the structure and she followed.

It was well after the regular workday had ended, and they were alone. There was wood dust everywhere, and tools were tucked out of the way, ready for the next day's use. Walls were partially built and not all the windows had been installed yet, but she could see the vision behind the structure, and it was brilliant and elegant.

The stone-carved entryway was ornately beautiful and welcoming. Inside, high-vaulted ceilings let in plenty of natural sunlight, and small glass enclosed alcoves created corners for reading or studying. Caeli was more than impressed. Daniel pointed things out to her and explained what would be where eventually, his voice animated and his excitement contagious.

As they wandered deeper into the building, her mind drifted back to the place it had been earlier, when he was still working in the last bit of sunlight. She thought about the sweat all over his body. He was still talking, but she was no longer listening.

"Daniel," she stopped him with a word. "Please."

He turned and looked at her. The intensity in his eyes was familiar and belonged to the boy she once knew, but his movements were more deliberate and sure. In one step he was in front of her, and then he was kissing her, and then his hands were on her body.

She pulled him closer, her fingers tangled in his thick, blond hair. Her pulse raced as heat spread through her belly. She ran her hands appreciatively down the smooth muscles of his back and felt his damp, hot skin.

"This isn't exactly how I imagined things," he said pushing her up against a dusty wall.

"This is how *I* imagined things," she whispered and threw an image directly into his mind.

"I think we can manage that," he answered.

Later, as they lay panting on the dirty floor, he laughed lightly and said, "You didn't get to see what I wanted to show you."

"I got to see it alright," she joked.

"I have something else to show you then." He kissed her forehead.

They awkwardly got up and readjusted their clothes, laughing and brushing wood dust off each other. He walked her over to a side room that had been framed out with high ceilings but no windows. "This is going to be the conservation room for recovered texts. We're dedicating the space to your parents," he said.

Tears welled up, and for a moment Caeli couldn't speak. Daniel had found the perfect way to honor her parents. "They would love this. 'Thank you' doesn't even come close," she said, resting her head on his chest.

"I've missed you Caeli." He kissed the tear off her cheek. "I've just been waiting for you to come back."

"I'm back," she said. "Sorry it took me so long."

# CHAPTER 8

They had been teenagers when they first fell in love. Now they had years to make up for, and neither wanted to waste a moment. One day spilled into another, and gradually their separate lives began to merge. At dinner one evening, Daniel asked her to go away with him for a few days. Neither had taken any time off in months, and Daniel's library project was finally nearing completion.

"After the dedication ceremony, let's hike into the mountains for a few days," he offered. "I'm sure Sam and the new students can hold their own." He waited expectantly for her answer, knowing how difficult it was for her to leave her work behind.

"Yes, let's do it," she answered him with resolve and smiled at the thought of what they'd do when they were alone.

A week later they were hiking through the dense forest toward the lower peaks of the northern mountain range. The weather was beautiful and sunny, as it generally was during the summer season, and they soon found a shady clearing to leave their packs. "Set up first, or start climbing?" Daniel inquired.

"What would Charlie say?" she laughed, referring to the camp counselor who had accompanied them on many expeditions in their teenage years. "You'll be too tired at the end of the day for these kinds of chores," she mimicked. "Better to prepare ahead of time."

By late morning they were on the side of the mountain. The route Daniel chose was part hike, part scramble, and part technical climb and took them about three hours to complete. Other than occasionally checking in with one another, they ascended in silence. Finding secure footholds, managing the cables, and the sheer physical challenge of the climb required all of Caeli's concentration.

When they finally reached the summit, the view was spectacular. To the north was the jagged mountain range, majestic with white caps and clouds skimming the higher peaks. To the east, in the distance, was the bright blue ocean, sparkling in the sunlight, and as far south and west as they could see were green, lush forests. Flowing streams cut curving patterns through the trees as the water made its way toward the ocean.

Caeli breathed in the pure air and stretched out on the gritty rock, smiling. Her muscles were fatigued, she was drenched with sweat, and she was utterly content. Daniel leaned back next to her and took her hand.

Her eyes fluttered closed, but a shift in Daniel's mood brought her out of her daydreams. He stopped rubbing her hand and sat up on his elbows. The tenor of his thoughts changed too. He suddenly seemed pensive and anxious. Caeli turned toward him with curiosity.

"Can't really hide anything from you can I?" he smiled.

"No. Out with it," she commanded.

He took a breath and said, "I want to build us a house."

She just stared at him, so he continued, "I know you love your childhood home, and I'd understand if you wanted to stay there, but I was hoping we could have our own home. And I was hoping it could be soon. I want to spend my life with you Caeli. I want to marry you, if you'll have me." His words rushed out, and he looked at her nervously.

"Of course I'll marry you!" she shouted, throwing her arms around him. "I can't think of anything I'd rather do." Touched by his nervousness, she kissed him and asked, "Did you actually think I'd say no?"

He laughed. "No. But you haven't answered me about the house. What do you think?"

"You'll design it?" she asked, more as a confirmation than a question.

"And build it," he answered.

"Then I will love it," she said, kissing his neck. "And I'm sure another young family will love my parents' home and make a wonderful life in it."

That night, as she and Daniel lay tangled in their sleeping bag under the starry sky, she whispered, "What do you think it's like out there?"

"I don't know," he said, following her gaze upward. "But I'd like to find out."

They were quiet for a moment, and then Daniel spoke again. "We're one very small civilization—well, two, really—sharing a relatively healthy planet in the middle of a huge, populated galaxy. We used to be part of that, and I think we should be again. Or at least we should be considering the possibility. We could probably learn from whoever is out there, and I think we'd have something to offer as well."

She leaned onto her side so she could look at him. "I didn't know you felt this way." They'd never really talked about it before.

He shrugged, "I wish the Council wasn't so immovable on the issue."

"They must still believe we'd be in danger," Caeli suggested.

"How do they really know? It's been so long."

"I wish I'd paid more attention to my parents' work," she sighed. "They spent their lives trying to give us back our history."

Daniel pulled her closer and said gently, "A lot of their research is being moved into the library. The Restoration Society still uses it. You can always go take a look."

She smiled at him. "Maybe I will."

"Anyway," he continued, "I'm not suggesting we behave recklessly and throw open our doors, so to speak. I think we should create some kind of long-term plan that includes the Amathi."

"I still don't understand why we've allowed this separation to go on for so long," Caeli said.

"The Council is well-meaning. I don't doubt that," Daniel answered. "But they are a like-minded group without enough perspective and with a very particular idea of how things should be done."

"Well, there's a forum coming up this fall. You should say something," she encouraged.

"Maybe I will," he grinned, echoing her words.

"Shake things up a little," she teased.

He laughed and then added more seriously, "Someone needs to."

***

A month later, Daniel's plans for the house were nearly finished. They sat together after breakfast one morning and enthusiastically added final touches to the drawing. Their wedding was now only weeks away.

Wedding celebrations were lively, anticipated community events that lasted late into the evening. Lia's family was helping to organize the neighbors who would bring piles of food, flowers for decoration, and instruments to make music.

Lia was designing Caeli's dress. Caeli had never been all that interested in clothing, but the pale-blue creation, hand embroidered with delicate flowers and trimmed with silver thread, was so stunning that she couldn't wait to wear it. She felt beautiful in it. And she wanted to look beautiful for Daniel.

During the ceremony she and Daniel would speak their vows to one another. Caeli had been nervously scribbling her thoughts down for days now, never quite satisfied with the results and sure they couldn't convey the depth of her feelings.

After the ceremony, the newly married couple was provided with all the leftover food and not expected to emerge from their home for days. Caeli was looking forward to this part almost as much as the ceremony, and she would often find herself grinning in the middle of some mundane task just thinking about it.

"I'm going to add another window here," Daniel said, interrupting her wandering imagination. Caeli nodded.

She got up from the table to fill her glass with water when they heard the first explosion. The house shook violently, and the water glass fell from her hand and shattered on the floor.

They looked at one another, stunned. Daniel was out the door first. A plume of smoke rose into the sky from the center of the settlement.

"That could be the Council building." He stared in the direction of the smoke. "I'm pretty sure they're in session today. I'm going to check it out."

She did not want him to go. Tentacles of icy fear crept up her spine, and her stomach twisted with dread. But her own sense of responsibility forced her to say, "I'm going to the clinic in case people are injured. Be careful!" she yelled after him as he began to run toward the town center.

Stretching her mind out toward the Council building, she was horrified to feel absolutely nothing. As she hurried toward the clinic, she swept her consciousness out in a broader circle and felt a rising panic from her people. Another explosion nearly knocked her off her feet, this time from an entirely different section of the town. Fear became blind terror as she raced forward.

Suddenly, she felt the wound to Daniel's chest as if it were her own and, gasping for breath, fell to her knees.

"Daniel, no!" she screamed out loud and in her mind.

Frantically she tried to get to her feet. She knew he was already at the Council building, and she couldn't make herself move fast enough.

"Please no," she pleaded. "I'm coming."

His life was bleeding out of him, and she would not get there in time. She collapsed to her knees. Then, laying her face on the ground, she let her consciousness completely merge with his. Time slowed.

"Don't leave me," she begged.

But he was slipping away.

"I love you." His voice echoed in her mind.

"Please, please no," she begged again.

She couldn't hold onto him. His voice was fading. The pain was fading.

"Caeli, survive this," he insisted. "Live."

She knew the second he was gone. An aching, gaping void replaced his consciousness. Weapon fire sounded around her, explosions rocked the buildings, and people ran through the streets in panic, but it was quiet in her mind as she lay unmoving on the ground.

*Live,* he had gently commanded.

*No. No, I don't want to,* she argued with him silently, *not without you.*

"Daniel," she whispered into emptiness.

When she finally lifted her head, the destruction around her came into sharp focus. Buildings had turned to rubble, and homes were burning. The world shook. People screamed.

Dazed, she staggered to her feet. A shred of survival instinct propelled her toward the clinic. Sam. She had to get to Sam. They could help. They could do *something.* As she stumbled forward, she stretched her mind out again in all directions and felt the terror and confusion in the minds of her people. And death, there was so much death.

She was several yards away when an explosion blew the doors off the clinic and threw her backwards onto the ground, unconscious.

# DEREK

## CHAPTER 9

Derek's heart hammered in his chest and he could feel the adrenaline coursing through his body. Caeli sat across from him, gazing vacantly out at the ocean, still swaying lightly to her own internal rhythm of grief.

"They're dead. They're all dead," she repeated, rocking back and forth with her arms wrapped tightly around her knees. "Daniel, Sam, Lia's family . . ." Tears streamed down her cheeks.

At first he couldn't move to comfort her, but when he regained control of his limbs, he leaned forward and pulled her into his arms. She closed her eyes and sighed.

"I'm tired," she whispered.

"I know." He stroked her back. "I'm so sorry," he said. They were inadequate words, and he wished he had better. Silently they walked back to the camp.

He convinced her to rest for a while, promising he would too, but his mind raced as he tried to untangle his own memories from hers. She settled herself on the hammock, and after a few shuddering sighs, her breathing became measured in sleep.

Derek leaned his head against a tree and felt the pain of her loss still echoing in his psyche. When he tried to close his eyes, another city with bombs falling and missiles flying filled his thoughts.

***

"Come on, come on!" he shouted over the deafening sound of exploding concrete and shattering glass. "Kat, move these people!"

He provided cover fire while Kat coaxed a terrified group of civilians out from a bunker and toward the waiting shuttle. They weren't pinned down yet, but they would be in about three minutes, Derek knew, just as soon as the Drokaran firing at them from the tower called in their position.

As they sprinted toward the ship, the starboard door slid open, and Kat herded the group inside. Derek followed behind. Once inside, he hit the sensor panel and the door slammed at his heels.

"Collins, go! Now!" he ordered his pilot.

"No!" Kat shouted, grabbing his arm. "The second group! We have to go back for them!"

The shuttle was only half full.

"Engage the shields and get us out," he reiterated to Collins, ignoring Kat and strapping himself into the copilot seat to bring the weapons system online.

"Derek, there are at least thirty people in that bunker," Kat pleaded.

"Kat, sit," he growled.

She threw herself into the jump seat and pulled the harness over her head. As the shuttle lifted off the ground, Derek locked onto the tower and fired, blowing the building into a mess of fiery rubble.

Then, just over the tree line, he saw the Drokaran drone.

He tried to get the weapons system to lock onto it, but it was moving too fast.

"Fuck, I don't have a shot!" he cursed as the small, deadly craft darted in and out of his grid. He fired anyway. Trees burst into flames, but the drone advanced through the smoke and debris. Derek slammed his fist into the side of the instrument panel.

The shuttle was gaining altitude quickly, but he could clearly see the drone as it approached the bunker. When it sent a payload of missiles directly into the structure, the shock wave from the blast jolted the ship. Derek squeezed his eyes shut, and behind him, Kat let out a small, pained sound.

Back on *Horizon* a day later, he found Kat in the gym, running as if her life depended on it. He leaned against the far wall and waited for her to notice him. When she finally finished her workout and stood in front of him, dark circles rimmed her eyes.

"They're dead. They're all dead," she said in a flat voice.

Twenty-two Mirans were being cared for in *Horizon*'s sickbay, but Derek just shook his head and whispered, "I know."

\*\*\*

Caeli yawned and stretched and then sat up, bleary-eyed.

"Did you have a nice nap?" Derek asked.

"I did," she nodded. Then she scowled at him. "But you didn't."

He shrugged and stared up at the clouds.

"Are you okay?" she asked gently, busying herself by stacking pieces of wood in the fire pit.

"Yeah, I'm fine," he nodded, but he was distracted. Caeli left him to his thoughts and went about her chores. A few minutes later she sat beside him and handed him a steaming bowl.

"Tea," she said, taking a sip of hers. "Medicinal, but also comforting and sweet." She smiled gently. "My mom used to make it for me."

He was about to say something when her expression changed. She put her bowl on the ground and sat up straight, tilting her head as if she were listening to something. He felt the hair on the back of his neck stand up, and he reached for his weapon.

"What's wrong?" he asked.

She glanced back at him. "Amathi. They're closer than they've been since I made camp here."

She stood up and so did he. "It's okay." She stopped him. "But I need to go see what they're doing."

"I want to come with you."

"Derek, you can't make the climb. There's a plateau just on the other side of the brook, but the path is steep and I have to go quickly." She was already lacing up her boots. He exhaled in frustration.

"Be careful," he said touching her arm. She gave him a tight grin and answered, "Don't worry. They won't see me." Then she slipped off into the woods behind the cave and out of sight.

Derek hated waiting. He paced around the fire pit, worried as he watched the movement of the sun across the sky. She was right, though. He couldn't have kept up with her. But being stuck back at the camp was maddening, and he couldn't sit still.

Wandering the short distance to the brook, he leaned against a rock and tossed pebbles into the water. He knew Caeli hadn't told him everything yet. When he let her memories settle next to the most violent of his own, shadow images still hovered at the edge of his consciousness. If he tried to pull one into focus, it dissolved. Finally, he gave up trying to sort them out and waited for her.

It was early evening when she found him still sitting by the brook. He couldn't read her expression.

"Sorry I was gone for so long. I got a few things for dinner." She shook her backpack lightly and turned to go back to camp. He followed.

"Caeli, is everything okay?" he asked while they sat by the fire and she prepared their food.

She didn't look at him but nodded. "It was a small group of Amathi soldiers. They were on the other side of the river coming through a pass, but heading in the opposite direction."

"Do you think they might be looking for my ship?" Derek asked, a knot of dread forming.

"It's possible," Caeli acknowledged hesitantly.

"Shit," he cursed under his breath.

"Or they could just be looking for ore deposits. Anyway, it would take some effort for them to get to this side of the river. It's why I chose to make camp here. We're okay. At least for a while."

*I don't want to run anymore.* Caeli didn't speak out loud, but Derek heard her as clearly as if she did. Her face held a haunted look he hadn't seen before, and despite her reassuring words, he knew she was more worried than she was letting on.

She passed him a bowl but didn't take one for herself. Anxiety poured off her, and he didn't have to be empathic to feel it.

Carefully, he put his bowl aside and turned to face her. "Caeli, how did you escape from Novalis?"

She looked in his eyes and then dropped her gaze to the ground. "I didn't."

# AFTER

## CHAPTER 10

A painful throbbing in her side pulled her out of the darkness. Someone was kicking her. She struggled to bring herself back from the fog of unconsciousness, but it was difficult. Her mind was hazy and her body felt heavy. A sharp burning smell seared her lungs and the metallic taste of blood filled her mouth.

The prodding in her ribs continued until she finally opened her eyes. After a moment of total confusion, the reality of what was happening, of what *had* happened, came crashing back. Caeli looked at the man kicking her. "Get up," he ordered harshly. She tried to comply, and when she wasn't fast enough, he grabbed her by the hair and pulled her to her feet. Pointing his weapon at her, he gestured with his head. "Move over there."

She staggered over to the small group of survivors who had been gathered together. They were seated on the ground, surrounded by several armed men. Caeli knew the men were Amathi by their accents. Her cloudy brain recognized that they were in uniform, a dark green color that would have camouflaged them in the surrounding forests. They were soldiers. An army of soldiers. And they had destroyed her home.

As soon as she reached the group, she sank to her knees and vomited. A searing pain tore through her skull, and when she reached around to touch the back of her head, her fingers came away bloody.

Familiar hands gently brushed the hair out of her face, and it seemed a small miracle that, amidst the destruction and death, Lia was at her side. They held hands tightly while silent tears spilled down their cheeks and Caeli retched the contents of her stomach out onto the dirty, bloody ground.

When the waves of nausea had passed enough for her to sit up and look around, she was struck by the silence. The huddled group was largely still. It was a pitifully small number of people, and if they were the only survivors, then the scope of destruction and loss was truly horrific. By Caeli's estimate, of the thousands of people in Novalis, only a few dozen remained.

The soldiers were working with efficient purpose. Some were standing guard, others were searching through buildings and rubble, and others were moving motorized vehicles into the streets surrounding the decimated town center. The only building still standing in the immediate area was the school. The attack had happened during the day. Most of the children were in school.

While she watched with increasing alarm, several soldiers opened the doors to the building, and hundreds of children were herded out of the structure into the waiting trucks. They moved in stunned silence. At least they were alive, Caeli tried to reassure herself. But a dark foreboding made her shiver, and she felt bile rise in the back of her throat again.

She struggled to her feet and, in a quiet but insistent voice, spoke to the soldier closest to her, "What are you doing with our children?"

He turned and pointed his weapon at her. "Sit back down."

She moved back to Lia but stretched her mind out to the children in an attempt to offer them some comfort. Their terror surged back at her, and she felt completely helpless.

When the children were loaded into the trucks, the convoy moved out of the settlement. About twenty soldiers remained behind with the small group of survivors.

As the hours passed, very few people were added to the group, and Caeli bitterly wondered why anyone had been saved at all. The Council members were all dead, and as she surveyed the people around her, she realized that most of the older and skilled members of her society were also gone.

Her thoughts began to disconnect from reality. A soothing numbness washed over her. On some level she knew she was in shock, and by the dazed faces of those around her, she recognized they were too. Anyone left alive had lost everything.

As the last bit of daylight filtered through the trees, she began an inner dialogue with herself, dispassionately weighing the pros and cons of staying alive. It would be easy enough to end her own life. With her mind, she could open a major artery and quickly bleed to death. It would be over before anyone else noticed, and both her people and the others would likely attribute it to injuries she received during the attack.

Ultimately she knew she should choose to live, but the fact that it was a choice, and at any time she could make a different one, was darkly comforting. She held the idea close.

When night fell, the soldiers ordered the group into the school. Several guards stood inside at the doors while voices and activity could be heard coming from outside. Numb and exhausted, the survivors huddled together and attempted to sleep, desperately needing the rest, but terrified of what the morning would bring. Curled next to Lia for both warmth and comfort, Caeli dozed fitfully.

*** 

The soldiers woke them at dawn. Caeli's first thought, when she felt the unforgiving floor of the schoolhouse beneath her instead of the enveloping warmth of her bed, was that Daniel was dead. He was dead, and his torn body lay cold and abandoned in the dirt. She whispered his name over and over in her mind until Lia caught her in an embrace. Her chest heaved, but it seemed all her tears had dried up and the only sound she could make was a low, strangled moan. Burying her head in Lia's shoulder, she struggled to breathe.

When the ragged group was ordered into the courtyard outside the school, Caeli and Lia stumbled to their feet. A few soldiers loaded supply vehicles, but most were packing their own gear and checking their weapons. When the men were ready, they marched their prisoners out of the settlement and onto the dusty road.

The pace was brisk and the day was warm. They became fatigued quickly but were not allowed to stop for several hours and only then for a hurried drink of water.

The soldiers had minimum contact with them at first, and when they did, it was with cold disdain, as if the survivors were somehow less than human. When someone stumbled, they were prodded up with a harsh word or the muzzle of a gun. No one was allowed to speak.

Caeli observed the soldiers without emotion, collecting information almost as if she were outside of her body but without the energy or interest in processing what it might mean. Many were young men in their late teens or early twenties. They were a highly disciplined group, well equipped for the trek with light packs, sturdy boots, and plentiful water.

As the day wore on, she noticed they were taking more of an interest in her people. Some of the young men glanced at them with what appeared to be simple curiosity, but others made her deeply uncomfortable. Their stares were filled with something darker that made her avoid eye contact and retreat within herself as much as possible.

By late in the afternoon, many Novali were near the point of collapse, and one young woman stumbled, painfully twisting her ankle. Caeli moved to the girl's side and knelt down next to her. "I can help you," she said, her instinct and training taking over. Laying her hands on the girl's ankle she could see an injury to the ligaments of the joint. The sprain would be easy to fix empathically, but Caeli wouldn't overtly show her gift in front of the Amathi.

Two soldiers were already behind her. One pointed his weapon at her head and demanded she move. Caeli stood to face him and, with the calm poise of someone with nothing left to lose, said, "I am going to stabilize her leg. If you want to stop me, shoot me."

A flicker of surprise passed over his face and was replaced quickly by anger. Before he could act, the other soldier ordered, "Give them five minutes." Both men moved back to the front of the convoy, and Caeli knelt down again.

A small group stood around Caeli and the injured woman. Someone was wearing a tunic style shirt. "Could you tear a long strip off your shirt?" Caeli asked. "I can make a binding with that."

The woman nodded and began to tease apart the hem to create a bandage while Caeli discreetly put her hands on the injured ankle and coaxed the tissue to heal. "Don't let on," she whispered and received a small nod in return.

Once the ankle was efficiently bound, Caeli helped the girl to her feet, supported her weight for a moment, and then stepped back. The girl walked forward with a slight limp, and then the whole group began to move again.

*\*\*\**

Caeli's aching head was still making her nauseous, and the suffocating heat of the day didn't help. When the late-afternoon sun finally began to sink, the cooling air was a welcome relief.

The convoy stopped at a clearing, and the supply vehicles formed a semicircle. The group was directed into the center of the circle and ordered to sit. A few guards stood up against the trucks and a few more created a perimeter on the open side. The rest began to unload supplies and set up a rudimentary camp.

She watched as they started a cooking fire and filled a large metal pot with water. While it rarely rained at this time of year, they set up a tarp and dropped their packs into neat rows underneath. Wooden boxes with food supplies came out of the truck bed, and vegetables and grains went into the pot, quickly filling the camp with the aroma of soup.

Caeli's stomach growled despite the nausea that had plagued her earlier. Her people were starving, but as the soldiers took turns serving themselves, nothing was offered to them.

Finally, several loaves of bread were unpacked and tossed to the hungry prisoners, with the warning that this was the meal for the night. Everyone had only a small piece. When the bread was gone, a bucket was filled with water and they were told to line up for a drink. A tin cup was tossed in, and the group quietly queued to have their share.

One soldier took a head count while Caeli waited. The same man who had given her a five minute break to care for the girl with the ankle injury now spoke in a dispassionate voice, "For any person missing in the morning, one from the group will be shot."

When Caeli put the cup back into the water after taking her turn and started back to her place in the clearing, the soldier she'd challenged earlier in the day blocked her path. His anger had cooled and was replaced by a chilling grin.

Caeli froze. A drop of sweat trickled down her back between her shoulder blades, and her mouth was suddenly dry despite the water she had just finished.

He grabbed her roughly by the arm and pulled her back behind the trucks into the woods a short distance away. Her eyes darted to the expanse of forest behind them.

"Go ahead, run," he taunted her.

But she couldn't run. She couldn't be responsible for someone else's death.

Her heart raced, and her stomach knotted with dread. He ran his thumb along the hammering pulse in her throat. She twisted away from him, and he grabbed a fistful of hair at the nape of her neck.

Her thoughts were panicked. She couldn't kill him or even render him unconscious and give away the secret of her gift. The soldiers would learn that she was dangerous. She would just make it worse for them all.

Revulsion filled her as he pushed her onto the ground. With all her being she wanted to fight him, but she forced herself to be still. The pungent smell of his sweat and her own fear stung her nostrils. When she felt his hot breath on her cheek, she turned her head away from him, closed her eyes, and retreated deep within her own mind.

# CHAPTER 11

After five days of grueling travel, the ragged survivors arrived at the Amathi settlement, half-starved and exhausted. As they walked toward the town center, they passed large fields of ripening grain and people with simple machinery working in the afternoon sun. Many stopped and stared with open curiosity.

Small but well-constructed houses increased in number, and they appeared neat and in good repair. Most had small gardens and many had children playing outside. This Caeli noticed particularly. The children laughed and played, and the sight of them shocked her in its normalcy. *How could these children be safe*, she raged in her mind, *when the children of Novalis had been ripped from their decimated homes?* She felt an indiscriminate anger twist in her gut, not at the children, but at the soldiers, the Amathi, the Novali Council, anyone and everyone who held responsibility for the horror that had happened.

The soldiers formed a loose perimeter and kept Caeli and the other prisoners moving. Buildings grew taller; some were several floors high, and they were efficiently arranged in city blocks. As she stared at the regular, rectangular shapes, Caeli thought of Daniel's library and how beautiful and elegant it was. Nothing here seemed beautiful. It was all functional and solid, but missing something she couldn't easily describe.

When she imagined the structure Daniel had so lovingly created shattered into rubble, her chest ached.

The group stopped in front of a large building constructed of solid cement blocks and were herded through the main entrance. As soon as Caeli was inside, she recognized that it was a hospital. The order and efficiency were familiar and comforting, and Caeli felt her body relax for the first time since the attack. The soldier who appeared to be in charge spoke for several minutes to one of the hospital staff and then ordered his men out of the building.

When the soldiers were gone, an older man addressed the survivors, scowling at them. Caeli wondered if his sour expression was because he did not want to interact with her people or because he did not like the condition of the group that had arrived on his doorstep.

"Our cafeteria space is being cleared, and we will provide each of you with a pallet and blanket. Shortly, my staff will examine you and treat any injuries. We'll prepare food and then someone from the general's office will be here to register your names and occupations." He motioned to a group of younger people and said, "Please follow my staff members. They will help get you set up."

His voice was controlled and his demeanor authoritative. The medical teams were already hurrying to follow his orders and accommodate their new charges, but Caeli got the impression they had been unprepared.

She moved numbly forward, following the medical staff down a long corridor, past exam rooms and workstations, and into the empty cafeteria. The smell of baking bread made her mouth water. There was a large cooking area off to her left, and when the group entered, the kitchen workers stopped what they were doing and stared. She caught the eye of one young woman, who looked down nervously and then returned to chopping.

Caeli took a blanket and sat in a corner with Lia. She wrapped herself in its warmth and leaned stiffly against the wall, watching the activity around her with detachment. Her eyelids grew heavy, but before she could doze, one of the cooks announced that food was ready. "Let's make a line here," he instructed. "Take a bowl and spoon, and then come to the counter for your dinner." His voice was gentle, and when it was Caeli's turn to take a bowl, she looked into his eyes and he didn't look away. She whispered a thank you and he nodded.

The bread was soft and warm and the stew thick with vegetables and grains. She had to force herself to eat it slowly so she wouldn't get sick. After the meal she and Lia found their place again in the corner. Neither of them had any words to offer the other.

*** 

Caeli awoke with a start, in a panic. Someone was gently shaking her arm. She jerked it away and sat up, sweating and gasping for breath. A startled young woman stammered an apology and whispered, "It's time for your examination."

She was at a hospital, not sleeping in the dirt. It was a young woman trying to help, not a soldier putting his hands on her in the middle of the night. It took Caeli a moment to get her breathing under control. Her heart hammered loudly in her chest, but finally she got up and followed. The young woman escorted her to one of the small rooms off the main corridor.

She waited only a few minutes before the man who had met them at the hospital entrance earlier in the day came into the room. He still wore his displeased expression, and just as before, Caeli couldn't tell why. He introduced himself as Dr. Kellan and invited her to sit on the examination table. He sat down opposite her in a chair, and the other young woman stood in the corner, prepared to take notes.

"Will you tell me your name?" he asked.

She wondered what the consequences of not answering would be, but somewhere inside she understood that this was her new reality. The control she'd had over her own life was gone. Defiance flared up in her, but she quickly batted it down. She was too exhausted, mentally and physically, to offer any resistance. "Caeli Crys," she answered.

"Caeli, are you injured?" Dr. Kellan asked her in a professional, but calming voice. She recognized the tone from her own interactions with patients and was comforted by this similarity.

"I had a head injury from an explosion, but it's fine now." She ran her hand through the tangled mess of hair on the back of her head and knew there was still dried blood matted in with the dirt.

"May I look?" he inquired, and she nodded.

He gently probed the back of her head with his hand. There was no evidence left of the injury save for the crusted blood. "It seems to have healed well. Are you having any blurred vision or headaches?"

"No," she answered.

"Okay. I'd like to do a more thorough exam now, so if you could change into this . . ." He pointed at a hospital gown folded on the counter. "Jana will help you." He motioned to the young woman in the corner.

"No," Caeli answered quickly, holding onto the edge of the examination table. The thought of it made her physically ill. Her heart began to race again, and she had to focus on breathing slowly and steadily to stop the rising panic.

"That's fine," he said without question or argument. "Maybe I could check you out a little just like this?"

She nodded, and he stood in front of her. "I'm going to listen to your heart and breathing with this."

She nodded again as he placed the end of the stethoscope over her heart and put the other end into his ears. She remembered reading about this type of tool in her medical books. Her people no longer needed these kinds of devices. If she wanted to, she could see and hear Dr. Kellan's heart with her mind. This simple thought gave her something to focus on while he took her pulse and shined a light in her eyes and ears.

"What do you see?" she asked before thinking about the question.

The doctor looked at her curiously. "I'm looking for fluid or infection in your ear, and checking to see that your vision is tracking and there are no issues with your eyes. Everything seems very normal."

It wasn't quite what she meant, but she didn't clarify her question.

"Could I feel your belly?" he asked. "Would you lie back for a moment?"

Reluctantly she did, and he gently pressed into her abdomen. She knew he was feeling for rigidity from internal bleeding. Next he pressed on her rib cage, and she winced. She hadn't been able to expend the energy to expedite the healing of her bruised ribs, and they were still sore.

"Your ribs could be broken," he said, looking concerned.

"They aren't," she answered with certainty.

He raised his eyebrows, skeptical, but nodded and said, "I have something that will help the pain."

"Thank you." She exhaled deeply and felt a wave of gratitude for his intuition and competence. He sent Jana off to get the remedy and sat back down opposite her, picking up the notes left on the counter.

"After we're finished here, Jana will take you to register with the general's office. How old are you, Caeli?" he asked with his professional voice again, taking notes.

"Twenty-four," she answered.

"Have you recently been in good health?"

"Yes."

"Is there anything I should know about your medical history?"

"No." She looked at the doctor and very much wanted to reach into his mind and understand his intentions. He was a perceptive man, and the facts were what they were. His people had nearly annihilated hers. He must know this. Maybe he was a good man, he probably was, but nothing would change that reality.

She was suddenly sure he was thinking the same thing, and the atmosphere in the room shifted uncomfortably. He opened his mouth to speak but hesitated. Then Jana entered the room and the moment passed. Caeli stood.

"Let me help you with this," Jana offered, holding a small vile of ointment.

She nodded, and as Jana approached, she lifted the right side of her shirt to reveal the faded purple bruises where days earlier the soldier had kicked her into consciousness. Jana gently rubbed the warm, soothing salve into her skin. With surprise, Caeli recognized the remedy from her own clinic.

"Thank you," she said and readjusted her clothing. "Where do I go next?"

Jana started toward the door and said, "Follow me. I'll take you there."

Jana led Caeli back down the hall to a small office. A young woman was seated behind the desk. She was attractive, with dark hair and eyes. Her hands moved constantly, brisk and efficient. "Name and occupation?" she asked.

"Caeli Crys, physician." She could appreciate not wasting words.

The woman looked at her and raised her eyebrows but didn't comment. After recording the information, she continued, "You will be housed with Nina Johanson and her family. After the general speaks tomorrow, you'll be escorted there." The woman looked down and continued with her note taking.

Caeli knew she was being dismissed, but she stayed. "Where are our children?"

The woman looked back up at her and answered curtly, "They've all been placed."

"With families?" she persisted.

"Yes."

"They had families," she said and walked out the door.

# CHAPTER 12

The next morning, Caeli felt more awake and alert than she had in the days since the attack. After breakfast, the prisoners were gathered together and escorted to the large town square by a small group of soldiers. There, Caeli noticed details that she hadn't the day before. This settlement was in a valley on the south side of a large mountain range. She knew they had traveled north and inland and wondered briefly if the winters here were colder than where she had grown up. The town itself was considerably more developed and populated than Novalis.

Hundreds of Amathi were already assembled outside. A high platform was set up in front of a barrack-type building, and there were soldiers positioned at the corners. The prisoners were kept together in the far corner of the square, behind the rest of the audience. Within moments the general appeared, surrounded by armed guards, and a regiment of soldiers stood at attention beside the stage facing the podium.

Caeli was not surprised to find that the "general" was Marcus. He looked somewhat older and leaner than the last time she had seen him, seven years ago at the last delegates meeting in Novalis, but his presence still made her deeply uneasy. She also noticed that his brother was absent.

His guards moved to his side as he stepped to the center of the platform, and the crowd went silent. *Interesting that he feels the need to be surrounded by armed men in his own settlement*, Caeli thought to herself.

"My people, good morning," he began with a somber voice. "It is with a heavy heart that I tell you a battle has occurred." There was absolute silence in the courtyard.

"I have suspected for some time that the Novali were preparing to invade our settlement and reintegrate us into their culture," he continued. The assembled crowd emitted a collective gasp.

*What?* Caeli looked around, appalled. Could the Amathi actually believe such a thing about her peaceful people?

Marcus paused and nodded at the murmuring crowd, then held up a hand to silence them once more.

"But our army has prevailed!" he shouted with a jubilant smile on his face. On cue, the regiment of decorated soldiers pivoted in unison to face the crowd and the mass of people erupted into cheers.

A first glimmer of rage now competed with the other emotions Caeli was so desperately trying to hold at bay, and her fists clenched in frustration. But when she looked around, not everyone in the audience was cheering with enthusiasm. Some of the faces around her were tight with fear and suspicion.

Marcus raised a triumphant fist in the air and continued, "Those who wished to subjugate us have been beaten! Those who tried to keep us from achieving our greatness as a civilization have been beaten!"

The crowd was frenzied now, stomping and clapping. Marcus allowed them several moments of celebration before he held up his hands and recaptured their attention.

"War is an ugly business," he continued, his smile now gone and his tone serious, almost regretful. "But we have done our best to save the innocent. Hundreds of small children were rescued from the battle. As we speak they are being placed with loving Amathi families." The crowd nodded its approval.

Then Marcus gestured at her small, pathetic group. "These young survivors are victims as well." He paused and shook his head in dismay. "For generations the Novali leaders have been deceiving their young people, filling their heads with lies about us."

Caeli could feel the eyes of the crowd boring into her. Marcus continued speaking, "The youth of Novali think we are inferior. They have been taught to fear and hate us. We must show them that we are not the enemy."

Caeli wanted to cry out in frustration. She wanted to scream that Marcus was a dangerous, vile criminal, and it was the Amathi who were being lied to. Her people had been slaughtered! She wanted to announce the truth to the whole crowd. But as quickly as her righteous anger flared up, it dissipated. What good would it do to speak the truth? Who would believe her? *And besides, the truth wouldn't change a thing,* she thought bitterly. *It wouldn't bring back the dead.*

She realized Marcus was still speaking and caught his final words. "We only did what was necessary to protect ourselves and our way of life. Be at ease! The threat that has loomed over us for so many years is over!" He smiled at the crowd and then turned and walked off the stage with his guards following closely.

Slowly the crowd began to disperse, and her group was escorted back to the hospital, where the woman who had registered their names the evening before waited. She wore a uniform similar in color and design to that of the general.

What seemed just a style choice the night before now had a new meaning. This woman was part of the military, part of the organization that had destroyed her home and her life. Caeli's anger was becoming a familiar, consoling presence.

The small group was seated. As they waited to be called individually to meet their host family, Caeli found Lia again. "Let me know you're okay?" Lia pleaded. She could feel her friend's panic at the thought of being separated.

"I will," Caeli promised.

When her name was called, she stood and went forward. There was a young woman waiting with three small children in tow. "I'm Nina," the woman offered, her expression blank. "These are my children: Cory, Micah, and Lily."

"Hello," Caeli answered. The two older boys observed her with open curiosity, and she forced herself to smile at them. They were beautiful, with dark, softly curling hair and wide, brown eyes.

She and Daniel would *never* have children. The unbidden thought nearly brought her to her knees and she had to look away. Swallowing, she took a deep breath and tried to regain control of her emotions. Nina stood silently, and her face visibly softened.

"Let me take you to my home," Nina suggested graciously.

They walked for almost a mile away from the center of the town and arrived at a cluster of small houses. Each had space in the yard for a small garden and plenty of room for children to play. Cory and Micah ran ahead to their own front door and tumbled inside.

Just before Caeli entered the house, she thought, *How can this be?* Everything had changed. Her home was destroyed, her dreams for the future were gone, and everyone she'd ever loved, except for Lia, no longer existed. The disorientation was staggering, and she could barely put one foot in front of the other to walk inside. She did not notice her surroundings.

Nina put the sleeping baby she was carrying into a large basket in the kitchen and turned toward her with concern. "Let me take you to your bed to rest. I'll show you the washroom as well. Please?" Nina started down the hall, and Caeli numbly followed.

"Here is the washroom, and this is the bedroom. The older children sleep in one room, but I thought you would prefer to be in here with me. We only have two bedrooms," Nina said apologetically, "and the children tend to be in and out of theirs to play, so I thought . . ." Her voice trailed off.

"This will be fine. Thank you," Caeli answered. Suddenly she wanted nothing more than to be alone. She could feel despair closing in around her, despair much darker and deeper than what she had experienced after the death of her parents. It was all consuming and threatened her very sanity. She sank down onto the bed set in the corner of the room and stared into nothing. Nina discreetly left the room, closing the door behind her.

Over the next few days, Caeli was only dimly aware of Nina coming and going, sometimes with the baby and sometimes without. Once, the older children followed their mother into the room, only to be gently turned out.

It was dark and then it was light. Nina would bring her food, which was left untouched, and then quietly remove it again before it spoiled. Caeli couldn't bring herself to drink the water, and she became feverish and dehydrated. Her loss felt so great, it was an abyss, and when she looked at it, it threatened to pull her into blackness.

The only other thing she felt was a blinding rage equally as intense as her grief. She wanted to wreak as much destruction as *they* had. She would pace the room contemplating the ways she could reach Marcus and kill him, or she would imagine the entire army burning inside their barracks. The madness of her own thoughts horrified her, but she had no control over it. Then all emotion would leave her, and she would be exhausted, nearly incapacitated.

Finally, one afternoon, Nina came and sat on the edge of the bed. "Do you want to live?" she asked with firm directness.

"I don't know," Caeli answered truthfully.

"Let's just start with today." Nina looked into her eyes. "Do you want to live *today*?"

She nodded at Nina and whispered, "Yes," and at once this became the truth. She became aware of the condition of her body: dirty, depleted, and weak. Then other small realities from the outside world began to filter in. She heard the children's voices as they played in the yard, she smelled the food cooking in the kitchen, she looked down at the baby cooing to herself in her basket by the bed, and she felt life begin to reassert itself.

Caeli looked at Nina's concerned face and realized that for days this woman had been quietly attempting to care for her. She was a stranger in Nina's home, and yet there seemed to be no resentment or fear. She felt a wave of gratitude and opened herself to the simple human compassion that she was receiving. When she tried to sit up, she was immediately dizzy. Nina reached out to her and then said, "I've filled the bath. Let me help you."

Nodding, she allowed herself to be guided into the next room. She could barely move, and Nina had to help her out of her filthy clothes and into the tub. The water was warm and a cake of aromatic soap sat on the ledge. Caeli breathed in the sweet scent of wild flowers. She had nearly forgotten that pleasure of any kind existed and sank into the water with relief. Nina gathered the clothes from the floor and said, "I'll bring a towel and fresh clothes for you. Please take as long as you like."

Caeli used the soap generously to wash her hair and scrub her body. She felt a twinge of embarrassment at how dirty she had been, and how incapacitated, but she was part of Nina's household now, and this gave her something to cling to. *One moment at a time*, she coaxed herself, *one breath at a time*. And Daniel's voice echoed again in her mind: *live, Caeli*.

She finished washing and carefully climbed out of the tub. Afterward, still weak and dizzy, she made her way to the kitchen. Nina smiled at her and placed a plate and cup in front of her. She hadn't been interested in food for days, but suddenly she wanted nothing more.

The children were at the table, quiet but squirming with excitement. Caeli waited for her host to sit down before picking up her spoon. Her own manners were deeply ingrained, and she wanted to see if there were any rituals that the family practiced before meals. They held hands for a moment in silence and then began to eat.

Caeli tried to help Nina clean up afterwards but was firmly sent back to bed. Stretching out her mind to find Lia, she offered a peaceful image of this home and the children to her friend before drifting off. For the first time in days, she actually slept soundly.

*\*\*\**

The next morning they began what would become a routine over the next few weeks. She would prepare breakfast for the older children while Nina fed the baby. They would all dress and then walk Cory to school. Caeli would continue on, taking Micah and the baby for a long morning walk while Nina went back home to tend to her chores. The smell of the baby's clean hair; Micah's laughter as he explored the landscape and looked for tiny animals, stones, and other treasures; and the fresh morning air were all simple things she looked forward to each day.

She began to pay attention to details about this civilization. She learned that large families were encouraged and children greatly celebrated. These children began their formal education at four years old in a school administered by the government.

The government likewise controlled most of the food supply. She would pass by the large-scale fields and farms during her daily walks. While small kitchen gardens were common around the homes, most food had to be purchased at carefully regulated markets.

Dressed in Nina's clothing and caring for the children, Caeli was able to wander about relatively unnoticed. The people seemed hard working and industrious, and when she passed a group in the fields or at the markets, they would wave and smile before returning to their tasks. They were more physically diverse than the Novali, who tended to mostly be fair haired and blue eyed, but otherwise, from the outside, there was nothing to distinguish one group from the other.

Occasionally she would come upon someone from her home. She would feel them in her mind, their whispering voices gently humming in her consciousness. Uncertain what to do when they encountered each other, they would simply find comfort in their connection.

At ease in the countryside or on the wooded paths of the forest, Caeli rarely ventured near the town center. It made her deeply uncomfortable to be anywhere near Marcus and his army. She knew this was irrational. They could be anywhere and everywhere, but she still had to avoid the barracks, factories, and other military facilities.

Instinctively she began to take note of various plants and herbs on her walks, and she reviewed their medicinal uses in her mind. There were many she did not recognize, and she itched to research them.

In the late morning, while the children napped, she would help Nina in her garden, with the wash, or with any of the other endless domestic chores. She was careful at first not to talk about home, but over time they began to share small pieces of personal information with each other. Nina's husband had been killed eighteen months earlier in a farming accident, and he had never met his daughter. Because she had been left alone with three small children, Nina received food and clothing vouchers from the government, and she wasn't required to work outside the home until the baby went to school.

Nina had family nearby, and they shared a meal together once a week. Nina insisted that Caeli come to these gatherings. The first time, the conversations were strained and the family was very cautious around her, but they were a close, warm group, and that quality soon outweighed any suspicions they might have had.

One afternoon during the weekly family meal, she offered to watch the children play outside while some of the other adults cleaned the kitchen. The extended family rotated houses for these gatherings, and this one was at Nina's brother Jon's home. She was surprised when he joined her outside and sat on the bench next to her.

"I don't want to make you uncomfortable," he began, "but I'd like to ask you a question."

She didn't answer but turned to look at him.

"What does the *change* enable you to do?" he asked with a calm directness.

She had to make a decision. Should she evade the question completely or trust him with some information? Did he have some purpose, other than curiosity, in asking her this? Would she be putting her people at risk if she shared anything? She couldn't sense any deception or malice coming from him, but without prying further into his mind, she couldn't be sure. And she *wouldn't* violate his thoughts. Possibly, this wasn't a wise choice anymore, she knew, but her moral code was just too deeply ingrained.

Sensing her discomfort and indecision, he added, "I think there have been some inaccuracies spread about your people." This was a gross understatement, but maybe she could plant some small seeds of truth. Maybe some of these people would be willing to hear them.

"I am a healer," she offered. "I can use my mind to see inside the human body and make diagnoses, and sometimes I can use it to actually effect a change." Facing him she added, "I'm not sure I feel comfortable with anyone else knowing this."

He nodded. "The general is trying to learn all he can about your people, and I'm sure his purposes are not altruistic."

She understood that Jon was reciprocating her trust with this piece of information. It also fed her suspicion that Marcus had an insidious purpose for the Novali survivors. She doubted her people had been brought here only to seamlessly disappear into Amathi society.

Jon continued with another question, "Are you able to use any sort of mind control?"

She raised her eyebrows with surprise and answered, "No, of course not. None of my people could do anything like that.

And even if we could, we would never use our gift in that way." She hoped she sounded reassuring, not indignant.

"I suspected as much." He looked at the children playing in the yard. "I want a future for them," he said, and his voice was filled with unspoken meaning.

"I'd like that for *our* children too," she added, her voice breaking.

"I'm so very sorry." He looked out at the mountain range. They sat for a few moments in silence, and then he went back inside.

# CHAPTER 13

One morning after returning from her walk with the children, she stood at the kitchen sink washing and chopping vegetables from the garden. The front door was open to let the breeze in, and also so she and Nina could hear Micah playing on the front steps. Suddenly, the little boy burst into the house and shouted with excitement, "There's a soldier coming!"

Caeli stood frozen at the sink, and the knife in her hand clattered to the ground. Paralyzed with terror, she began to shake uncontrollably. Nina led her to the table and sat her in a chair. "I'll go see what he wants."

She could hear Nina speaking with the man in a voice that sounded concerned but not afraid. Nina returned to the kitchen and sat in the opposite chair. "Caeli, I know this soldier. His name is Finn. I've known him since we were children, and he's a good man. He's coming to take you to the infirmary. You're going to start working there."

She tried to process this information while attempting to get her heart rate under control. "Okay," she whispered. Then, "I feel sick."

"Let me get you some water," Nina offered, and she nodded.

Her hands were trembling so badly she could barely hold the cup and Nina had to help her so it wouldn't fall to the ground and shatter. She could hear Micah talking animatedly to the soldier outside, and she had to force herself to get up and walk to the door. She did not want this man to see that she had very nearly just fallen apart, but it was all she could do to keep from running into the bedroom and hiding like a child.

She looked desperately at Nina, who took her hand and squeezed. "I know," Nina said. "I promise it will be okay." *That's a promise no one can keep*, Caeli thought to herself, but there wasn't a choice, and so they walked to the door together.

The young man was dressed in the impressive uniform of the Amathi military and wore his weapon comfortably slung over his shoulder. He had light brown hair that was cut short, like all the soldiers she had encountered, and hazel eyes. He was of average height and solidly built, and his skin was a few shades darker than hers. She did not recognize him, and this fact provided so much relief that she nearly cried.

When she stepped outside, his playful demeanor with Micah changed noticeably and he greeted her with professionalism. "Good morning, ma'am. I'm Lieutenant Finn Braden, and I'd like to escort you to the infirmary."

She nodded, unable to find her voice. Nina squeezed her arm gently. "Finn says this is just an orientation today, so I'll see you in a few hours."

Caeli leaned down reflexively to give Micah a hug. The little boy planted a sloppy kiss on her cheek and ran off to play, leaving her with nothing to do but follow the man in front of her.

Finn seemed to genuinely want to put her at ease. He tried to make casual conversation while still maintaining his respectful, professional tone, but she could only utter one-word answers at best. Walking alone with him, she could barely keep her panic under control. She reminded herself that Nina trusted him and she trusted Nina, but his uniform, his weapon, and her memories kept her on edge.

Finally he stopped talking and just walked beside her. As they approached the town center, her anxiety level began to rise again, and she stopped moving altogether when they were in sight of the barracks. He turned to her and coaxed her forward with a low, gentle voice that one might use for frightened children or skittish animals. "The hospital is right here. I'll walk you in. I know Dr. Kellan is eager to work with you."

They entered the infirmary building, and the familiar setting immediately put her at ease. *This* she knew. *This* she could manage. She turned to Finn and tried to see through his uniform and simply respond to his kindness. "Thank you," she said.

He nodded earnestly and then handed her off to Dr. Kellan, promising to return later in the day to escort her back.

Kellan wore his displeased expression, and Caeli had to wonder if gruff was just his natural state. She tried to be as unassuming as possible, since there was a good chance she would be spending a significant amount of time with this man.

"Are you feeling well?" he inquired. "No headaches, ribs all healed?" She was surprised he remembered her initial injuries so accurately. Maybe he'd reviewed his files before she arrived.

"Yes, thank you," she replied.

"Today, I thought we'd get you acclimated with the physical facility. I'm going to have Jana, one of my medical students, show you around a bit. Do you remember Jana?"

"Yes, I do," she smiled at Jana, who had appeared from one of the exam rooms.

"Bring her to my office when you've finished." He nodded at them and walked briskly away.

They were awkward with one another at first, but soon her comfort with all things medical, and Jana's forthcoming and efficient demeanor, put them at ease. The building was logically organized into an emergency wing, wards for critically ill patients, a pharmacy, a surgical suite, and an area for routine care and exams.

The emergency area was buzzing with activity when they entered, and no one gave them a second glance.

"This is the only major hospital in Alamath," Jana explained. "We handle all the emergencies from the army barracks, the outlying farming towns, and the city proper. There are other small clinics, but they can't manage major trauma or illness, so we get it all here."

Caeli shook her head, momentarily disoriented by the sheer size of the space and the frenetic energy swirling around her.

Jana noticed Caeli's stunned expression. "You'll get used to it," she said.

When they entered the pharmacy, Caeli's interest was piqued, and when Jana couldn't thoroughly answer her all questions, they spoke with one of the other doctors. Medicine here seemed more specialized, Caeli observed. At home she prepared her own remedies, dealt with any trauma, and also followed the wellness care of all her patients.

Jana explained that here, the medical students had a solid understanding of all parts of the practice, and would then choose an area on which to focus.

"Dr. Kellan's in charge of the whole facility, but he specializes as a surgeon. I'm mostly interested in emergency care," Jana explained.

Caeli had never thought about choosing only one area to focus on and hoped she wouldn't have to right away.

The critical care ward was quiet; the silence punctuated by the soft beeping and hissing of machinery. Caeli's eyes widened at the array of monitors and devices used to gather information, and at the number of people so grievously ill or injured. She suspected her practice here was going to be dramatically different from what she did at home, and she felt slightly overwhelmed again.

When they finished their tour, Jana dropped her at Dr. Kellan's office. He was seated at his desk, engrossed in reviewing his notes. He glanced up when they entered and then returned to his notes. "Thank you, Jana. Please sit down, Caeli," he ordered without looking at them. Jana left the room, and Caeli sat and waited patiently for the doctor's attention.

Several long moments later, he put down the papers and looked at her. "This is what I'm thinking. I don't know your skill level or training, I don't know how people here will feel about being treated by you even if you are competent, and truthfully I have more students than I can manage right now," he stated bluntly. "However, we certainly need the extra hands, and I have a professional curiosity about how your people practice medicine, so I'm going to have you shadow me. Speak up if you have questions, don't get in the way, but also talk to me about what you would do if you were at home. Just do that part discreetly, okay?"

She was startled by his directness, but also pleased by it. She knew where she stood at least. "I can do that," she answered.

"Generally, I start my day reviewing the care of our critically ill patients, but then I leave it to their team. I'm involved in any serious emergencies, and I still take on the more complicated surgical cases. Your picture of things will be a little skewed by my own specialty, but I'll make sure you get a little time in the pharmacy and doing some wellness care. Now in two minutes or less, tell me what your typical day was like in your clinic," he demanded.

She raised her eyebrows and wondered how much information to reveal. It seemed that Dr. Kellan's only agenda was caring for patients and running his hospital, but she really didn't know him at all. She kept her response truthful but simple. "Our medicine is much more integrated, and most of our care is about health and wellness. We have very few trauma cases and virtually no long-term, critically ill patients. I generally spend my day consulting with patients about their health, researching pharmacology, and occasionally responding to emergencies . . ."

When she noticed that she was speaking about her work in the present tense, she became silent. The crush of loss threatened again, not as intensely as it had in weeks past, but in a different way. She suddenly missed Sam profoundly. She gripped the sides of the chair until her knuckles turned white in an attempt to keep her emotions under control. Unable to speak, she looked away and focused on her breath.

Dr. Kellan cleared his throat, obviously sensing her distress. "Well, I look forward to hearing more. Are you able to be here at six a.m. tomorrow?"

She nodded, rising from the chair. Dr. Kellan also rose and walked around the desk. "Follow me. I believe the good lieutenant is waiting to take you home."

She went outside into the afternoon sun and found Finn waiting for her. She felt more at ease in his presence now, relatively certain he was simply going to walk her home, but she was still wary. Somewhere close by were the soldiers who had destroyed her civilization and murdered her people. Was

Finn part of that? She couldn't ask, and in truth, she didn't really want to know. Nina had used the words *good man* when describing him. Could a good man be party to that?

Her head swam with contradictions. Most of the people she had met so far *were* good people. Fundamentally they seemed to value the same things she did: a love for their children and families, a desire to do their work well, a sense of community. And yet Marcus had engendered enough fear and hatred in enough young men to convince them to commit atrocities. She didn't understand and thought that maybe she never would.

When they arrived back at Nina's house, a wave of comfort washed over her. It was beginning to feel a little bit like her home too, and this realization filled her with gratitude. In the six weeks she had been here, she had grown to love Nina and her children. She wanted them to have a future. She wanted there to be hope.

***

In the following days, a new routine was established. She would leave the house in the morning just as the children were waking up and head to the hospital. For a week or so, Finn would be waiting to walk her there and back, but soon she was left to make her own way.

Her days began just as Dr. Kellan had described, by reviewing the most critically ill patients. She struggled with the fact that she could significantly accelerate their healing if she chose, but she was reluctant to express the full extent of her empathic skill. Often, during each day, there were more emergencies than the staff could manage at once and their finely tuned triage skills were put to the test.

Dr. Kellan did not need to perform surgeries every day, but he, and therefore she, would often observe his staff during interesting or complicated cases. She knew she was gaining the doctor's respect. Her questions were thoughtful, and they revealed her extensive knowledge of human anatomy; her diagnostic skills were strong even without using her inner vision; and her curiosity about their remedies, tools, and procedures highlighted her keen intellect.

One early morning, after she had been working at the clinic for just over a month, a frantic mother came into the emergency unit with her toddler. The boy could not stand up straight as he was experiencing severe abdominal pain. With one touch, she knew the cause. "Get Dr. Kellan quickly!" she demanded of the unit assistant. The urgency in Caeli's voice made the startled assistant scurry out of the room, returning moments later with the doctor.

"Intussusception," Caeli said to him quietly under her breath. In her mind's eye, she could see the child's twisted intestine as clearly as she could see his tormented face. Kellan looked at her sharply and began his exam, gently asking the mother about the boy's last several hours.

"Rebound tenderness, loss of appetite, fever. Appendicitis," he declared.

"I promise you I'm right," she argued insistently, but softly. She had never challenged his judgment before. He was an excellent doctor and was nearly always correct, but not his time. She could not let this child die, and that was a real possibility if he didn't listen to her. "Please, trust me," she begged.

"He'll need surgery either way. Let's prep. Caeli, scrub in," he ordered.

She did as she was told and was ready in the surgical suite when they brought in the unconscious boy. Dr. Kellan looked pointedly at Caeli and made a midline incision. She exhaled with relief knowing he was treating intussusception. After the initial tension that generally existed among the team members in the operating room before they got into a rhythm, the surgery was unremarkable and they finished with relative ease.

Once the boy was resting comfortably, his grateful mother at his side, Dr. Kellan asked Caeli to join him in his office. "Shut the door," he said when she entered.

"How did you know with such certainty?" He got right to the point.

She looked down and knew that he was too astute to settle for anything but the truth. Working with him these past several weeks, she knew all he wanted was to take care of people in the most efficient, professional, competent, and compassionate way possible.

She had to trust someone. She cared about these people, and she needed to speak the truth. "Seeing inside the human body is part of my skill. It's a well-developed skill, and I can diagnose almost anything with it."

"Is that all?" he asked, his face blank.

"I can heal with my mind, but even if I were at home, I wouldn't do that very often. It requires quite a lot of energy," she finished.

He raised his eyebrows. "I understand why you might want to keep that hidden here."

"Please know that I *will* use it if I have to. I couldn't let someone else die to keep my secret," she said earnestly.

"That will be entirely your decision. I won't ask that of you, ever." There was deeper meaning behind his words and she understood that he was committing to protect her. She looked at him and whispered a heartfelt thank you and then stood up to leave. There was always so much to do, and if others were busy, she needed to be as well.

"Caeli, this is a dangerous place. Take care," he warned her in a low, serious voice.

She nodded and went back to work.

# CHAPTER 14

Caeli and Nina were in the kitchen preparing for the weekly family gathering, filling jars with fruit preserves. Even though Caeli had been working long hours, she still tried to find time to take walks with Micah, Lily, and Cory as often as she could. On one of their excursions they found a berry patch and gathered a generous amount to take back home. The late berries would be a welcome treat in the coming winter months.

In her new home, the winters were long and cold. This day, six months after her arrival, had a crisp feel to it and she knew that the fall season was quickly turning to winter. She had to admit, she was looking forward to the snow. Once, during a hike in her teenage years, her group trekked far enough north to experience real cold, and she had played in the snow like a child.

Her memories of home were at times vividly clear, and on other days seemed as if they belonged to another lifetime. When Nina's extended family began to arrive for their weekly dinner, Caeli was in a quiet mood. Lost in her thoughts, she stirred the jam. Her own family, Sam and Daniel especially, felt so close today that she expected to see them walk through the door, and when they didn't the ache in her chest took her breath away.

After dinner, Caeli, the children, and Nina's brother Jon went for a walk. When they reached an isolated field some distance from the house, they stopped to let the children run and play chase, then found a long, solid log and sat down.

Jon began to speak right away, "Caeli, there are people here who understand how dangerous Marcus is and who also believe that what was done to your people was horrific. This is not the kind of world most of us want. Some of us are trying to make changes." He had her full attention.

"No one talks about it." She turned to him and waited for more.

He sighed. "Marcus has created a culture of fear. People who disagree with him or speak out openly tend to disappear. He's smart, though. He supports families, he makes sure there is enough food, he keeps the infrastructure functioning, he speaks about this idealistic, technologically advanced civilization he imagines for our future, *and* he's built a strong, well trained, extremely loyal army."

"Why destroy my people? We never posed any kind of threat to you." Her voice sounded pleading.

"There is not, nor will there ever be, justification for that," Jon answered emphatically. "Marcus played on our own fears. You have abilities that we don't. We had to trust that your people would never misuse them. Over time Marcus spread what I suspect were mostly rumors. Tales of the delegates' minds being read against their will while they were visiting, a plan for reintegrating our peoples that completely subjugated the Amathi, your Council using mind control on his brother Dimitri to influence decisions. There's more, but I think you get the picture. Marcus's close circle would lie and kill for him. In fact, they have," he said pointedly.

"I would say so," she acknowledged.

"Even before the attack on your settlement, we suspect he actually killed his brother. Or had him killed," Jon admitted.

She was not entirely surprised by this piece of information. She'd wondered about Dimitri and assumed that somehow Marcus had wrestled control from him. It didn't seem too much of a stretch to imagine Marcus had actually murdered his own brother.

"Marcus returned from the last Council meeting seven years ago and said your people had detained Dimitri. He said he continued to try and negotiate for Dimitri's release until he learned of his death about a year later." Jon looked at her pointedly. "I doubt that Dimitri was ever detained at your settlement?" It was not really a question.

"No, of course not," she confirmed. "I was there when the last delegates' meeting ended, and the Amathi left all together. Dimitri was alive and well."

Jon nodded. "I wish we had been able to see Marcus for who and what he was much sooner, because now he has a very solid base of power and a very clear agenda that he seems to be implementing step by step."

There wasn't much she could say in response to this. Nothing could change the events of the last six months now.

"A group of us have been meeting, very quietly, to explore possibilities," Jon looked at her intently. "We would like for you to join us."

"Who is *we*?" she asked immediately.

"I can't tell you that. You would have to take the same vow and agree not to reveal the identities of anyone in the group for any reason. I *can* say that there will be some familiar faces," he added. "You must understand how imperative it is that we protect ourselves."

"Yes, I understand that. How will I know what to do, where to go?" she asked.

"So you are interested in joining us?" He obviously needed her word before giving out any other information.

"I am," she said, knowing she had just committed to something very dangerous and certainly much bigger than herself. But it felt right.

Jon nodded. "We are meeting at midnight tonight at the Stefans' barn. Do you know where that is?"

"No." She shook her head.

"Then come to my house a little before and we'll walk together," he offered.

"Does Nina know about this?" she asked.

"She suspects, but she's not part of the group, so she has no real information," he sighed. "She's pretty sheltered out here on her farming homestead. She's been well taken care of since her husband's death. He was a man who kept his nose down and did his work. I don't know what it would have taken to get him involved. Maybe you," he shrugged.

"Why me?" she asked.

"You're real. Your very presence speaks a truth that many people over here would rather ignore. Aaron—that was Nina's husband—was a fair man and a good father. I think he might have eventually taken a stand," Jon said.

"Is that why you want me to join your group? I'm the evidence?"

"No. We're already convinced. You can provide pieces of information, fill in some of the gaps in our knowledge probably, but we have enough of our own evidence. We want you because you're strong, a survivor, and I think you want a better future for all our people. I think you would be willing to stand up for that." He got up. The children had tired of their game, and it was time to start back.

"I'll be there," she promised.

***

That night she left the house silently. Caeli's stomach was in knots and she was shivering from the cool air when she arrived at Jon's. The night was dark and silent. In years past, she had enjoyed sitting outside in the stillness. She'd look up at the stars, feel the vastness of the sky, and still have confidence in her own sense of place. Now that the security of home had been torn away, the experience was different. As she walked under the glittering canopy of stars, she felt very much alone.

Jon was waiting for her in the front yard. They greeted each other quietly and began to walk. The Stefan family barn was less than a mile away, and they arrived shortly. A young man she didn't know was standing by the door. He greeted Jon with a nod and let them inside. It was dark in the barn, but Jon, familiar with the space, led her behind a hayloft ladder and knocked three times on the floor. He pulled on a rope fastened to a metal bracket and lifted a well-camouflaged trap door. He motioned for her to go first, and she carefully climbed down another ladder into the underground space. Her hands shook, and despite the chilly air, sweat prickled her forehead and the back of her neck. Jon followed, supporting the trap door with his left arm so it would close quietly on top of them.

The room looked like a root cellar. There were herbs hanging from the rafters, barrels neatly stacked in corners, and shelves filled with preserved fruits and vegetables. Lanterns also hung from the rafters and gave the space a warm glow. About twenty people were already seated on hay bales talking softly with one another. When she and Jon entered, all conversation stopped.

Immediately she recognized Finn and Dr. Kellan, and she also noticed the cook from the hospital. While she didn't know his name, she remembered his kindness to her people when they first arrived months ago. A few faces were familiar, probably from the clinic, but otherwise the rest were strangers. Jon motioned for her to sit next to Finn, who smiled gently at her and moved over to share his hay bale. She noticed he was dressed in civilian clothing.

"Hello everyone," Jon began, and she knew right away that he was the leader of this small group. Soft, friendly greetings echoed back at him and then he continued, "Tonight we have a new member. Some of you already know Caeli Crys. She is a physician and has been working with Dr. Kellan for several months. As our process requires, she was recommended by me and confirmed by both Lieutenant Braden and Dr. Kellan. I am sure we all have many questions for her and she for us, but let's begin with our agenda for the evening. Are there any new members to be presented for recommendation tonight?" He looked around the room, and he gestured at a young woman who had raised her hand. "Shannon?"

"I propose Anya Jansen. She's been a close friend of mine since childhood, and she's an engineer. She is not in the army, but she works on special projects like vehicle design and energy. She has no children of her own, but she's become very close to Caleb."

Jon interrupted and explained, "Caleb is the Novali boy who was placed with Shannon."

Shannon continued, "Anya's alluded to disturbing incidents at the research facility, and she has openly said to me that she is afraid. She says colleagues have disappeared and the military is almost always present. I think she could be an asset to us because of the access she has to research and development."

"Okay, let's open the floor for questions and discussion," Jon invited.

"We have to talk about strength of character," an older man spoke. "Many people are afraid, and they choose to do nothing. Are you convinced she'd want to get involved? How do you know she would be willing to risk herself for our ideals? Will she protect the group?"

There was no animosity in the questioning. Clearly the group was used to vetting potential members this way, and Shannon answered, "I know her well and I will vouch for her character. I believe she would welcome the chance to join us."

The other man nodded, and Jon said, "We need two more people willing to vouch for Anya before Shannon can approach her. Does anyone else know this woman?"

The hospital cook raised his hand, "She's related to me through marriage. I don't know her well, but I know the family and they are good people."

"Okay," Jon said, "We need one more, and I don't think anyone else knows her personally. Can anyone make a connection?"

Finn raised his hand, "I'm in and out of that facility. I'll make contact. It'll take me a few weeks to feel comfortable supporting a recommendation."

"Fine," Jon continued, "Finn's on it. We'll review this petition in three weeks time. Thank you, Shannon. Does anyone else feel ready to put a name forward?" No one raised a hand. "Let's move to the next order of business then. Finn and Jason have intelligence reports."

All attention turned first to Finn, who stood and faced the group. "We know that Marcus has several mining operations currently in process. He has teams working locally in the Orainos range, and he has additional teams scouting hundreds of miles away for metals. Some of the supply is being used for current research and development, but quite a lot is being stockpiled. I think that's worth noting."

Finn sat back down, and Jon called Jason to speak. Caeli did not recognize Jason, but he had the look and mannerisms that she associated with the military. He was concise in his report, but what he had to say was equally as interesting. "Long range communication signals are being intermittently sent out in multiple directions from the base at Deira Point."

"Sent out *where*?" someone from the group asked.

"Into space, I would imagine," Jason answered and sat down again.

Jon stepped to the front of the room again and began to speak, "Here's where some sharing of history might be helpful. The Amathi are taught that we were once a great, technological civilization. We've recovered some of that technology, and we integrate it into our society today. We also suspect that Marcus and the government are making rapid advances and that much is not being shared with the general population. Caeli, what do your people know of our history?"

She looked around the room and took a deep breath. She had hoped to just listen and observe tonight, but this was an area in which she actually had some knowledge, so she spoke. "My parents were archeologists and historians. They were part of a group who studied the last civilization. Our evidence also supports the fact that we were, at one time, very technologically advanced. The planet was highly populated with many cities.

We've never been able to determine if we evolved on this planet or came from somewhere else. I'm sure our ancestors knew, but so much information was lost during the war and our study of paleontology was in its infancy, so no answers were found there. But we do know we've had contact with other worlds. There's evidence that we did so during the height of our last civilization, and there is more evidence that there was contact after the war, but before the Novali and Amathi societies split. The last interaction caused my people to "shield" the planet. I don't know who found us, but I think they were only interested in exploiting our resources. We were too fragile at the time to defend ourselves, so everyone, the Amathi included, believed that was the best course of action."

She looked at Jon and then Finn. "I suspect one of the reasons Marcus attacked us was to eliminate our ability to stay invisible."

"I agree," Finn added. "He wants to make contact with whoever is out there. That's part of his vision to achieve greatness." His voice held a touch of sarcasm.

"Let me be honest," she continued. "Our Council was not willing to negotiate that point, and not all of us agreed that it was the best choice anymore. However, my gut tells me Marcus's decision is a reckless and dangerous one, even if the means he used had not been," she paused searching for the right words, "barbaric."

There was silence when she finished speaking, and Jon gently put a hand on her shoulder. After a moment he spoke again. "Marcus is a dictator. He is ruthless, dangerous and highly intelligent. It would be a mistake to underestimate him. Yet we must find a way to stand against him, or our society will *never* represent the best of us. We cannot continue to live in fear, we cannot stand by and allow horrors to be committed in our names, and we *must* have a voice in creating our own future."

Caeli was moved by his words. The task ahead of them was daunting, and as she sat in this small room, hidden in the root cellar of a barn, she understood that it might cost them their lives.

\*\*\*

When the meeting concluded, Finn volunteered to walk her home and she agreed. Before the group left for the night, it was explained to her how the next meeting would be called and what everyone was tasked with doing until then. The current host would choose the time and place. He would release this information one day before the scheduled time and then, using a predetermined communication chain, each person would hear the information from one member of the group and be responsible for communicating it to another member. The idea was to keep suspicious conversations to a minimum and keep the date and location unknown for as long as possible.

Generally meetings occurred once every seven to ten days, providing enough time for some work to be accomplished in between. In the coming week or so she would hear from Finn and pass the information on to Dr. Kellan. Although she didn't have a particular task to accomplish in the meantime, Jon asked that she be prepared to speak next time about her people's unique skills and how they were used in her society.

She had much to think about on the walk home, and she still had so many questions. "You vouched for me to the group. Why? You hardly know me," she asked Finn, curious.

"Jon met you before you started working at the clinic, through his family. You must have made a good impression, because he asked me to try and spend some time with you. I assigned myself the job of escorting you to and from the hospital those first few weeks. I know we didn't talk much, but I think I'm right about you. You care deeply about Nina's family, you have a strong sense of justice, and the losses you've suffered have made you a fighter, not literally, but you've made a place in this society already. You're scared but that won't stop you from doing what you think is right, and you will put the good of others above your own wellbeing. Is that a pretty good assessment?"

They were walking along a path through the woods and Finn stopped and turned to look at her. It was dark, but she could see his eyes and they were searching hers for a reaction.

She gave a slight nod. "And Dr. Kellan? I didn't think he really liked me at first." She remembered how his permanent scowl and brisk demeanor had confused her.

"He liked you fine, and he's come to deeply respect you as a colleague," Finn offered.

"Tonight was interesting," she said, taking the conversation in a different direction. "I understand we are gathering people and intelligence right now, but have you laid out a plan? Marcus will not go quietly."

"Well, right now we are a very small group. We have to find a way to exponentially increase. The problem with that, as I'm sure you can figure, is the more people involved, the more risk of exposure. But without widespread support, when we do make a move, we won't have any traction," Finn answered.

"Some people don't want to see the ugliness right in front of them," she mused. "And some have so much to lose. I'm thinking of Nina and people like her. What would convince Nina to risk the lives of her children?" In her mind, this was the dilemma. Nina would give her life for her children, but Marcus would use those children against her if it were to his advantage. He would sacrifice them if needed. Of this fact, she was sure.

"I don't know, Caeli, but I think when she sees her sons changing, when they begin to talk about wanting to join Marcus's army, when they start to lose their innocence and humanity—because that *is* what's going to happen—maybe she would take a stand. Our children are slowly and insidiously being indoctrinated. Our government has always controlled the educational programs and the curriculum, but in the last seven years under Marcus's reign, the schools have been a recruiting ground for the army."

He continued, and his voice filled with controlled rage. "Other people's sons were convinced to destroy your home and kill thousands of innocent people. They were ordered to gather up terrified children, whose parents had been murdered, and bring them back to be studied. They were ordered to rape and torture the survivors so they would be broken and desperate when they arrived here."

His voice was low and hoarse, and she understood that this was a confession. "I knew it was wrong. I should have done something, *anything* to try and stop it. I should have died trying."

He leaned back against a tree and slid down to the ground with his head in his hands. "I'm sorry," he whispered.

She knelt in front of him and reached out to touch his arm. He was as damaged by what he had done as she was by what had been done to her. "On the first day that you came to take me to the clinic, Nina said you were a good man. I didn't recognize you, so I knew you weren't part of the group that brought us over here, but I knew you had to have been part of the attack." She took his hand. "I was afraid of you, and I wanted to hate you. But just like you have a pretty good measure of my character, I think I have a good measure of yours. And Finn, I believe you *are* a good man." She moved so she was sitting next to him.

He looked over at her and, taking a deep breath, began to speak again, "I've known Dr. Kellan for almost my whole life. When I got back afterwards, I started having nightmares, the shakes. I couldn't eat. I had to hold it together in front of my unit, and I couldn't let my superiors know what was going on, so I went to Kellan. I was hoping for some drugs to help me sleep at least, but he knew that wasn't a real solution. He was sick about the attack. Most of the population here had no idea it was going to happen until it was over. He and Jon had already been working to quietly organize a resistance movement for a while, and he asked if I would join him. I think that saved my life, or at least my soul."

They sat quietly for a few minutes, and then Finn said, "If you ever want to talk about home . . . If you need to share your memories with someone, I'll listen."

"Someday I might be able to do that," she answered, and they stood up to finish walking back.

# CHAPTER 15

Over the following weeks, the group continued to meet regularly. She learned that the Amathi had, in fact, implemented some of the ideas her people valued in areas such as sustainable energy, agriculture, and medicine. But the Amathi also invested considerable time and resources into weapons development, communications, and mining.

While the Novali had focused on slowly and carefully rebuilding their civilization, the Amathi were mostly interested in recovering technology. She learned about the immediate history of Alamath under Dimitri and then Marcus, and how Marcus was more radical, ruthless, and brilliant than his brother had ever been.

She shared the nature of the Novali's unique change and the various abilities it conveyed to individuals. She tried to offer a picture of her society, their ideals, and what they had been trying to create for their future. And slowly she began to think of this group not only as revolutionaries, but also as her friends.

As far as anyone knew, the Novali children were being well cared for. They were scattered throughout the community, and those old enough attended school. Their host families were required to bring them for a monthly check-in with a government official, but according to Shannon, the hour-long meetings didn't seem to bother Caleb. No one had a good feeling about Marcus's intentions for the children, but there was nothing definitive on which to base that assumption yet. However, they made it part of their task over the next few weeks to gather the names and locations of as many of the children as possible. Caeli was especially committed to this.

Work at the hospital, Nina's family, and her own involvement with the resistance group kept her busy. Weeks were passing, and winter had taken hold. She had not seen Lia for almost a month, but one morning her friend was waiting in an exam room at the clinic. When she walked into the room, Lia stood, smiling widely, and they embraced. As soon as Caeli touched Lia, she knew.

"Oh!" she exclaimed and her eyes filled with tears. She placed her hand over Lia's belly and stood for a moment in pure wonder. She remembered the first baby she'd felt as a child so many years ago.

"You're happy?" she asked Lia, but she knew the answer already. Lia was glowing.

Taking her hand Lia said, "Let's go for a walk."

Caeli checked in with one of the medical students, grabbed her coat, and they left. They meandered away from town toward one of the many rivers that cut through the landscape. The icy water flowing down from the mountains roared, and they stopped to sit on a rock near the edge. She knew Lia was in love with Ben, the oldest son of her host family, but it was a relatively new relationship, so she asked, "Is Ben happy?"

"Very. You know how it is here. Everyone rejoices about children. The whole family has been wonderful," Lia answered, then continued, "A part of me feels like I'm betraying our people by finding such happiness, but I want this child and I love Ben."

"Love is a wonderful thing," she smiled at Lia. "I am truly happy for you."

"That means everything," Lia said simply.

They sat together for a moment, and she knew her friend had more to say, so she waited. Finally Lia spoke again, "I need to move forward. This is our home now. What about you, Caeli? I remember it was years after your parents' death before you fully engaged with life again. How are you doing, really?"

Caeli paused and thought how best to answer. She didn't want Lia to think she judged her for her choices or begrudged her this happiness, but she wasn't in that place herself. Honesty seemed best, and so she tried to explain, "I can't forget that we had another life once, a beautiful one. I can't move forward without some kind of justice for our people. I don't know what that looks like yet, but the Amathi army *destroyed* our civilization. Most of these people want to behave as if that never happened. They don't even want to acknowledge it."

She continued and had to work to control the anger in her voice. "Marcus is a dangerous fanatic. He was a danger to our people, and he is a danger to his own. Some Amathi see that and are afraid. Some simply don't care enough. But some do, and more will."

Lia understood the implication of her words immediately. "What do you hope to accomplish?" she inquired.

"I don't know yet, but I have to keep telling the truth at least," she answered.

"Please be careful," Lia pleaded emphatically.

"I know. I will be."

Lia sighed, "No, I don't think you will be, but I really need you to be there when my baby comes. None of this *Amathi* medicine," she added with a small laugh, but she very much meant her words.

"I wouldn't miss it." She smiled at Lia and hoped this was a promise she could keep.

She and Lia returned to the clinic together, and Lia had her first prenatal exam. They talked about morning sickness and exercise and the need for plenty of rest. As a physician, Caeli had already attended several Amathi births. Like her people, they considered the process healthy and natural, and babies were generally born in the family home unless there was a serious complication. Lia looked and felt healthy and beautiful, and she left promising to return for the next scheduled visit.

\*\*\*

When Caeli arrived back at Nina's that evening, her mood had turned melancholic. When Nina asked her what was on her mind, she burst into tears, something she hadn't done in months.

"I miss him so much. It's like there's this gaping hole and, no matter what I do, I can't ever really fill it," she sobbed. Sometimes she would imagine a parallel life, one where there had been no attack, where her home was still intact, and where she and Daniel were making their own family.

Nina held her and said softly, "I know."

While Nina had not lost her whole community, she *had* lost her husband, the father of her children, and she did know about grief. Nina's quiet, resilient strength was something Caeli had come to admire.

"Tell me about him," Nina gently requested.

Caeli had not spoken about Daniel to anyone since she'd been here. She needed to keep that part of her memory sacred and close, but now she wanted Nina to know him. She wanted her to understand what an incredible man he had been and how her world was a darker place without him in it. So she shared as much about him as she could, the color of his hair, the feel of his kiss, the beautiful buildings he created. She talked about how they met as teenagers, and how he had found her years later. She talked about their wedding plans.

She tried to recount all the small details that made up their life together, walking to work in the mornings, making dinner together in the evenings, swimming in the ocean, and doing the laundry. Some of those memories were fading, and she desperately needed them to stay vivid in her mind. She did not want to let him go. And yet she had to.

Nina held her and brushed the hair out of her face, just as she would do with her children to comfort them. Finally, when she was cried out and exhausted, Nina wrapped her in a blanket, made her a cup of tea, and sent her to bed.

# CHAPTER 16

The resistance group was growing. They were beginning to create a structure so that different, independent teams gathered on their own. Each team was tasked with a particular job and would send a representative to the central meeting to report and interface. This meant that members of one group might not recognize members from another and that most people now only had information about the activity for which they were responsible.

Caeli knew that weapons stockpiling and increased intelligence gathering were major tasks. As the group became more active, the risk level increased, and every member had been instructed to have a survival bag and weapon easily accessible in case they were compromised and had to run. There was still no cohesive plan in place to implement a radical change, but Jon and Dr. Kellan were encouraged by the sheer number of people who were waking up to reality and were willing to stand behind the resistance movement.

The days at the hospital were always busy. The relatively small medical staff had difficulty keeping up with the needs of the ever-growing population. More students were being trained, but the current situation required that everyone work hard and often for long hours. It was satisfying to Caeli though, and she loved her work there as much as she had at home. For this she was truly grateful.

Late one afternoon, she was closing up a routine surgical procedure when the ground shook beneath her. The staff looked up at one another, alarmed. "Let's finish here, and then we'll see what that was about," she said calmly to the team. She fought to keep her hands steady, remembering the last time the earth shook. Her heart raced and panic danced around the edges of her mind, but she stayed focused on her patient. The team responded to her mood and was able to quickly finish the surgery and move the patient along to recovery.

When Caeli left the surgical suite, the tension in the hospital was palpable and the activity level was high. People raced through the corridors gathering supplies and shouting instructions to one another. She stopped one of the medical students to ask what was going on.

"There was an explosion at the barracks in one of the research facilities. We're preparing here to receive multiple casualties, but other teams are assembling in the cafeteria to head over," he explained rapidly.

She took off for the cafeteria at a run. When she arrived, she found Dr. Kellan, several other physicians, medical students and assistants loading stretchers with equipment. He stopped briefly when he saw her. "It's bad." His voice was low and tense.

"I'll go now. I don't need any of this." She gestured to the medical supplies that were being sorted and packed all around her.

"They're soldiers," he said quietly, only to her. "You don't have to do this."

Caeli hesitated, and then shook her head. "I have to be able to live with myself tomorrow," she answered.

"Come over with us, then. You'll draw less attention to yourself, at least," he suggested. "The first team is ready to go."

She nodded and helped finish loading the stretcher. The site of the explosion was chaos. Soldiers were carrying other soldiers out of the crumbling structure. As soon as she arrived, she frantically began to look for Finn, who appeared moments later, bloody, but helping another person out of the building. Caeli hurried to his side. "Are you hurt?" she asked reaching out to touch him.

"No, I'm okay, just banged up." He was out of breath, but his injuries seemed superficial. She put her hand on his shoulder and scanned his body with her mind anyway. Breathing a sigh of relief, she turned her attention to the young woman he was supporting.

"This is Anya." He handed her over to a medical assistant and said, "I don't think she's bad either, but I'm not sure." Another quick scan indicated that she had no internal damage, only a minor head injury and a fractured wrist.

"She'll be okay. Get one of the soldiers to escort her to the clinic."

He did as she asked and then, "What else can I do?"

"We'll need extra hands, so just stay close," she answered.

As more wounded arrived, Dr. Kellan began to bark instructions. "Bring the injured here, and we'll set up triage in this section of the yard. I want the most serious injuries on this side." He gestured to the western corner of the grounds outside the building and continued, "Send the moderate but not life-threatening over here. The walking wounded we'll get to when we can, and the deceased we'll move to that area there." He pointed to the stage where Marcus often spoke to the people. The cold and snow would complicate things. They'd need to move the injured back to the hospital as quickly as possible.

The soldiers seemed relieved to have some direction and began to transport the injured to the designated sites. Dr. Kellan turned to her and asked, "Do you want to work with the most critical?"

"It's where I'll be most useful," she said and he nodded in agreement. "But I'll eventually be so exhausted I *won't* be able to do any more." She looked at him meaningfully.

"When you need to, go back to my office and lock yourself in. I have a key, but no one else will bother you. You can rest and recover there," he ordered.

"Thank you," she said with appreciation, and then her attention was diverted to her first patient.

The young man was severely burned. His uniform was seared to his skin, he was moaning in agony, and he was going into shock. Another was bleeding from his head and most likely had internal injuries. She took a breath and then ordered one of the medical students to cool the burn victim with clean snow, get an intravenous line established, load him onto a stretcher, and wait for her.

She stood over the second patient. Placing her hands lightly on his chest she used her inner vision to find his injuries. His spleen was ruptured, his ribs were broken, and his liver was lacerated. He was bleeding out internally. She closed her eyes and coaxed the tear in his spleen to knit back together. Then she turned her attention to his ribs, which had punctured the liver. She drew the bones back into place with her mind and repaired the shredded liver much the same way she had with his spleen. He had already lost a significant amount of blood, so she ordered an intravenous line on him as well and told an assistant to get him to the hospital.

The burn victim required more energy. His blood pressure had dropped significantly, and his throat was swelling shut from the damage near his face and neck. She decided to take the conventional approach first and intubated him. Oozing, angry burns covered half his body, so she used her mind to coax the tissue to heal itself. The intravenous solution would build his fluid volume back and an extremely powerful antibiotic salve would be applied all over his body once the dead tissue was removed. She hoped this would be enough.

More were coming. There were severe burns, shrapnel wounds from flying pieces of metal, internal injuries, head injuries, and some amputations. She kept herself calm and continued to act as quickly as she could, using as little empathic medicine as possible. The more she worked conventionally, the longer she would last. Suddenly, a panicked soldier came running out of the wreckage to Dr. Kellan, who motioned her over. Finn followed.

"They need us inside," Kellan said gravely, and they hurried towards the rubble. The soldier brought them to a section of the building that was blown apart by the blast. In one corner, impaled on a jagged piece of metal, was a young man. He was conscious but in shock. The metal pipe had passed through his abdomen and was protruding out the front of his body. Finn exhaled loudly, and Caeli winced at the gruesome display.

She knelt by the young man's side and put her hand on his shoulder. The object had severed the abdominal aorta and passed through his stomach. The only reason he hadn't bled to death already was that the pipe was acting as a stopper and had temporarily staunched the blood flow. Even if they could leave the object inside his body and perform surgery in the operating room, there would be little chance they could repair it quickly enough.

She looked at Dr. Kellan. "I think I can do it," she whispered to him. He nodded at her.

First, she took the boy's hand and looked into his terrified face. "I am not going to let you die." She spoke to him with more confidence than she actually felt. His eyes held desperation. "What's his name?" She looked to the soldier who had led them inside.

"Jonah," he answered.

She turned her attention back to the patient. "Jonah, I have to work on you here, so we'll need to move you. Do you understand?" His nod was barely perceptible, but she knew he was scared because he gripped her hand hard.

She touched his face and said gently, "It's going to be all right." Then to Finn and Dr. Kellan, "Let's do this."

There were several soldiers with horrified looks on their faces standing nearby. She moved out of the way and Finn squatted by Jonah's left side and then commanded, "I want someone on his right shoulder and then someone on each side by his legs. We need to extricate him in one motion."

No one moved. "Now!" he ordered, and they jumped to attention. When everyone was in position she said, "Once you lay him on the ground, move out of the way quickly."

Finn nodded at her and then looked back at the other men, "On three, straight up until we clear the bar, then move left. One, two, three!" The soldiers lifted and Jonah's shrill scream filled the air. As soon as he was freed from the object, they placed him on the ground. Blood poured from his abdomen in spurting red currents. He gasped for breath and instinctively clutched at his gaping belly.

As soon as the soldiers left his side, Caeli was there. She couldn't take the time to comfort him and had to pry his hands off his abdomen. But she quickly found the rupture with her mind and moved the pieces of the vessel back into alignment.

She visualized them knitting together and knew when the repair took hold. She then turned her attention to his stomach.

By the time she finished, he was unconscious and she was exhausted. "He needs fluid volume rapidly," she said to Dr. Kellan. "He's still alive, but barely."

Dr. Kellan got the soldiers organized and moving, carrying Jonah between them as gently as they could. He stood up to follow the patient and realized that Caeli hadn't moved off the ground. In fact, she had leaned forward onto her hands and knees and felt very much as if she were going to pass out. He squatted back down next to her, concerned. "What can I do?" he asked quietly.

"I need to get out of the way and rest," she said. "I won't be any use now for hours. I'm sorry," she added, heartfelt.

Dr. Kellan just shook his head at her. "Finn, get her to my office and make sure no one bothers her."

Finn nodded. Dr. Kellan touched her shoulder and said, "Excellent work today." He stood back up and hurried off.

"Let's get you out of here," Finn said gently, helping her stand. She leaned on him, utterly spent.

He half led, half carried her back to the hospital. No one paid them any attention. She was covered in Jonah's blood, and it looked like a soldier carrying an injured patient to the hospital. He found Dr. Kellan's office quickly and sat her in a chair. "Give me a second. I'll be right back." He left, closing the door behind him. She nodded and put her head down on the desk.

He was back within moments carrying a pillow and blanket. Dr. Kellan's office wasn't an exam room, and there was no table or stretcher, so Finn laid the blanket and pillow in one corner on the floor. Then he easily lifted her off the chair and tucked her into the makeshift bed on the ground.

"Thank you," she whispered, her eyes already closing. "Will you check on Jonah and Anya? And there was a really bad burn victim. Will you see how he's doing? I haven't seen Jason today either. And you need to get that arm stitched up. Don't think I didn't notice." She disliked being incapacitated this way when so many people needed help.

Finn laughed and shook his head. "Just rest. I'll check on you in a few hours, and I promise to have information." He sat with her until she fell into a deep sleep.

***

She woke up groggy. Finn was sitting next to her with a glass of juice and a plate of food. Sitting up slowly, she rubbed her eyes. "Have you been here the whole time?"

"No," he answered. "I've been out there helping as much as I can and checking on your list." He handed her the glass of juice. "Drink up." She knew she needed it, so she finished the glass quickly, started on the food, and looked at him expectantly.

"Anya's fine. She has a concussion and a wrist fracture. Jonah's still critical, but he's alive and that's something. Jason wasn't at the factory. My arm is stitched." He held it out for her to inspect the repair. "And there were several burn victims, so I'm not sure which one you were asking about."

"How long have I been asleep?" she asked.

"Only four hours. All of the critical patients have been transported here now, but everyone is still running around like crazy."

She started to get up and Finn put a hand out to stop her. "Wait a minute. That wasn't an invitation. You need to eat and then you need to convince me that you can stay on your feet. Dr. Kellan's orders," he finished emphatically.

She took a deep, exasperated breath, but she knew he was right. The amount of rest probably wasn't enough, but she wasn't on the verge of collapse either. She continued to eat and then asked, "How many dead?"

"Forty-two," he answered gravely, "and over fifty injured."

"Oh no." She felt sickened by the loss. "What happened?"

Finn's voice had a bitter edge. "There is a real push to finish a fuel cell design, but it's an extremely volatile piece of tech and we just aren't there yet. Marcus is anxious for results, so he was leaning on the team hard, and they'd started making mistakes. This was a big one, and it took out the whole building and most of the engineers who were working on it. This wasn't Anya's project, but she knew about it and passed along the information. I wonder how Marcus is going to spin this little disaster?"

She had no answer for that, so she continued to eat. "How are you feeling?" he asked, with genuine concern in his voice.

"Getting there." She took a last bite and then said, "I really need to wash and change my clothes. Maybe I could use the bathroom and you could get my things from my locker?"

"Sure," he said, standing. "Meet you at the bathroom, and if you don't look comatose after that, I'll let you go back to work." He smiled at her, lightening the mood a little.

"Okay, boss," she grinned back. She was unsteady as she got to her feet, but once she started moving, she began to feel more like herself.

Finn was waiting for her when she came out of the bathroom, washed and changed into clean clothes. "At least I won't scare anyone now," she said to him.

"Are you really okay?" He was walking next to her as she made her way to the emergency unit.

"I could probably sleep for a few days straight, but I won't be able to rest now anyway, knowing this is all going on around me. I can work for a few more hours. Thank you, Finn," she said sincerely.

They parted company, and she headed for the emergency unit where she thought she might find Dr. Kellan. He wasn't there, but there was plenty to do, and it was hours before she was able to get any sleep again.

# CHAPTER 17

In the following few days the entire staff stayed in the building, organized by a rotating sleep schedule and hiding out in quiet offices or bathrooms to get a few hours of fitful rest whenever they could. Since most of the critical care was done, Caeli didn't need to use her gift very often and worked the same long hours as everyone else.

Three days after the accident, she was pleased to find a conscious Jonah sitting up in his bed, sipping water out of a cup. An image of him screaming in pain and clutching the gaping hole in his stomach passed through her mind, but she blinked it away and smiled at him. His eyes widened when she walked into the room.

"Good morning. You're looking much better. I'm Caeli Crys." She never introduced herself as Dr. Crys. *Doctor* wasn't what the Novali called their healers, and she just couldn't get used to the title.

"I recognize you. I should be dead," Jonah said, and his eyes held a question. "You aren't Amathi, are you?"

"No," she answered simply. "Our medicine is a little different."

He looked nervous, so she said, "I just wanted to make sure you were okay," and turned to leave.

"Wait," he stopped her, his voice unsure and wavering.

"Why did you save my life? I'm glad you did, but I'm not sure I would have if I were you." He looked down, twisting the corner of his sheet.

She really didn't have an answer for him, but she said, "I'm glad I did too," and it was the truth.

Caeli left the ward and was making her way to her next patient when one of the medical students redirected her outside the emergency unit. A soldier was waiting for her.

She recognized him immediately. He was the soldier who'd been in charge of leading the group of survivors to Alamath after the attack. He had given the order to shoot one of her people if anyone went missing. He was part of the general's inner circle. Her pulse raced and she stumbled backward, steadying herself against the wall behind her.

She was sure he recognized her. With the same cold, detached voice she had heard him use before he said, "Please come with me. The general would like a word."

Silently she followed, calm and composed on the outside, but a bundle of nerves on the inside. She would *not* let Marcus see her fear.

The bunker was a nondescript, industrial-looking building. When they entered, an automatic lift carried them a significant distance down, and the doors opened into an underground research facility. The size of the space stunned her, and she looked around, wide-eyed. She estimated that the ceiling was at least a hundred feet up to accommodated the machinery housed inside. Equipment hummed and engineers and scientists shouted instructions at one another.

They continued down a dimly lit hallway, past uniformed staff members who paid them little attention, and finally stopped in front of a closed door with a soldier standing guard outside. The soldier saluted and stepped aside.

The general stood when she entered the room and gave her a charming, terrifying smile. "I see you've met Captain James." He nodded to the captain, who stepped back but not out of the room.

Marcus came around his desk, and Caeli took an involuntary step backwards. If he noticed, he didn't comment, and she forced herself to hold her ground and look him in the eye.

"I remember you, actually," he began, "from Novalis, the last time we were there. Of course I didn't know who you were then and you were younger, but one notices a pretty girl." He smiled at her again.

"Dr. Caeli Crys," he continued. There was a hint of menace in his voice now that he wasn't trying to hide, "you are quite the talented physician, I understand."

She swallowed hard but continued to stare at him, unflinching.

"*You* have been holding out on us," he said accusingly, with the same cold grin on his face. Her anger flared to the surface and momentarily blotted out her fear.

"*You* ordered a genocide," she countered, her voice clear and bold. The smile finally disappeared from his face.

"No, I overthrew our oppressors," he snarled.

"Please don't bother with that charade," she responded, and he raised his eyebrows at her reply.

"Fine then." The smile was back. "I heard about a miraculous event after the terrible accident last week. What *can* you do?" he asked.

There was no point in deception. Too many people had witnessed her saving Jonah with her gift. Certain Marcus knew this already she answered, "I can heal people with my mind. I don't like to because it exhausts me, but I will. Mostly I use the skill to see into the body and make very accurate diagnoses. I'm also trained in conventional medicine: anatomy, pharmacology, surgery, wellness, and pediatrics."

"Well, this is one of the more useful skills I've seen from your people. Most of them can only talk to plants, or sense each other's deepest feelings." His voice dripped with sarcasm.

"You killed the rest," she commented attempting to keep her voice steady and emotionless. But a vision of Daniel bleeding to death in the dirt flashed through her mind and her hands clenched into fists.

"So I did." He tilted his head to the side, considering her.

"Is there anything else?" she asked. "I really should get back to the hospital. There are so many injuries from the explosion." She stared at him, unflinching.

"By all means, go take care of my soldiers." He looked at her knowingly and a small, vicious grin curled the corners of his mouth. She swallowed back the bile that stung her throat. Finally he gestured toward Captain James. "Please escort Dr. Crys to the hospital facility."

The captain nodded and opened the door. "And Caeli," Marcus called after her, his tone deadly, "I hope you aren't hiding anything else."

She didn't look back.

***

They walked silently to the hospital, and when they reached the entrance to the emergency department, James stopped her and said, "Private Matthews wants you to know how much he enjoyed his time with you. He sends his regards." And suddenly a name belonged to the face that still haunted her nightmares. Her stomach clenched, but she didn't react until the door was closed behind her. Then she ran into the nearest bathroom and was sick into the washbasin.

About an hour later Dr. Kellan found her curled up in the corner of the bathroom, drenched with sweat and shaking.

"What happened?" he asked alarmed, but she couldn't answer. He guided her into an empty exam room, wrapped her with a blanket, and closed the door behind them.

Haltingly, she began to relay her meeting, describing every detail in a dull, flat tone.

"I think he's going to have me watched now. I'm putting you all in danger," she finished.

"You've just come to his attention, so until now he's had no idea where you go, who you're friends with, or what a normal day looks like for you. I don't think you can attend meetings right now in case he does have you followed, but I'll keep you informed," Dr. Kellan offered, his voice soothing.

"You've got to let Finn know. He has to stay away. He'd have the most explaining to do if we were seen together."

"I'll tell him," Dr. Kellan promised. He put a comforting hand on Caeli's arm. "I think for now the best thing to do is go about your life. If you notice you are being followed, don't let on, but take note. Do what you normally do. I'll be the link between you and the group and I'll let Finn know what's going on."

"I was starting to feel safe here, and now I don't," Caeli said, sighing heavily. "But I guess none of us are really safe."

"No," Dr. Kellan agreed, "we aren't."

***

In the coming weeks, Caeli noticed she was being watched right away. She continued on with her daily life, ignoring the soldiers who barely tried to hide their presence. She suspected that Marcus wanted her to know he was ever-present, and could at any moment demand her attention or disrupt her life. Nervous and edgy, she felt it was impacting her ability to care for patients. However, Dr. Kellan kept her grounded and on task at the hospital, and Jon reassured her during family gatherings that things were progressing positively with the resistance. She just needed to be patient and act naturally.

Winter gave way to spring. Lia's prenatal visits to the clinic became the best part of her week. While she never spoke to her friend about the resistance, her encounter with Marcus, or any of her fears, their natural empathic connection allowed her to truly let down her guard. It was the only time she could.

The baby was growing healthy and strong, and Lia's new family eagerly awaited his birth. She and Lia took walks together and talked about normal, wonderful things like what to name the baby and how anxious Ben was about changing diapers. For a few moments she could forget the horror that had happened in the last year.

And once, Finn even managed to stop by the hospital, claiming he'd been experiencing acute headaches. He spent the appointment checking up on her and assuring her that the members of the resistance were all being extremely careful. They'd made progress stockpiling weapons and mapping the complicated infrastructure of Marcus's underground bunkers. Caeli was pleased, but couldn't shake the sense of foreboding in her gut, so she did what she always did during stressful times and worked herself to exhaustion.

# CHAPTER 18

When the soldiers came for her this time, there were three of them. Captain James was waiting outside the hospital exit, flanked by two younger men who trained their weapons on her the moment she emerged from the door. It was dark and she was leaving the clinic alone.

"This way, please. The general has need of you." The polite tone of his voice sent chills up her spine.

He led her to the same bunker but brought her down a different corridor in the depths of the building. The walls were grey cement blocks and the doors were made of heavy metal with locks on the outside. Icy dread crept up her spine, and her shirt clung to her body with nervous sweat as they made their way deeper into the building. Finally they arrived at a guarded door.

"Let the general know we're here, please," Captain James ordered. The guard saluted and then pressed a button on a panel next to the door. Less than a minute later, the door slid open.

Captain James shoved her roughly inside. Her mind took in several things at once. The room held four people. Marcus was standing at the far end with his arms folded over his chest. A soldier in full uniform stood in the opposite corner with his weapon at the ready. Another man, sleeves rolled and shirt covered in blood, was sorting through instruments on a table.

The final occupant was naked from the waist up and chained to the ceiling in the center of the room. His arms were stretched painfully over his head, supporting the full weight of his body, and a dirty rag was stuffed in his mouth. Caeli could not take her eyes off this boy. She did not know him, but he looked about twenty years old, and he was barely conscious. Judging from the blood and bruises all over his body, he'd been horribly tortured.

"Let's close the door and continue, shall we?" Marcus smiled and nodded to the soldier standing in front of the prisoner.

A single, bright artificial light hung over the table. The soldier chose an instrument that looked like a simple metal pole with a forked end and approached the barely conscious boy. When he touched the metal to the boy's naked side, muffled screams echoed through the chamber as the boy's body jerked involuntarily from the current passing through it.

Caeli wanted to scream. As the soldier tormented the boy over and over, she bit her lip until it bloodied and tears streamed down her cheeks.

Marcus held his hand up. "Let's take a break for a moment." The soldier put the metal pipe back down on the table and stepped aside.

Marcus moved toward Caeli and sighed. "You're probably wondering why you're here, yes?" he asked. She remained silent, and he continued, "Well, this is my dilemma. I'm hoping you can help." He gestured at the boy who was now completely unconscious. "This young man has been accused of stealing arms from my supply. Such a crime is a capital offense here, especially because he's a soldier himself. Now, the problem is we only have circumstantial evidence against him. I'd really hate to kill him if he just happened to be in the wrong place at the wrong time. We've tried to persuade him to tell the truth, but he hasn't changed his story, so . . ." he paused, "I'm at somewhat of an impasse."

Her heart was beating so loudly in her chest she thought the whole room could hear it. Marcus took another step toward her, and this time she backed away and swallowed hard.

He smiled wickedly and continued, "Then I had a brilliant idea!" He clapped his hands and she startled at the sound. "We've been watching the Novali children to see what interesting talents might be developing. You can imagine how delighted I was to learn that some of them can do more than sense emotions and grow trees! Some of them can actually read the thoughts right out of another person's head."

His gaze was deadly now. He lowered his voice and continued, "They're mostly very young and untrained. It will be a while before I can count on their skill."

Moving directly in front of her, he reached out to take a strand of her hair between his fingers. When he touched her face, she began to shake. The same trapped, helpless feeling she'd had months ago, on the brutal march to Alamath, now gripped her again so fiercely she could barely breath. Darkness hovered in her peripheral vision, and she swayed on her feet.

"But I know someone who has a very well trained mind, one of the most powerful I've ever seen," Marcus continued. "And remember, I've been dealing with the Novali for a long time, so I do know what I'm talking about." He raised his eyebrows and moved away from her toward the boy.

"Kristof, wake him up," Marcus commanded, and Caeli's clouded mind snapped back to attention. The soldier took a small jar off the table and waved it under the boy's nose. The young man jerked his head up and opened his eyes, panicked.

"So here is your choice. You can deny that you have this skill. Who knows, maybe I'm wrong?" he shrugged. "If that's the case, I'm going to blow this boy's brains all over the floor right now because I won't take the chance that he's stealing my weapons." Marcus removed his sidearm from its holster, stepped behind the boy, and placed the muzzle against the back of his head. "Or, you can find out if he's telling the truth." The young man moaned and squeezed his eyes shut.

She had never violated another person's mind for any reason. The thought of it made her sick to her stomach. It was the gravest of offenses. But this boy would be dead if she didn't. He could be a resistance member and she wouldn't know it. There were so many now. But what if he wasn't? What if he was truly an innocent? She could save his life.

Marcus spoke again, "Let's move along the decision making, shall we? I'll give you three seconds to make up your mind," he grinned, "One . . ."

She moved quickly to the young man and put her hand on his chest. He looked at her desperately and shook his head no. "I'm sorry," she whispered.

She closed her eyes and pushed her consciousness into his. With the first image, she knew. This boy wasn't being tortured so that he would confess to stealing weapons. He'd been caught doing it. Marcus was torturing him to find out who else was a part of it, because so far this young man hadn't talked.

With one cunning move, Marcus forced her to show the full extent of her powers. He had revealed her unwillingness to sacrifice an innocent, a vulnerability to be exploited, and she had just obtained the very information he couldn't get himself. Now she had a picture in her mind of the resistance members from this boy's group, the jobs they had been tasked with, the places they met in secret, and where they were hiding the stolen weapons.

Her eyes flew open and looked into his. She could hear his thoughts. "Don't give them up," he pleaded.

When she thought of Finn, Dr. Kellan, Jon and all the other people she had grown to love, she understood his desperation. "I will protect them with my life," she promised.

She could feel his relief, and then his thought, "I'm already dead."

She knew this was true and the tears spilled down her face, "You won't be alone. I'll stay. You'll feel me here." It was all she could offer.

"Thank you. Tell them I'm not sorry. I'd die for them again if I had to."

"What's your name?" She needed to know.

"Connor Mason." She kept eye contact with him as she stepped away.

She didn't break the empathic connection, and when Marcus stepped back behind him, put the gun to his head and pulled the trigger, she felt his fleeting, blinding pain. She screamed as blood and brain matter sprayed over the front of her, and then she sank to her knees.

*** 

She sat on the floor in a corner of the cell. The only contents of the frigid room were a cot with a threadbare blanket and a bucket, which she assumed was to be used if she needed to relieve herself. The blood spatter had dried to a crusty mess on her clothing and face, and was matted into her hair.

They'd left her alone and she had lost all sense of time, but she knew they would be coming for her. Marcus wanted the information in her head. She was a liability to the whole group now, not only for what she knew, but also for how she could be used. She understood that she would have a limit. She would protect the resistance with her life, but Marcus was creative. If he put his gun to the head of a child, what would she do? Her mind was racing with unspeakable possibilities. She had to get away.

When she heard the door begin to open sometime later, she already had a plan. A single soldier entered the cell carrying water and food. She lay unmoving on the concrete floor and didn't respond when he called to her. She heard him swear under his breath and put the tray down to approach her. When he knelt beside her and put his hand out, presumably to check her pulse, she grabbed his wrist. Startled, he tried to pull back, but she had already pushed her consciousness into his.

His eyes widened with surprise and then fear as she used her mind to constrict the blood vessels traveling to his brain until he was unconscious. She dragged him into one corner of the cell, took his weapon, and after checking the hallway, closed the cell door behind her. The corridor was dimly lit. It was quiet and empty as she quickly made her way to the lift. Her heart pounded in her chest as the machine rose steadily and finally came to a stop aboveground.

There were people on this level, soldiers and researchers working in the facility, and she knew she would need all her concentration to get out of this building. When the door opened, she created a mental image of herself as a shadow and projected this image into the room in all directions. On a very small scale, this was similar to what her people had done to hide the planet, but Caeli had no idea if she possessed the skill or if she had enough energy left to do it.

Sweat dripped between her shoulder blades and down her back as she crept into the room. When her stolen gun bounced against a metal railing with a loud clang, she froze, her heart hammering madly in her chest. An older man looked up from his project, and stared directly at her and then, with a puzzled look and a shake of his head, went back to work.

She exhaled the breath she'd been holding and continued on. When she finally came to the exit, an armed soldier stood guard at the door. He wasn't aware of her, but now she was stuck, huddled against the wall. *He* had to open the door so she could slip out, and she had no idea how to make that happen.

Willing herself not to panic and inadvertently release the shadow image, she squatted low. Maybe if the guard thought something was happening outside, he might open the door to investigate. From her own memory, she recalled the first shattering explosion that had rocked her home almost a year ago. She remembered every detail, from the deafening blast to the way the ground had trembled beneath her feet. Gathering the whole experience in her thoughts, she threw it into the guard's mind. He jerked in alarm and pulled the door open. Caeli slipped outside.

It was dark. There was maybe an hour before dawn would begin to break over the mountain peaks. The streets were empty, and she was able to run home to Nina's quickly. Adrenaline was the only thing propelling her forward now. Entering the silent house she found the pack she'd hidden under her bed at Jon's urging, and put it over her shoulder, adjusting the stolen weapon to the other side. She wished for time to change her clothes, but the soldier she had rendered unconscious wouldn't be out for long. She had to be gone before he sounded any kind of alarm.

It was hard to leave. She stood by Nina for a moment. This woman had saved her life, and there was no way she could ever repay the kindness she had been shown. The best she could do was leave so Marcus couldn't use the people she loved. She hoped somehow Nina would come to understand this.

Using all the skill she had been taught as a child, she blended seamlessly into the landscape and left little trace of herself behind. She stashed her pack and weapon under thick brush in the woods and then headed toward the river. She found an ideal spot quickly. It was a steep ledge overlooking a deep and rushing part of the wide Nama River, about a half-mile from where it poured into the Kalanama Lake. The spring thaw was underway and the water melting from the glacial peaks in the Orainos range caused powerful rapids.

Her breath caught in her throat as she peered over the ledge. She didn't actually want to die, just make it look as if she had, but if she miscalculated the jump and hit a rock, or if the current was too powerful and she was swept under, then she really would be dead. If Marcus suspected she had simply run, though, he would track her down relentlessly. No matter how good she was in the wilderness, he probably had soldiers who were better. She had to take this chance.

She stripped off her clothes and shoes and threw them into the river below, hoping they would become caught up on branches or rocks and found later as evidence. When she stood naked and shivering in the dim light of the breaking dawn, she stretched her consciousness out to find Finn and touched her mind to his.

Recreating the events of the last several hours as carefully and with as much detail as she could, she projected them from her mind to his. He would understand that a young man named

Connor had died to protect them. He would understand that the danger was close and they needed to be ready. He would understand why she had to run.

The last thought she sent to him was of complete and total forgiveness. She knew he carried a terrible weight, and nothing could change what had already been done, but Finn made her believe in redemption. He needed to know that too.

When she finished, she broke off that connection and made one more. She stood balanced on the ledge and projected her thoughts to Marcus. She knew he could see exactly where she was, and that he would know her genuine fear.

"You will *not* win. I'll die first," she thought defiantly and jumped. She let him feel her stomach drop as she plunged off the side, the sting of the frigid water as it covered her, and the rush of the current pulling her down. She let her body relax and go limp, and then abruptly severed the connection.

# DEREK

## CHAPTER 19

Just as abruptly as Caeli had severed the connection with Marcus, she severed it with Derek and then leaned heavily into his arms. He felt her exhaustion. Hell, he was exhausted. They had been sitting outside the cave for hours, and there was a chill in the late night air. The campfire had long since gone out, and the only light around them came from a few glowing embers.

Just like before, Caeli's experiences felt very real to him. He might even be able to walk down a street in Alamath without getting lost. And there were definitely people he would kill without hesitation. Marcus of course, the sociopath Captain James, and that fuck Matthews were all on the top of his list.

She blinked up at him.

"Hey," he said.

She gave him a weary half smile.

He had no words to offer, so he just sat quietly with her for a while longer, but his mind was racing. When she began to shiver, he suggested they move into the cave and get a few hours of sleep. She nodded.

Gesturing at his bowl on the ground she said, "I'm sorry you didn't get to finish dinner."

"I won't starve," he said lightly, helping her inside.

"No, but you need more food than you're getting. Right now your body is using a lot of energy to heal, so it needs extra." She sounded worried about him. Strangely, he liked that.

But he was also worried about her, and as he tucked her under the blanket on the pallet, he brushed the hair off her face and said quietly, "You're not alone anymore."

She gave him a small nod and her eyes fluttered closed.

He actually *was* starving, but he ignored the feeling, drank a good amount of water from the bottle, and sat down next to her. Not ready to sleep yet, he thought about what was happening on this planet. A small-scale civil war could be erupting just across the mountains. A genetic variation had appeared in some of the human population that was unlike anything he had ever experienced. And a fanatical dictator was sending out signals to attract attention to this very vulnerable world without any idea of the disaster that might rain down on it. Derek had to force the image of a Drokaran invasion fleet from his mind.

He looked at Caeli and thought about how much damage had been done in such a short amount of time, and the danger that was still close by. The protectiveness he'd felt toward her just after she'd healed him now made sense. He agreed with her friend Finn's assessment that she was a survivor, but some things took a long time to heal—if they ever really did.

Caeli wasn't safe from the Amathi, and this entire planet wasn't safe from threats it didn't even know existed. He closed his eyes and leaned back against the cave wall, frustrated by his inability to do anything about any of it.

***

He woke to Caeli frantically shaking him. His heart pounded as he sat up blinking.

"They're on this side of the river. They crossed down by the beach." Her voice was tight and controlled, but her eyes betrayed her growing panic.

"The Amathi patrol?" Derek asked, trying to clear his head.

She nodded. "If they keep following the beach south, they're going to find your ship."

He took a deep breath, attempting to form a coherent thought. "And if they find my ship with no bodies, they're going to search this entire area."

She didn't answer.

He stood, reached for his sidearm, and tucked it into the back of his pants. "How many are there?"

"Six," she answered.

They would have the element of surprise on their side, but still, six to one odds didn't fill him with confidence.

"Even if you take out the whole patrol, they'll be missed eventually," Caeli said. "Marcus will send more."

He knew this was true, but he didn't have a better idea. Surprise was their only advantage.

"If I get to your ship before they do, I might be able to hide it," Caeli said, touching his arm.

It was a good idea. If the Amathi didn't see the ship, hopefully they'd move on and have no need to return to the area any time soon. He wasn't sure if hiding his ship would be more of a challenge for Caeli than escaping from the military prison, but it was worth a shot. "Okay. Let's try that first."

"We have to hurry," Caeli said, tightening the laces on her boots.

She was quick and agile, moving easily along the forest path, but within a few minutes his chest and left leg began to throb.

Sweat trickled down his back. He knew she sensed his growing discomfort when she slowed her pace.

"No, Caeli," he said. "Run."

When the forest ended and they reached the stretch of brush near the beach, he was gasping for breath, his recently damaged lungs heaving in protest. They slowed down to navigate the wild brambles, and soon the charred path leading to his ship came into view. Caeli stopped and squatted low.

"We need to find a place to hide." She surveyed the area and pointed to a dense flowering bush about a hundred yards from the aft section of the ship. "We'll be able to see them approach from there."

He nodded. Still crouching, they made their way over. From his position tucked behind the bush, he could part the branches and have a clear view of his ship, the burned trail, and a good expanse of the beach. There was no sign yet of the Amathi patrol.

His heart was pounding, and he still couldn't take a deep breath. The throbbing in his ribcage and left leg had now turned into a sharp, stabbing pain. He let go of the branches in his hand and sat back on his heels, feeling nauseous and dizzy, and trying very hard not to fall over.

Caeli eyed him with concern.

"I'm fine," he lied.

She started to argue with him but stopped abruptly, turning back toward the beach. "They're coming. I have to do this now."

She crept to the edge of the bush and studied the decimated area around the ship. Then she took a deep breath and whispered, "You'll be able to see the effect too."

As he stared in amazement, the blackened ground began to fill in with brown branches and green brush. Blue sky appeared where seconds before the metallic hull of his ship jutted up over the vegetation. It was as if an invisible paintbrush was blotting out the destruction and replacing it with what *should* have been there.

Distant human voices grabbed his attention, and he peered toward the beach. The Amathi patrol were tiny specks against the white sand. Pulling his weapon out, he held it low against his thigh.

He and Caeli were pressed so close together in the small shelter of the bush that he could feel her body tense and her breathing speed up. Her gaze was fixed on the altered landscape in front of them, and the image of it remained unwavering to his eye. As the Amathi patrol got closer, she began to shake, and beads of sweat ran down her temples. He wanted to reassure her but not disrupt her concentration, so very gently he touched his free hand to hers. She inhaled a shuddering breath and squeezed him back so hard his knuckles turned white.

The minutes crept by as the patrol approached. With his heart thudding in his chest and his fingers growing numb in Caeli's grip, Derek watched them visually scan the area around his ship. Their demeanor didn't change and they didn't stop.

In a quarter hour the soldiers were almost out of sight at the other end of the beach. When they disappeared into the woods, Caeli finally let go of the vision and sat back with her eyes closed. Derek let out a painful breath.

"They think your ship must have crashed into the ocean," Caeli said, wiping her forehead with the back of her hand. "They're going back to Alamath."

Derek tried to grin. "Did they have some help with that idea?" he asked.

Caeli nodded weakly back, "Maybe a little."

When she opened her eyes a moment later, she frowned. He must have looked like shit. Without asking, she put her hands on his chest.

"You've reinjured some of your soft tissue, and the fractures weren't nearly ready for this kind of stress. We need to get you back to camp," she said, reaching to help him stand.

"I can make it. I just need to go slow," he assured her, although he had some doubts.

By the time they returned to the cave, his shirt was drenched and he could barely put weight on his left leg. He stumbled onto the sleeping pallet with a groan. They shared the water in her bottle, and she helped him out of his shirt. Her hands on his body were warm and gentle, and the tingling sensation felt comfortingly pleasant. He passed out with strange visions of disappearing ships in his mind.

Sometime around dusk, she gently prodded him awake to feed him some broth and tea. Bluish circles rimmed her eyes and, even in the diminishing light, her skin looked pale.

"Caeli, you're exhausted. Please sleep. I promise I won't die in the night."

She nodded reluctantly, stacked the dishes, and lay down next to him. This time she reached for his hand.

***

Her nightmare woke him. The blanket was tangled around her, and she was thrashing about, desperately trying to free herself. He sat up and shook her gently, pulling the blanket off.

"Hey, it's okay. You're okay," he whispered, as she sat up with a cry, panting and backing away from him into the wall.

In the seconds before she was fully awake, the force of her

thoughts hit him. He felt a hand gripping her hair and the weight of a body pinning her down.

"You're safe, Caeli," he repeated over and over, until finally she whispered, "Derek?"

In the dark of the cave, he could barely see her silhouette against the rock, but he could see her shoulders heave as she sobbed silently. In that moment, he wished he'd killed every one of the Amathi soldiers they'd seen at the beach.

He moved closer and gently touched the side of her face. "I'm here," he said.

She leaned her head on his chest, and he held her until she was ready to sleep again.

# CHAPTER 20

When he emerged from the cave the next morning, Caeli was already up and busy. The fire was going, the pot was full, and she sat carving something out of a chunk of wood with her utility knife.

He sat down next to her. After a moment he asked, "Are you okay?"

She paused and nodded. Derek tried to assess whether she was being completely truthful. He noticed that the dark circles under her eyes had faded, but her mood was subdued.

"It was brave, what you did yesterday," he said.

At first she didn't answer. Small slivers of wood fell to the ground as the knife flashed in her steady hands. He studied her face in the morning light, wishing he had even a fraction of her empathic skill.

"I didn't feel very brave," she admitted.

"No, but you did it anyway."

She gave a slight nod and then looked up at him. "Thank you. For being there."

He knew she didn't only mean with the Amathi patrol at the beach. Last night she'd stayed curled in his arms with her head on his chest. He remembered the smell of her hair and the feel of her body against his. He'd gently stroked her back while her heart thudded against his chest, and he knew the moment her breathing finally slowed and she'd fallen asleep.

His feelings for her were far stronger than they should have been in such a short amount of time. But it was like he'd known her all his life. Really, it was like he'd known her all *her* life.

He wanted to pull her back into his arms, but instead he nodded at the block of wood and asked, "What are you carving?"

"Spoons," she replied, holding up what was actually beginning to look like a utensil. "It's been on my to-do list for a while. I can show you how to make one."

He raised his eyebrows at her. "I might cut my own fingers off."

"I promise you won't," she said as she went into the cave and returned with another knife and chunk of wood. "Picture the shape you want, carve away from yourself, and always hold the knife like this," she instructed. "Breakfast will be ready in a few minutes."

As if on cue, his stomach growled loudly. "This is why I feel the need to feed you constantly," she teased. "But seriously, I have to stock up on supplies today. If you're feeling up to it, we could do some fishing."

*What a big career change*, he thought, mildly amused. "I feel much better than yesterday, and fishing sounds fun, actually," he said, and it did. He lived on a ship, and sometimes he didn't breathe anything but recycled air for weeks at a time. This planet was beautiful, pristine almost, with very little evidence of whatever catastrophe had taken place on it centuries ago. He was eager to explore.

"Keep working. I'll get our breakfast," she said, folding her knife and tucking it into her pocket.

She added a few more ingredients to the pot and, when she seemed satisfied with the results, served him a steaming bowl.

He inhaled the nutty aroma appreciatively, thinking how much he enjoyed her simple meals.

"Thank you," she answered, even though he hadn't spoken aloud.

He laughed.

She looked up, startled, and then realized what she'd done. "I'm sorry. My people can always feel each other," she hurried to explain. "But it's only like background noise. After we make a deeper connection, like I did with you, it becomes easier to hear one another."

"Please don't be sorry," he said emphatically.

They ate together in silence until his bowl was almost empty. When he found himself cleaning the bottom with his fingers, he joked, "Those spoons will really be useful." And he was rewarded by her smile.

***

After breakfast, they headed to the river. "I'm thinking we'll hike down to the lake. This river empties into it, and we should be able to catch something there. The view of the mountains is spectacular too," Caeli said as they walked through the woods. Derek knew she was keeping the pace intentionally slow.

In about an hour they arrived, and the view was as amazing as she said it would be. The lake was still and blue, and the mountains rose majestically in the distance on the opposite shore. He breathed in the tangy sweetness of the leafy trees and, for just a moment, allowed himself to believe that everything would be all right.

Caeli set down her backpack and satchel. He put down the crudely fashioned sticks that would act as fishing poles and the interesting net that she'd made out of flexible branches and woven vine. As she squatted down near the edge of the lake to bait the line, he sat and watched her work.

His sudden urge to touch her was overwhelming. He wanted to feel her body pressed against his and taste the saltiness of her skin. He could imagine the shape of her face with his eyes closed, and he very much wanted to kiss her. But as soon as the thought formed in his mind, he frantically tried to trap it inside.

Caeli glanced up at him, eyes wide. He looked out over the water, forcing his expression to remain neutral. She tilted her head and stared at him for a moment, then finished what she was doing.

When she had the line set, she handed it to him. A memory of fishing with his father as a child flashed through his mind, and when he felt a tug at the end of his line, he smiled.

"This lake is so populated; we should have a good catch." And sure enough, in less than an hour they had plenty. She expertly placed them in the net and secured it in the water so the fish would stay alive until they were ready to leave, then sat down next to him.

"How are you feeling? Yesterday was a bit of a setback."

"Not quite myself, but getting there," he answered, and that was pretty accurate.

"I'd like to check you out before we start back," she said.

"Have at it." She knelt in front of him and placed her hand lightly on his chest. Right away he could feel the familiar tingling sensation. After a moment she sat back on her heels and said, "Everything's healing up nicely. Are you a little tired?" She knew he was, so he answered honestly.

"That's pretty normal. Let's sit here for a while." She stretched out on the mossy bank and shaded her eyes from the sun. He did the same.

"Can I ask you a question?" she asked.

"Sure."

"What's it like out there?" she gestured upward, toward the sky.

He thought about where to begin and what would be most meaningful to her. He remembered that her parents were historians, so he decided to give that perspective first. "Once our original human civilization became spacefaring, we began to colonize other habitable worlds, so there are literally hundreds of planets with human populations on them. Naturally the cultures evolved very differently over time, but biologically we're all pretty similar."

She interrupted, "It would make sense that this planet was colonized too, wouldn't it?"

"The population here is human," he agreed. It would be interesting to see if there was evidence of this in any historical archives. Likely some of the older colonies would have records, but since he wasn't sure they would ever get off this planet to check, he didn't bother to mention it.

"What's your world like?" she asked, turning toward him.

He propped himself on his elbow. "It's a planet about this size called Erithos. It's a beautiful world, with lakes like this one, and even oceans like yours. We have big cities too. And orbiting cities," he added, grinning at her wide-eyed response.

Then she turned her face back toward the sun and asked quietly, "Is it peaceful there?"

"Yes," he answered. "But it wasn't always. For generations, at any given time, one world would be at war with another, Erithos included. We fought over resources, territory, whatever. It was a pretty deadly time for all the colonies. Eventually though, coalitions formed, diplomacy and cooperation became more the rule than the exception. Now in most regions, each planet has its own defense and independent government and is also part of the larger Inter-Planetary Alliance. The military branch of this Alliance is called the Inter-Allied Forces and until very recently, I've been deployed for them on a ship called *Horizon*." He stopped for a minute.

"How did you end up here?" she asked.

"*Horizon* heard the signal. Marcus's signal," he explained. "It's not a form of communication we use regularly anymore, but we did pick it up. This planet wasn't on our charts, even though the system was. Your people did a very good job hiding it," he added then continued, "My scout ship was sent out to simply drop a sensor marker so we could keep track of the signal and any activity in the area and also update our charts for this region. We weren't planning on engaging the population yet, if there was one."

"Your ship was attacked?" It wasn't really a question. He looked up in surprise.

"That's one of the images I picked up very clearly when I was repairing your brain injury, probably because it was so recent and such an intense memory," she explained.

He nodded in agreement. "Not everyone out there is part of our Alliance, and not everyone wants to be. I think the ship that fired on us were mercenaries. Without the data from *Equinox*, I don't know for sure, but it's my best guess. These rogue ships and their crews don't form allegiances with anyone. For the most part, they will buy or sell weapons, tech, and information to the highest bidder. Some are thieves and even assassins," he explained.

He didn't want to say the next part, but he knew she would probably work it out in her mind anyway. "I think they probably heard the signal too and were coming to check it out."

She took a second to digest this piece of information, and before she could form another question he added, "On the upside, we destroyed their ship. It doesn't mean no one else will come looking, but at least for now, one threat's been eliminated." He knew it was only a matter of time, though.

Her worried expression told him she was probably thinking the same thing, but he couldn't offer her any real words of reassurance.

***

He was nearly dozing in the afternoon sun when she sat up and said, "I'm going to go look for some more food. I think there's quite a lot in this area. Do you want to come with me or stay and rest?"

He was so relaxed and felt so warm and comfortable lying on the soft banks of the lake that he could have stayed there for the rest of the day, but he wanted to be with her. "I'd like to come."

Very quickly she found berry bushes and filled the bottom of the satchel with the sweet, little fruits. They snacked as they went along; picking green, fern-like plants, nuts from various trees, and mushrooms from shady patches under the brush.

Her bag was full to capacity when she was finally satisfied that they'd gathered enough. He was quite certain he would enjoy dinner tonight. They went back to the lake and she cleaned the fish then put them back in the net for the trek home.

They walked in companionable silence and arrived back at the camp in the late afternoon. She made him lie down on the hammock while she sorted, unpacked, and organized all the supplies they'd collected. He tried to protest, but she gave him a stern look and wouldn't allow him to help. "Just talk to me while I make dinner," she requested.

"Sure," he acquiesced. "What do you want to talk about?"

"Tell me what you do on *Horizon*."

"Well, I'm a pilot and I have command of *Horizon*'s fighter squadron, but we aren't in open combat all that often. Remember I said that not everyone is part of our Alliance?" he asked, and she nodded. "There are certain requirements for participation. They're pretty basic things like you can't invade another planet for their resources and you have to have some semblance of a functioning government that guarantees basic human rights for your citizens. The Alliance doesn't micromanage and mostly stays out of the local politics, but we have certain principles we all agree on."

"That makes sense," she said.

"But some cultures are aggressive and imperialistic. So while each world has its own defenses, the Inter-Allied military will assist if they're being significantly threatened," he explained. *Lately, we've gotten our asses kicked*, he thought, remembering the Alliance's failure to protect Mira from the Drokarans.

Caeli looked at him questioningly. He was sure she'd seen some of that horror when she was healing him, but it wasn't a battle he wanted to relive again, so he pushed it from his mind.

"*Horizon* is an intelligence vessel," he continued. "Our missions are generally covert. It's our job to stay ahead of anyone who wants to cause trouble or do harm to our allies." Now that the Alliance had a better handle on the Drokarans' approach to territorial expansion, every agent and every intelligence vessel in the fleet was working to prevent another disaster from happening on their watch.

He stopped talking for a moment and wondered whether or not he should say anything else. Sometimes the things he and his team did looked very much like the things the bad guys were doing, and the only way you'd know the difference is if you understood their intentions. Sometimes the ends *did* justify the means, and that was hard to explain to an outsider.

For him, trusting that the mission of the Inter-Planetary Alliance was to protect its member worlds and trusting the integrity of anyone directly above him in the chain of command were the things that made it possible for him to do his job.

He stared up at the trees swaying in the gentle breeze and tried not to think about some of the decisions he'd had to make over the years. Sometimes it was a matter of making the best awful choice out of only awful choices.

Caeli stopped what she was doing and gently put a hand on his shoulder. The tension in his body eased at her touch. "Close your eyes. Dinner will be ready in about an hour. You can rest for a little while."

He didn't protest. And then, in what felt like a minute, she was gently shaking him awake. "Hungry?" she asked.

"Always," he answered, a little groggy. He moved himself off the hammock and sat down next to her. She had skewered large chunks of white fish and whole mushrooms on pointed sticks and had them roasting over the fire. It smelled heavenly.

She handed him the first one. He could barely wait for it to cool, but it was worth it. The fish was tender and flaky and the mushrooms plump and earthy. He had never eaten anything this good in his life. He told her so, and she smiled shyly at him. "I think you'll like this too."

She had already crushed some of the nuts into soft flour and then added enough water to make it into a batter. Pouring small circles of the mixture onto a flat, heated slate stone, she added berries to the top of each little cake and let them cook until they were golden brown. After they had cooled enough to be removed, she handed him one. He closed his eyes, groaned out loud, and finished it in two bites.

She put a small pile of the cakes in front of him and then began to clean up. In a few minutes she was back next to him with their half-finished spoons and the utility knives. She handed him his chunk and said, "Don't worry about carving the bowl of the spoon out. I'll show you how to do that. Just finish the overall shape."

She had a way of instructing that was confident yet not overbearing. He thought about how she had managed to find a place in the Amathi society, in their resistance movement even, in such a very short amount of time. She was a natural leader. Not the kind who called attention to themselves with eloquent words and a charismatic personality, but the kind that people followed because they were strong and brave and capable.

As he sat carving, he realized that he knew this woman more intimately in three days than he had ever known *anyone*.

"Have you got enough of the shape?" Her voice pulled him out of his thoughts and back to the task at hand.

"I don't know, do I?" He held his crude utensil out to show her.

"That will work," she nodded. Using her knife and a small stick, she removed a glowing red ember from the fire and placed it on one end of her spoon. "The ember cools quickly, so you have to keep blowing on it."

He watched as she carefully centered the ember on the wood and pressed it down with the stick, while simultaneously keeping its fiery glow with her soft breath. She moved the ember in a slow circle, burning out a depression in the spoon. When she was finished she tossed the ember back into the fire pit and began to carve out the burnt wood with her knife.

"Your turn," she said. "I'll find you a good one." She repeated the same process to get him started.

He was completely absorbed in what he was doing. "Totally satisfying for such a simple project, isn't it?" she commented, and he just nodded, occupied. "I got obsessed the same way making bowls. Therapeutic, I think," she admitted casually.

"We all need something," he agreed and kept working.

***

The sun had long set, and she was sitting quietly next to him with her knees drawn up and her arms wrapped around herself. He realized she had stopped working, and he put down his project, yawning.

"Let's go to bed," she said, and as soon as the words were out, she sat very still. He knew she meant sleep, but this time he gave up trying to hide the thoughts that ran through his mind.

Her stillness was absolute, like an animal protecting itself, so he moved in front of her on his knees and sat back on his heels. Gently he ran his finger down her cheek. His touch sent a shiver through her body, and from the way she leaned slightly into him, he knew it was a good shiver. Cupping her face with his hands he kissed her. Her lips moved tentatively against his, and when his hand brushed against the side of her neck, he felt her rapid pulse.

Afraid he would push her too far, he backed away and asked, "Is this okay? Just say so and I'll stop."

She shook her head, "No, I don't want you to stop." Her eyes were wide and her expression almost pleading. "I want a new memory."

Taking her hand, he led her into the cave.

Her skin was hot to the touch, and he could feel her heart racing. She tilted her head back, exposing her neck, and he trailed his mouth over the soft skin until she was panting. They sank onto the sleeping pallet.

Sitting back, he pulled his shirt over his head and she reached for him, gently running her hand down his chest. He sat still and let her explore his body. Her touch was light and soft, but when she leaned back in, their kiss turned from careful and tentative to deep and urgent.

"Let me feel what you feel," he said, sliding his hands up the smooth skin of her back.

She closed her eyes, and she was there with him. He felt her vulnerability and the traces of lingering fear, but he also felt her desire building. He knew exactly what she wanted and how. When he got it right, he could feel her response in his own body, and her urgency just added to his own. Her eyes opened and locked on his, reflecting back the same intensity.

They moved with each other, building on each other's pleasure, until neither could hold back. His release was so powerful it felt like his body had splintered into a million pieces.

Afterward, he lifted himself onto one forearm and with the other hand brushed her damp hair out of her face. They were both sweaty and still slightly out of breath. "That was . . ." he searched around in his head for the right words and then settled for saying, "It's just never been that good."

# CAELI

## CHAPTER 21

Caeli woke before Derek, as she had for the last several mornings, but this time she didn't rush to get up. The sun's morning glow cast dancing shadows over his still form, and she smiled at how young he looked with his face relaxed in sleep.

A gentle memory of lying in bed with Daniel flashed through her mind, and a wave of sadness washed over her. Early mornings had been their favorite time, before the rest of the world woke and the demands of the day began. Sometimes they would talk, and other times they didn't need words. She knew she would carry the ache of his loss for a long time, but as much as she wanted to hold onto him, she was letting go.

Turning toward Derek's warmth, she spent the next few minutes tracing her fingers gently along the fading bruises on his forehead and down the strong line of his jaw. The physical intensity she felt for him was like nothing she'd ever experienced. Last night, he had been careful and gentle with her, at least until she didn't want him to be anymore.

Her heart rate quickened at the memory, and she took a deep breath, trailing her hand over his chest to the sprinkling of dark hair just below his belly button. When she worked her way back up again, he was awake, and they began the day in a different way.

Afterward, as they lay tangled around each other, she leaned over and kissed him. "Thank you."

He looked up at her questioningly. "Why are you thanking me?" Then he grinned, "For my superior skills in the bedroom?"

"Well, yes actually . . ."

And she laughed with a lightness she hadn't felt in a long time.

*** 

It was late morning before they stumbled outside. After breakfast, they swam and lounged on the sand. When their skin began to burn in the sun, they retreated back to the edge of the woods to spread the blanket under the shade of a tree.

He was lying on his back, and she was on her side with her head on his chest when he asked her quietly, "What are you planning to do?"

She didn't answer for a moment, and when she did her voice was tentative. "I'll try to go back to Alamath eventually, but I have to give it enough time for something to happen with the resistance, otherwise nothing's changed."

He turned toward her and said, "If *Horizon* finds me, I want you to come."

She stared at him, taken aback, and didn't answer.

"You can't guarantee that the resistance will make any progress. And we both know what the Amathi will do to you if they catch you," he pressed.

"But I can't abandon my world," she argued, shaking her head.

"Caeli, your world is going to be in even more danger. Someone else is going to find Almagest. It could be mercenaries"—he paused, and she tensed—"or worse."

She waited for him to explain. His expression was neutral, but his voice held an edge. "The biggest threat to the Alliance right now is a race called the Drokarans. They kept themselves isolated for generations, until about a decade ago, when they invaded the first Alliance planet."

"You think they'll find Almagest?" she asked.

"We did," he answered bluntly.

A chill worked its way up her spine. "Would the Alliance protect Almagest?"

"I honestly don't know," Derek answered. "But if you come with me, you can tell your story. We can at least keep track of what's happening here. And I can keep you safe," he finished softly.

Her own safety wasn't her primary concern. She hadn't left Alamath to protect herself. She'd left because she was a liability to the resistance. Should she go back and warn them of this new potential threat? But even if she did, they wouldn't be capable of defending the planet against an enemy like the Drokarans. Helplessness and frustration filled her.

Leaving with Derek felt like it would be a selfish choice, but maybe not. Right now, she wasn't helping anyone.

"Caeli, please come with me. It won't be forever," Derek pleaded.

"I'd have to come back," she insisted.

"I promise you. I'll find a way."

She put her head back down on the blanket and closed her eyes, the ease of the morning replaced by a gnawing sense of foreboding.

"What are you thinking? Tell me," he coaxed, brushing his hand along her cheek.

"I don't know what to do," she whispered. But the thought of being alone again made her sick with dread.

***

The ship arrived early the next morning. Caeli was already awake and knew they were close. Shaking Derek, she said, "Someone's coming. For you I think."

He was instantly wide-awake. "They'll try to land at the beach."

They hurried to the shore in time to watch the ship make its approach and gracefully land on the sandy expanse. Caeli stared at it in awe. Her first experience of a ship streaking across the sky had been colored by Derek's frenzied emotions coursing through her mind. Now she could appreciate its power and beauty, and its absolute *foreignness*. For the first time, she truly understood how different Derek's world must be from her own.

He held her gaze for a moment and said, "I wish we had more time."

"There's never enough time," she answered.

But as the ship powered down and the door slid open, he grinned broadly at the two people who emerged. They had weapons drawn, but when they saw him approach, they put them away.

"Commander, it's good to see you, sir." The man looked a little younger than Derek, tall and fair-haired. "We saw *Equinox* from orbit, and it didn't look good."

"It wasn't," Derek hesitated and then said, "Tommy's gone."

The young man's face fell, but he contained himself quickly and nodded. The other person, an attractive, dark-haired woman nearly as tall as the men, closed her eyes briefly. "Damn," she said under her breath and then softly, "I'm really sorry, Drew."

After a moment of silence, Derek said, "There's someone you need to meet." Caeli moved forward out of the woods to greet them.

"Caeli, this is Lieutenant Kat Rowe," he gestured at the woman, "and this is Lieutenant Drew Chase." He looked at her and said almost inaudibly, "Tommy was married to Drew's sister."

"I am so sorry for your loss," she offered.

Drew just nodded, swallowing. Derek continued, "Why don't we go back to the camp? We can talk and then go deal with *Equinox*."

Kat and Drew followed as they walked back to the campsite. Caeli could see they were looking around with interest. Derek invited them to sit down, and it sounded like an order. Trying to be as unobtrusive as possible, Caeli stepped softly into the cave to gather ingredients for breakfast and then efficiently started the cooking fire.

"We placed the sensor, took some data from the planet, and were on our way back. We didn't see them until they were right on top of us, and that makes me think they've got some kind of new tech," Derek explained and then added, "I'm pretty sure they were mercenary, not Drokaran."

Both Kat and Drew nodded, and a look of relief passed between all three.

Derek continued, "*Equinox* should have all the data intact. They took out the port engine and the stabilizers before we could get a shot off. Life support was failing, and it wasn't going to be enough to get us back to *Horizon*, so we tried to land here. Thankfully the shields held up, or we would've cooked entering the atmosphere. The last thing I remember was hitting the tree line, and then I woke up two days later right here," he finished.

Caeli felt them looking at her. Derek gave her a small nod and she took a breath, stirring the pot. "I heard the ship and was able to find the crash site quickly. Derek was alive, barely, and Tommy was already gone." She looked at Drew and hoped her next words were at least a little comforting, "His neck was broken. He died instantly. I went back later and performed our funeral rites for him. I can show you."

"Thank you," Drew said, a catch in his voice.

Kat looked at her questioningly, "How bad was Derek?"

"Skull fracture, bleeding in the brain, punctured lung and broken ribs, fractured humerus, scapula, and femur." Caeli felt the need to establish credibility with Kat quickly. "I'm a doctor," she added, using the word that would be most meaningful to them even though it still felt awkward to her.

Kat raised her eyebrows and looked over at the relatively uninjured Derek, who didn't comment. Caeli got up and went to find bowls to serve the food. When she came out, Derek had changed the subject and was back to talking about *Horizon*. "I'm assuming, since you found me, that *Horizon* got my last transmission?" Kat affirmed that they had. "What took you so long?" he asked.

"We got some intel that the research facility orbiting Telouros was being targeted," Kat offered. "We were close, so we provided support until one of the Allied cruisers could get there."

Drew looked up and said, "We volunteered to come and look for you while *Horizon* was at Telouros, but Donovan wouldn't let us send another ship into this region without *Horizon* right behind it."

"The whole squadron volunteered," Kat added.

"Thank you," Derek replied, moved.

During a lull in the conversation, Caeli spooned breakfast into the bowls and handed them around. Drew and Kat looked surprised, but Derek said, "You should eat. It's better than anything on *Horizon*," and he attacked his food with enthusiasm.

They looked skeptical but thanked her politely and ate. She was happy to notice that they finished every bite, and Drew was even using his finger to clean the bottom. She grinned at him and said, "There's more." He looked slightly embarrassed but didn't refuse.

When they were finished, she stacked the bowls and Derek said, "Let's go see *Equinox*."

Caeli led and they followed. As dawn broke fully, she wondered if this would be the last sunrise she would see on her planet. If she left her home and her people now, she would have to come back. But when and under what circumstances, even Derek couldn't say. Deep in thought, she almost didn't notice when the terrain shifted and they came within sight of the ship.

It was Kat's voice that caught her attention. "Shit," she said, as the magnitude of the damage became visible. "It completely broke apart."

Caeli stepped back as the other three wandered around *Equinox*, inside and out, and went to work removing the data recorder. Then they figured out how best to destroy the wreckage of the ship.

"Thermal charges," Drew said confidently. "We have enough on *Solstice* to do the job."

Derek nodded his agreement. "Let's do it."

Caeli sat on a small log and watched as they set the charges, and then together they moved deeper into the forest.

"Commander?" Drew looked over at Derek, who nodded. Drew hit the remote detonator and the world shook.

Suddenly Caeli was standing in her kitchen with Daniel on the morning of the Amathi attack, shattering her glass on the floor, and then she was running across town to get to the infirmary, and finally she was falling backward onto the ground as the building in front of her exploded. Frozen in her memories, she didn't hear Derek speaking to her, and when he touched her arm to get her attention, she jerked away in a panic.

"Caeli, look at me," he said, his voice soft and gentle.

Slowly she began to reorient herself to the present. She blinked at Derek and whispered, "That hasn't happened to me in a long time."

He moved so that he was kneeling in front of her sitting on his heels. "I'm sorry. I should have warned you," he said, looking distressed.

"I'm fine now," she tried to reassure him, even though she was shaking. She took a deep breath and could feel her heart rate returning to normal. Derek didn't look convinced but he stood up and she joined him. When they surveyed the results of their work, they were satisfied that what had once been the *Equinox* was now just a lump of charred metal, nothing recognizable or salvageable.

***

Afterwards, the group walked toward the beach. Derek turned to Caeli and said, "We need to say goodbye to Tommy."

Derek removed the medallion from around his neck and solemnly handed it to Drew. They stood for a while in front of the marker, and then Kat and Derek moved away.

"Thank you for doing this," Drew said to Caeli.

"I sang to him," she offered. "My people believe that the soul leaves the body but remains close by for a few days. We think singing helps to ease the transition from this state of being to the next. They can't really hear us, but they can," she searched for the right explanation, "feel our intentions for them."

"I hope that's true," Drew whispered. He looked at the ground, and she could see he was fighting back tears. "His daughter will never know him."

"You'll help her to know him." She gently touched his arm and then left him to grieve in private.

When she wandered over to Kat and Derek, the air was full of tension. Caeli caught the tail end of the conversation and heard Derek say, "I'm not asking your permission. Stay here with Drew."

He came to Caeli's side and said, "I want my spoon," and then began walking, stalking actually, toward the campsite. She raised her eyebrows and followed him.

When they were standing back outside the entrance to the cave, Derek turned to face her. "We have to go soon. I don't think it will take the Amathi long to get here. Please, Caeli, I can't leave you," he begged.

After a long moment, she nodded.

There wasn't much for her to pack. She'd taken only one change of clothes with her from Nina's, and as she sat down on a rock to put on her shoes, she realized she had essentially nothing to bring with her from her own world.

Sensing her distress, Derek sat next to her, tapping his spoon against his leg. She knew he was anxious to leave, but he waited.

The only things about his world that she knew were what he'd shared, and the only person she had a connection to was him. And once again she would be leaving the home she knew for one she didn't. The thought of it was suddenly overwhelming and exhausting.

"One moment at a time," he said, looking into her eyes and echoing the words she'd said to herself on more than one occasion. "One breath at a time."

She nodded, swung her backpack over her shoulder, and followed him back to the beach. Kat and Drew were already on the *Solstice* powering up the ship. She paused before stepping inside and turned to Derek, "Could I have a minute?"

He nodded and took her backpack. She made her way down the beach and looked out over the vast, blue ocean and into the distant horizon where sunlight was sparkling off the waves. Bending down, she touched her hand to the water. There were memories of the living and the dead that anchored her to this world, and it was difficult to say goodbye. But her future was not here, at least not right now, and so she turned, took one last breath of the salty air, and walked toward *Solstice*.

PART II – HORIZON

# DEREK

## CHAPTER 22

Caeli's eyes widened as *Horizon* grew larger and *Solstice* began its docking maneuvers. Derek watched their approach and tried to see the imposing ship through Caeli's eyes. Even with weapons retracted, it looked dangerous. Built for speed, agility, and tactical prowess, *Horizon*'s triangular body and curved nose appeared sleek and deadly. In stealth mode, it would blend into the background of space, but now light glittered through cabin windows, and Derek could see tiny figures moving in the forward bridge.

Kat guided the ship effortlessly into the launch bay and set her down with barely a bump. Derek complimented her as the door slid open and the four of them walked out onto the hanger deck. She only nodded, but he could tell she was pleased by the recognition. He also knew she was not happy that they had an extra passenger on board.

They were met enthusiastically by the deck crew and by all the other pilots in their squadron who had been waiting for their arrival in the bay. Derek's voice caught in his throat as he greeted them. They were grieving for Tommy and yet pleased to see him at the same time. It was as emotional a moment as this group of highly trained professionals would ever manage.

Derek was aware the instant they noticed Caeli. Except for Kat, all the other members of his squadron were men. He looked back at Caeli appreciatively. Her wavy, dark blonde hair had, in his opinion, a sexy, disheveled quality to it. There was a foreignness about her that was intriguing and appealing, and her wide blue eyes had a slightly fearful look that made him want to comfort her. His men were too well disciplined and too well mannered to be disrespectful, but they did appreciate a beautiful woman and they couldn't help but stare. He motioned her forward and introduced her to them. She smiled shyly and repeated everyone's name as they greeted her.

After their welcome, he led Caeli to the infirmary, as was protocol. She followed quietly, observing her surroundings. When they arrived, Dr. Gates and the medical team were waiting for them.

"Commander, it's good to have you back," Dr. Gates said with enthusiasm and then more somberly, "I'm so sorry to hear about Tommy."

Derek nodded and said, "I still can't believe he's really gone." Turning to Caeli, he held out his hand, "Dr. Gates, this is Dr. Caeli Crys. I think you'll be very interested in how her people practice medicine."

Gates raised his eyebrows and greeted her warmly, "Dr. Crys, it's a pleasure. I look forward to learning more. Right now, as a matter of protocol, I have to examine you both. Let's have you get comfortable in one of the exam rooms, and I'll be with you shortly."

Caeli nodded and Dr. Gates showed Derek into his own exam room, where he was scanned and prodded with what he thought might be every piece of medical equipment in the place.

"How is this possible?" Gates shook his head. "I can see how severely injured you were from these images. That was only a week ago, and there was no hospital in the woods where you crashed."

"I don't really understand either," Derek replied honestly. "You'll have to ask her."

"I look forward to that conversation," Gates answered, and Derek grinned at the enthusiasm in the doctor's voice. "I'm not going to clear you for another day or two. Get some rest and check in with me tomorrow," Gates finished.

"Yes, sir," Derek answered obediently. Technically the doctor didn't outrank him, but Gates assessment of his physical condition, or that of any crewmember, was the last word. He got up off the table and dressed.

He found Caeli seated on an exam table with one of the medical assistants already at work taking scans, drawing blood, and asking questions. He asked gently but firmly, "Could we have a minute?"

The assistant left the room, and Derek shut the door behind her. "Are you okay?"

Caeli nodded, smiling. "I'm a little overwhelmed, but all this technology is fascinating. I hope they let me back in here. I have so many questions."

"Well, they're fascinated by you too." He walked over and took her hand. "I have to go talk with the captain, and you'll need to stay here for a while. Dr. Gates will take good care of you. I trust him," he added then kissed her. "I'll be back as soon as I can."

She smiled again, and he left the room reluctantly.

***

Derek was seated in Captain Donovan's private quarters.

"What happened out there?" Donovan asked.

Derek shook his head. "Someone has new tech that we need to get a handle on. I didn't see them until they were locked on to us and firing. I tried to land in one piece, but there was so much damage . . ." Derek's voice trailed off, and he looked down at the table, the weight of Tommy's death constricting his lungs.

"It's never easy," Donovan said.

"No, it isn't," Derek agreed. They sat in silence for a few moments.

"And this young woman?" Donovan finally prompted.

"I couldn't leave her behind. She wasn't safe," Derek answered. His voice was steady and didn't betray a hint of emotion, but his commanding officer knew him well.

Donovan looked at him for a long moment and then said, "She needs asylum?"

"Yes, sir."

"What do I need to know?" Donovan asked, sitting back in his chair. Derek exhaled loudly, and the captain waited for him to collect his thoughts.

"Almagest is the name of Caeli's world," Derek began finally. "Her people have some kind of unique genetic mutation I've never seen before. Apparently it can be expressed differently in all of them. Caeli is powerfully empathic, and she's also a healer. She saved my life," he added quietly.

Donovan raised his eyebrows and nodded. "Gates tells me you shouldn't have survived that crash, and he's very curious how you're still in one piece. Incidentally, I'm glad that you are."

Derek gave the captain a halfhearted grin then continued more somberly, "After a pretty devastating war, the planet purposefully went dark and tried to recover. But the population had divided into two segments: the Novali, who have this change, and the Amathi, who don't." Derek paused and rubbed his hands over his face. "A little over a year ago, the Amathi nearly annihilated the Novali. Caeli is one of the few survivors."

Donovan didn't respond. He merely shook his head, looking appalled but not surprised.

"Caeli can give you a more detailed accounting," Derek continued. "There's still serious civil unrest on the planet, and a resistance group has already formed with the intention of overthrowing the current Amathi government."

"I'd like to speak to her directly," Donovan said.

"Yes, sir," Derek answered.

The captain pursed his lips. "I don't like having a civilian on board for any length of time, but we can't risk sending out a shuttle. When we dock at Aquila, I'll petition the Minister for asylum on Caeli's behalf, and you can make arrangements for her safe passage." Donovan paused and rubbed a hand over his chin. "With the mercenary activity in this area and the Drokarans ahead of us at every turn, Almagest is going to have a target on it soon."

"I know," Derek agreed.

"I'll report the situation to Alliance Command. Have Caeli here first thing in the morning," Donovan said, standing.

Derek was being dismissed. "Will do, sir."

"And, Commander," Donovan stopped him at the door. "It's good to have you back."

"Thank you, sir. It's good to be back."

Derek breathed a small sigh of relief as he made his way down the corridor and back to the infirmary.

Caeli was dressed, sitting up on the exam table, and talking quietly with the medical assistant. Before Derek could enter her room, Dr. Gates intercepted him. "There are no foreign pathogens that we need to worry about, and she's very healthy. You can take her to get settled. Will she be on the ship for a while?"

"We're not sending any shuttles out right now, so she'll be here until we dock at Aquila in a few weeks," Derek answered.

"Excellent," Gates replied. "I've invited her to come back as often as she'd like. Professional curiosity on my part, and she seems like a woman who'd want something to do besides wander the ship."

Derek smiled at the assessment. "You've got that right. And she is a really talented doctor."

"She must be," Gates looked at him pointedly. "Right now, though, you both need to go get some rest, doctor's orders. You've had a long few days."

"Roger that, sir," and he motioned for Caeli to join him.

He wanted to take her to her quarters and then, despite Gates's directive, go see what the analysts had recovered from his data recorder. He needed to know who had shot down his ship and if there were any clues as to how they had remained off the radar for so long.

He was distracted as he walked her to the room she'd been assigned and put the override code into the security panel on the door. "It has an automatic lock you can reprogram with your own code," he explained. When they entered, he shrugged apologetically, "It's really small, but there's a shower and a bed."

She tilted her head to the side and raised her eyebrows, "Derek, I've been living in a cave and sleeping on the ground."

"I guess this will be okay then," he grinned. "I don't want to leave you, but I need to check out a few things."

"I'm fine. I think a shower sounds lovely. Go," she encouraged and gave him a little shove back towards the door.

"I'll come back later and take you to dinner in the mess hall. Very romantic," he quipped, and she laughed.

\*\*\*

Before he went to the "tech deck," the space where the analysts worked their intelligence magic, he went to go find Kat. She was running diagnostics on one of the smaller fighters, but when she saw him she stopped what she was doing and climbed out of the ship.

He'd known Kat a long time. When he'd first transferred from the Erithos Air Defense to the Inter-Allied Forces, they'd worked security details and flight patrols, and eventually covert missions. Years later, when he received his commission on *Horizon*, he requested Kat for his team. Shrewd, skilled, and loyal, she'd become one of his best friends.

"Hey," he said by way of greeting. "How's Drew?"

She shook her head. "He talked to Dana about an hour ago. She's taking it badly, and he's pretty broken up. I wanted to give him a little time alone to process."

"Don't wait too long," he offered. "I think he probably needs you."

"Dating advice from you, Derek? That's rich," she snapped. Derek knew she got edgy when she was worried, and right now he suspected she was very worried about Drew. But he'd had a rough couple of days himself and wasn't feeling very patient.

"What's your problem?" he retorted.

Her expression tightened, and she turned back to the ship, but not before he noticed the hurt look in her eyes. Changing tactics, he continued in a gentler, teasing tone, "Well, I'm about to ask a favor that will probably piss you off some more. Can you check on Caeli in a while? Maybe bring her some clean clothes that fit, show her a little bit of the ship?"

Kat turned and said in earnest, "She shouldn't be on this ship."

"That wasn't your call to make," he answered. He might have been offended, but Kat's concern, as an officer on an intelligence vessel, was justified. To Kat, Caeli was an unknown who hadn't earned her trust. But Derek didn't have the energy to explain again. "Kat," he said wearily.

She looked up at him, and her expression softened.

"Please, will you check on Caeli?"

She nodded.

"And then go be with Drew."

She nodded again, then tilted her head and searched his face. "Are you okay?"

He shrugged and didn't answer.

# CAELI

## CHAPTER 23

Caeli had finished showering when there was a knock on the door. It seemed awfully quick for Derek to be back, and it didn't feel like him anyway. When she opened the door, she was surprised to find Kat standing there holding a pile of clothing.

"Lieutenant Rowe, come in," she offered.

"It's Kat, please. Derek asked me to bring you some clothes. The jumpsuit is what most of us wear off duty. It's the smallest size I could find." She could feel Kat's reservation toward her.

"Thank you. My things are so dirty and worn, I didn't even want to put them back on after the shower." She gratefully took the clean clothes from Kat.

"Would you like to have a quick tour of the ship when you're dressed?" Kat asked politely, if a little stiffly.

"That would be great. I'll just be a minute," Caeli said and pulled on the jumpsuit. She knew she was underweight, so the suit was a little loose around the waist, but it was clean and in good repair and she was grateful to have it. She wound her hair into a tight braid and came out of the bathroom. Kat was standing near the door.

They wandered the decks, and Caeli paid special attention to where things were. She didn't want to get lost on the ship. They walked back to the launch deck and then the infirmary and the mess hall. Kat led her through the ship's bridge, and they stopped in a more casual, comfortable space. People were sitting at tables and on couches. Some were socializing; others were alone reading or relaxing.

"We call this the rec deck," Kat explained. "Not much recreational activity going on, but when you're off duty, if you want to hang out somewhere other than your quarters or the mess hall, this is what we've got. They serve some drinks up front. There's no alcohol allowed on the ship, but it's still nice to come and sit at the bar."

Caeli nodded at Kat and noticed that nearly everyone in the room had stopped to look at her when they entered. She took a deep breath and said, "I feel like a lab specimen."

Kat gave a short laugh. "Well, we really don't have anyone on this ship but the crew. Once in a while we're asked to run a high-level security transport or something like that, but otherwise, it's just us." And then she added, "The work we do here is highly classified and dangerous. Anyone not part of our crew could potentially be a liability."

And there was the issue, or at least part of it, out in the open. "You feel like I'm a liability?" It really wasn't a question, but Caeli wanted to clear the air as soon as possible, if it was possible.

Kat looked over at her, surprised by her bluntness. "Let's sit for a minute." She motioned to an empty table.

They sat facing each other. Kat began, "I don't know you, and I don't know why you're here. Derek hasn't shared. That's not like him and I have to ask if he's really thinking clearly about this." Her tone was very matter-of-fact.

"I'll tell you anything you want to know," she responded with a similar, unemotional yet open manner.

"Let's start with why he brought you back with him," Kat suggested.

Caeli thought about how to answer, and was reminded of her father, who always found a simple but honest and direct way to address her constant questions. "On my world there are, *were*," she corrected, "only two societies left, the Amathi and the Novali. Recently, one attacked the other. My home and my people are mostly gone, and the few who remain were taken and integrated into the other settlement. The Amathi leader is a ruthless dictator. There are good people working to make changes, but it's been a slow and careful process. I can't be there anymore because I have too much information in my head about our resistance effort and Marcus, the Amathi leader, knows it. He would use me to get to them." She let that sink in for a moment and then added, "I staged my own suicide and ran away."

She paused and Kat looked at her with an expression somewhere between disbelief and respect. "Not what I expected," she said.

"Derek didn't want to leave me there." She shrugged and added quietly, "I probably could have survived for a while, maybe a long time, but it was hard. When he asked me to come, it seemed like a more promising option than the one I was facing."

"You're sleeping with him," Kat stated, and Caeli blinked at the abrupt change in the direction of the conversation.

"Yes," she answered.

"So your planet is a mess, you can't go home without endangering your friends, you saved Derek's ass, and he probably has feelings for you," Kat summarized.

"I'd say that's all true." She looked at Kat directly.

"Okay, I can live with that for now," Kat finished. Caeli was starting to like this woman.

"Thank you for taking the time to show me around and for the clothes," she said to Kat.

"No problem," Kat brushed it off.

"And Kat," she exhaled deeply, "I am very sorry about Tommy." Kat looked down and nodded.

"How is Drew? Derek said Tommy was family," she asked gently.

"More than that," Kat answered. "They were childhood friends, and then Tom married Dana, Drew's sister." She paused. "I don't know what to do for him." Caeli heard the vulnerability in Kat's voice and suspected there was more than a friendship between Kat and Drew.

"Maybe just be there?"

Kat nodded again, and then they both got up to leave.

***

Caeli had fallen asleep on the bunk in her quarters when Derek returned, knocking softly on the door. Disoriented, she sat up as he let himself in.

"Hi," she said rubbing her eyes. "What time is it?"

"Time for dinner as promised," he answered smiling. "I see you've got some new clothes." He raised his eyebrows. "Was Kat okay?"

"Yes definitely," she assured him, but Derek looked suspicious. "I like Kat," she added, and he looked even more skeptical.

"Hungry?" he asked.

"I am." She got up and went into the bathroom to splash

water on her face and straighten her hair. When she was finished, they left the room and headed to the mess hall.

"It's open all the time, but I don't think it'll be too crowded right now," he said when they arrived.

Nothing looked or smelled familiar, and she glanced over at him hoping for help. He piled one of everything onto a few trays. "This way you can see what you like," he suggested.

They sat down in a quiet corner and he looked up at her. "How are you doing?" he asked softly, and she knew it wasn't just a casual inquiry.

"Tired," she answered honestly, "and a little disoriented, but Dr. Gates said I could join them in the infirmary whenever I wanted, so after I get some more sleep, that's what I'll do." She took a bite of something on her plate and wrinkled her nose. "This is terrible," she said quietly.

"Yeah, I think you've ruined my taste for processed food forever," he agreed. "Try this." He pointed to something that looked like a piece of fruit, and then added, "the bread's okay, too."

She forced herself to finish a few more bites. "The Amathi practice a more technical, less intuitive kind of medicine like you do here, but what's on this ship is so much more advanced. I'm actually really excited to learn more," she said, and she was. She also knew that Gates was interested in running a detailed brain scan and DNA analysis.

Derek seemed pleased and then told her, "Captain Donovan wants to see you tomorrow morning. He's agreed to let you stay on the ship until we dock at Aquila. He's being very cautious about sending our smaller ships out after what just happened."

She nodded and then asked hesitantly, "What then?"

"I was thinking you could go to my home world," he suggested. "My family would help you get settled. I haven't really been able to think beyond that yet."

"Your home," she repeated. "I'd like to see your home. But you won't be there?" She knew the answer already.

"Not right away," he acknowledged and then added, "I have to finish my tour on *Horizon*, but I'll be able to keep track of Almagest from here."

Caeli knew she couldn't stay here with Derek, but as that reality began to sink in, a wave of panic gripped her. Her home, and everything she knew, was growing farther and farther away by the moment.

Derek reached across the table and squeezed her hands. "Everything will be okay. We'll figure it out."

Swallowing back her fear, she forced herself to nod. His assurance would have to be enough. She'd chosen her path, and now she had to live with it.

They finished their dinner, and he walked her back to her quarters. At the door, he kissed her deeply but then pulled away. "I'm going to leave now and let you get some real sleep. I'll come back in the morning when it's time to meet Captain Donovan." Hours passed before she finally drifted off to sleep.

*** 

Caeli's knees shook as she sat in Captain Donovan's small, well-appointed office. He immediately tried to put her at ease with the offer of tea. She accepted, smiling at this universal gesture of comfort.

"Are your quarters comfortable?" he inquired, sitting in a chair next to her and handing her a steaming cup.

"Yes, thank you," she answered.

"Good." He sat back and crossed his legs. "Derek's told me a little about Almagest's history, but I'd like to hear more about the current situation."

She put her teacup on the table and tried to begin, but to her embarrassment, her eyes filled. She opened her mouth and closed it again.

"I know this must be difficult," he said gently. "Make it as simple as possible. I need to hear what's going on to assess what action, if any, the Alliance may need to take."

She collected herself and gave him as dispassionate and factual an account of the attack on Novalis, and of the following months in Alamath, as she could manage.

When she finished, they sat in heavy silence. Finally the captain said, "Caeli, I'm truly sorry. Your loss is incalculable, and I assure you the Alliance will grant you asylum."

"I appreciate that very much. At home, I'm a liability," she said, pausing. "But it's very hard not to be there."

"I understand," he answered.

"Will the Alliance be able to do anything?" she inquired, hopeful.

"An internal conflict on a non-member world is not something the Alliance would normally get involved with. But if anything changes and there are larger implications, we'll assess," Donovan answered. She didn't understand enough of the political climate or the function of the Alliance to know what he meant by larger implications, but at least someone was paying attention.

She nodded and he continued, "We now have sensors in the region so we'll know if anyone approaches the planet. Almagest is too vulnerable to defend itself. Your people were right about that."

He paused and leaned forward slightly. "Caeli, I promise you, if anything changes, whether or not the Alliance takes action, I'll inform you."

She knew he meant it. Breathing a small sigh of relief, she thanked him.

"Now," he said in a lighter tone, "may I suggest that you create a record of your planet's history, as much as you know, and certainly the most recent events? It will be useful for the Alliance to have that information."

She nodded and smiled. "My parents were archeological historians. They'd be very pleased. I never showed any interest in this kind of thing while I was in school, much to their disappointment."

"Are they still alive?" he asked carefully.

"No, they were killed several years ago in an accident." She tilted her head. "At the time I was devastated, but part of me is grateful they didn't have to experience the loss of our entire civilization."

He just nodded.

"I appreciate you letting me stay on *Horizon* for now. I know it's highly unusual to have a civilian here. I'll try to be useful," she said.

"I'm certain you will be." He smiled and stood up. "Thank you for saving Derek's life and for your care with Tommy. It means quite a lot to this crew and to his family," he finished.

"I wish I could have done more for him, but . . ." Her voice trailed off.

"Some things are beyond our control. We have to be able to let go when that's the case," he offered.

"Thank you, Captain." She sensed a deep compassion for his crew and a true commitment to his mission. She liked him.

\*\*\*

Over the next few days, Derek showed her how to access *Horizon*'s vast library through the portable tablet in her quarters. She spent several hours each day in the lounge getting familiar with the written language used by the Alliance planets. She also documented Almagest's history, just as Captain Donovan requested, and then translated the text to practice her fluency.

Derek tried to share at least one meal a day with her, and he would sometimes turn up in the infirmary to say hello. He joked that his pilots seemed to be suffering from any number of strange symptoms just to have an opportunity to visit the clinic. It was interesting to watch him in what she considered his "natural habitat."

She got to know some of the other crewmembers and soon, even when she went to the mess hall by herself, she felt comfortable joining a table. Occasionally Kat would come find her to check in.

The best part of her day, and the most interesting, was spent in the infirmary. She allowed *Horizon*'s team to run tests on her, and she demonstrated her empathic abilities. In turn, she learned things like microbiology, nanotechnology, and how different types of biotechnology integrated into their medical practice. If she stayed on this ship for years, she felt she still wouldn't be able to learn everything. Dr. Gates was an excellent teacher and an avid researcher himself and, like Sam and Dr. Kellan, he was competent, compassionate, and very practical.

The constant activity kept her moving. When she fell into bed at the end of each day, she was exhausted and grateful to have only limited energy available for her anxiety.

# DEREK

## CHAPTER 24

Once Gates cleared him for duty, Derek jumped back into it with the same intensity he'd always had. He spent a lot of time looking at the data from *Equinox* and reviewing information the analysts had extracted. It was definitely a mercenary ship that had fired on him, and they definitely had some kind of new stealth tech. Acquiring it was becoming a priority for him and for the Alliance.

He'd initiated contact with operatives stationed on both member and nonmember worlds, and was in the midst of his investigation, when Donovan called him into a briefing with Alliance Command.

"We have to put this search on hold," Donovan said.

"Yes, sir," Derek answered. It was unusual for *Horizon*'s mission to change abruptly, but if they were needed elsewhere, it was important.

"You'll be escorting a diplomatic team to Tharsis," the holographic image of Admiral Reyes informed them. "Normally we wouldn't use you as the transport, but the political unrest on the planet is escalating and the team is urgently needed."

The admiral paused and when he continued, his voice was

clipped. "We also have intel suggesting the Drokarans have targeted Tharsis. It could be nothing, but this is just the kind of situation they've taken advantage of before. Get our people safely to Tharsis, and once you arrive, find out if our concerns are justified."

"Yes, sir," Captain Donovan answered.

Captain Reyes's image dissolved and Donovan sank heavily into his chair. "Maybe we can get ahead of them this time," he said, running a hand over the top of his head. "Commander, you'll interface with Tharsis and run the advanced security detail for the diplomatic team. Once we arrive, we can assess the Drokaran threat," Donovan finished.

"Understood. Sir," Derek began hesitantly, "what about Caeli?"

Donovan sighed. "Obviously this changes our timeline for arriving at Aquila. Let her know we'll be delayed. I'm still not comfortable sending her on a transport from this region. It's too damn unpredictable."

Derek nodded. When he left the briefing, he was torn between worry that Caeli would be on the ship during a mission and guilty elation that he would be able to spend a little more time with her.

***

At dinner the evening before the delegation was due to board *Horizon*, Derek, Caeli, Kat, and Drew sat talking about the impending mission.

"Kat and I have done some work on Tharsis before," Derek explained to Caeli. "It's been one step away from anarchy for years. Resources are plentiful in some areas and in others they're running short. Infrastructure can't be built quickly enough to meet the demands of the population, so people are getting desperate. Mass riots against the existing government have already started. Not to mention the planet has a large criminal underworld."

"You think the diplomatic team can really help?" Caeli asked. "It seems like an enormous task."

"We have to try," Derek answered.

Kat nodded emphatically, "This is exactly the kind of situation the Drokarans will try to capitalize on."

Derek continued, "The Drokarans are a highly organized, militaristic, and powerful society. Until about a decade ago, they left Alliance planets alone. It's hard to know what's going on with them and why they changed tactics, but now they're attacking vulnerable Alliance worlds directly." He paused for a moment then continued in a somber tone, "When they attacked the first Allied planet, they used biological weapons and wiped out the entire population."

Caeli's eyes widened with horror.

"They rendered it useless for human occupancy, including their own. No one in the Alliance saw that coming," he added.

Kat and Drew wore grim expressions.

Derek continued, "Their technique is to look for worlds that are already unstable, mostly politically, and destabilize them some more. They assassinate leaders. They conduct large-scale terrorist activities on the ground. Really nasty shit. When everything is in total chaos, they send their military in, large scale, to restore order and then never leave. The Alliance lost two more planets this way."

They all sat silently for a few moments, and Derek was sure both Kat and Drew had similar nightmarish images running through their minds.

"Our best option is prevention," he explained. "Get in and provide support before they wreak total havoc and get the upper hand. It's why the intelligence work we do is such a priority. *Horizon* has near total independence to conduct operations as we see fit. The Alliance, especially the civil branch, has to walk the line between honoring a member planet's sovereignty and assuring the common ideals are met. The tricky part is when to get the military involved. Our job in intelligence is to provide enough information to help make that decision, and many times it's also to conduct operations that will prevent or mitigate an impending disaster."

"We've got our work cut out for us on this one," Kat said, shaking her head.

"Well, right now our only concern is to get this ship and our guests to Tharsis safely. One thing at a time," Derek advised, as much to himself as to them.

\*\*\*

He sat in his fighter waiting for clearance to launch. The on-board computer had preformed a retinal scan and greeted him in a friendly, near human voice. "Commander Markham, confirmed," it said, and then, "Launch sequence initiated." He grinned to himself as the launch bay doors opened. He loved flying. It was pure pleasure.

The delegation had already arrived and was safely aboard *Horizon*, which was now on approach to Tharsis. A fighter escort wasn't necessary while they were traveling at interplanetary speeds. No ship could track another going so fast. But now that they'd entered the system, they were more vulnerable. *Horizon* wouldn't be in orbit around Tharsis for another six hours, and a lot could happen in that time. He and three other pilots were taking the first rotation, and then Kat would be in command of the second team.

"Everyone all clear?" He checked in with his squadron, although he could already see them on the radar of his control panel. They all confirmed and moved into position flanking *Horizon*.

"*Horizon* control, all vectors are clear," he reported.

"Roger that, Commander. *Horizon* scopes read clear. Good flying," control answered back.

His team settled into a routine of monitoring their scopes and flying their ships. They exchanged an occasional bit of chatter over the com line, but not much. They were acutely aware that at any moment the situation could change drastically.

And it did. Derek's radar went from completely negative one moment to bright and flashing the next.

"Damn, they're right on top of us!" one of his pilots shouted into the com.

It was eerily similar to what had happened near Almagest on the *Equinox*, except this time there were two ships attacking. One headed straight toward *Horizon* while the other sent a burst of weapons fire at the fighter in the starboard, forward position.

"Kade, how bad?" Derek asked over the com, his voice tight with tension.

"I'm okay. Shields held and I got out of the way fast," Kade answered.

"Good. Kade, Maren, see if you can get that smaller ship away from *Horizon*." He knew *Horizon* would be able to get some shots off to help out, especially if they weren't so tight around her. "Alaric, on me. We'll go after the other one."

The mercenary ships were different models, which meant they were most likely two different crews. Someone was paying an awful lot to disrupt this mission, and Derek knew, almost without a doubt, that it had to be the Drokarans. While one part of his mind was working through the politics and implications of the situation, the other was focused on making tactical decisions and not getting blown out of the sky.

"*Horizon* control," he spoke calmly, "can you scramble the rest of the squadron?"

"Negative, Commander," control answered. "The launch bay sustained heavy damage."

"Roger that," he responded, his voice still even. *Shit*, he thought, *we're going to have quite a fight.*

Derek sent his ship into a steep dive under *Horizon*. Alaric followed him and the larger mercenary ship turned to make another run at them. Evading weapons fire, he allowed it to chase them until they'd cleared *Horizon*. Then he ordered, "Alaric, break hard left, I'll go right. He'll follow one of us."

"Roger that, sir," Alaric acknowledged.

As soon as they split up the mercenary ship followed Alaric. *Good*, Derek thought. He wanted to take the shot himself. Throttling back hard he brought his ship around, now behind the other two.

"He's on me tight." Alaric sounded panicked, and Derek could see the attacking ship closing in.

"On my mark, pull up!" Derek barked. "Three, two, one, now!"

Alaric's ship lifted quickly out of the way and Derek fired. The shots made good contact. Derek watched the damaged ship spin several times, finally correct itself, and change course away from *Horizon*.

"Nice shooting, Commander." Relief echoed in Alaric's voice. "Want me to go after him?"

Sweat dripped between Derek's shoulder blades. "Negative," he answered. "We have to protect *Horizon*."

They both headed back to the firefight, but there wasn't much left to do. Kade and Maren had kept the smaller ship busy, and just as Derek turned toward the action, *Horizon* fired. The remaining enemy ship exploded in a brilliant display of quick burning flame and flying metal.

# CAELI

## CHAPTER 25

Caeli was in the infirmary when the ship was hit, and she was knocked into the wall, stunned. Alarms began to sound and everyone around her moved with practiced, purposeful urgency. Her breathing was ragged and shallow as she fought to regain control of herself and not to slip into that dark place that rendered her immobile. She shook her head to clear it, and at that moment a voice spoke from the com system, "Casualties in the launch bay. Medical team needed. Status critical."

Her adrenaline surged as she took off toward the launch bay. She could feel a low, powerful vibration pulse through the ship. *Horizon* was firing its weapons. Her mind reached out to Derek as she ran. She allowed her consciousness to brush up against his just enough to sense that he was all right, and to let him know that she was as well, but not enough to distract him. She breathed a small sigh of relief.

That relief was short-lived, though, as she arrived at the launch bay. The area surrounding it was severely damaged, and there were officers clearing debris from the door and trying to gain access through a mangled passageway. She recognized two of the pilots from the squadron, and they looked more anxious than anyone else she had seen.

One of them looked up and saw her approach. "Our second team is trapped in there, along with the deck crew. They're injured," he informed her. "The atmospheric containment is holding, but the ship automatically locked down the area. The override command isn't responding. We have to break in manually."

"Can you open it enough for me to get through?" she asked. "If they're injured, I can start treating them right away, while you clear the space for the medical team."

He nodded at her and got the rest of the crew to work with him on the door. "Get as close as you can," he ordered her, and then to the others, "On three we pull."

They opened just enough space for her to turn sideways and squeeze through. She stumbled out the other side and into the launch bay. Blinking, she tried to reconcile this mess with what she knew it ought to look like. Thick smoke made her cough and blurred her vision, so she closed her eyes and reached out with her mind to find any signs of life. Seven. There were seven people alive in this room somewhere, and she knew right away that one of them was Kat.

She found her sitting upright against a back wall, semiconscious, with Drew on the ground next to her. Quickly she knelt at Kat's side and touched her lightly on the shoulder, scanning with her mind for injuries. She was bleeding profusely from her head and definitely had a serious concussion. Her left arm hung uselessly at her side and was broken in several places, and she also had rib fractures. While she was seriously injured, nothing was life threatening. Kat looked up at her with pain and panic in her eyes and tried to speak.

Communicating directly into Kat's mind she tried to reassure her, "You're going to be okay. I'm here, and the rest of the medical team is coming."

Kat nodded, barely. Her hand was on Drew and a tear escaped from the corner of her eye. "Please help him," she whispered.

Drew's chest was very nearly crushed, and he had severe head trauma. Caeli placed her hands on his shoulders and closed her eyes, shutting out the chaos around her. His heart was struggling to beat despite the viscous blood pooling around it. Caeli stopped the hemorrhaging and removed the most damaging bits of bone. It was only enough to stabilize him, but it would buy him time.

She spoke to Kat once more, "I've repaired his most critical injuries. We'll take care of you both as soon as we get you back to the infirmary. Right now there are more people alive in here and I need to go find them."

Kat nodded again and then gasped, "Collins was in his fighter doing a check, and a couple of the other guys were in the control room."

She got up and looked around at the wreckage more carefully. She could see the four fighters that were due to launch next, but they were badly damaged and she couldn't find any signs of life inside them. The control room was at the far end of the bay. Climbing over debris, she found the space still mostly intact, and when she slid the door open, she knew the occupants were alive. There were two crewmembers—engineers, if she remembered correctly—stunned on the ground but with only minor injuries. She went to each one and assured them that help was coming and to stay where they were, and then went back out to the launch bay. She could hear the pilots breaking through the main access way and hurried over to meet the medical team.

Dr. Gates was the first to come through the cleared entryway, pulling a stretcher loaded with equipment. She didn't waste any time and updated him, "Kat and Drew are back there," she pointed. "Kat is serious; Drew is critical but stabilized for the moment. There are two more with minor injuries in the control room, and I know that there are three more alive in here."

Gates nodded his head and assumed control of the situation, "Get them back to the infirmary," he ordered two of his team members. Then, to one of the pilots that had entered behind his team, "Escort the crew from the control room out." He turned to Caeli. "Find the other survivors. We'll be right behind you."

She stretched out her mind and located the faint traces of life that she knew were still in the room. Moving toward the opposite side of the bay, away from where she had found Kat and Drew, she found a body trapped beneath some heavy debris.

"Here," she called out, and Gates ordered more crew members to remove the obstruction. The body was slowly uncovered, and Caeli recognized him as another one of the squadron pilots.

Placing her hands on him, she scanned his body just as she had done for the others, but this time she spoke her findings out loud to Dr. Gates. "His left femur is fractured, pelvis too, ribs are damaged, and spleen is ruptured. I'll repair the spleen, and then you should be able to move him." She located the laceration and stopped the bleeding. When she finished, she nodded at Gates, who gave the order to move him.

Just as she was about to look for the last two injured bodies, another crewmember shouted, "I've got them over here," and both she and Gates hurried over. They were behind what looked like a storage locker. A heavy metal beam had fallen across the lower leg of one officer and was pinning her to the ground. She was conscious, and when they knelt beside her, she explained with frustration, "The damn thing knocked Evans out and then fell on me. I can't even budge it."

A string of profanity followed the explanation and Dr. Gates gave a short laugh. "We'll get you out of here." He motioned for some help moving the beam and then turned his attention to Evans, who was blinking himself back to consciousness.

"Dr. Crys, help him to the infirmary, and then we'll start working on our critical patients." She nodded and moved to get up, sending her mind out once more to make sure she hadn't missed anyone. Before leaving she spoke to Dr. Gates, "We've found all the living, but I think there were some fatalities. I won't be any help locating them." He acknowledged that piece of information with a slight nod and turned to speak to another officer about organizing a search and recovery operation.

Evans needed some help getting to his feet, and he was groggy as they walked out of the wreckage and toward the clinic. Caeli tried to keep him engaged in conversation while helping him stay upright and moving forward. He seemed alert by the time they reached the infirmary, and she knew he was going to be fine.

The space was filled with controlled chaos, and she was relieved when Dr. Gates arrived only moments later. "I don't think we have any more casualties coming in, so let's make a plan," he began. "You deal with Lieutenant Chase, and I've got Williams."

Drew was still unconscious when they arrived at his side. His skin was pale and his breathing shallow, but he was already receiving fluid replacements. She was grateful for the competent assistant. Most of the medical assistants on *Horizon* had been combat medics, and while they did not have the advanced science background of a physician, they were familiar with all the technology in the infirmary, had a solid working knowledge of human anatomy, and were highly skilled at dealing with trauma.

Caeli was confident she could treat Drew effectively, which was a very different experience from working with the Amathi on difficult cases or caring for Derek alone in the forest. Between her mind and the advanced technology on this ship, he had the best chance possible.

Kat was on the bed next to Drew's. Her broken bones were already being aligned and set, and her head wound was cleaned and repaired. She was staring at Drew, worried.

"Kat," Caeli called softly, "he'll be all right."

The scanning device projected a three-dimensional image of Drew's damaged chest into the space directly above his head. Caeli could see broken ribs and the fluid buildup in the pericardium, the sac surrounding his heart. She had stopped the active bleeding in the launch bay, but now the pressure needed to be released, and she had to be sure his heart wasn't damaged.

She inserted a syringe into the pericardium and slowly withdrew the fluid. Her eyes widened as she watched the scanned image above his head. It was almost exactly what she pictured in her own mind. Next, the assistant adjusted the scanner to image the heart directly. They were able to examine the heart muscle from all angles.

Caeli looked over at Kat. "There's no damage to his heart." Kat nodded with a small measure of relief.

"Okay, let's move up to his head," she instructed.

"We've already started him on diuretics and high-flow oxygen, and we're monitoring the pressure level," the assistant reported to her.

"Good," she answered as the image of his skull and brain appeared in place of the heart. She looked at the visual image and reached out with her mind. "That's a sizeable fracture, but it hasn't splintered into the brain. And there"—she pointed at a darkened spot on the scan—"that's where the brain matter hit up against the skull. There's probably a spot on the opposite side from the bounce-back." She rotated the image, and in fact there was similar damage to the other side. "What is your protocol for repairing this kind of injury?" she inquired.

"We have neuro-stimulating drugs that will coax the tissue to repair itself," was the answer.

"How fast-acting are they?" she asked.

"Very. They'll start working within hours."

That result was as good as her own empathic remedy and wouldn't leave her exhausted. "Excellent," she said. "Start a course, keep him in an induced coma, and monitor his pressure. Let me know if anything changes."

Before leaving to attend to the less-seriously injured crewmembers who she knew were waiting stoically elsewhere in the infirmary, she sat down on the edge of Kat's bed for a moment. "Is he really going to be okay?" Kat asked. The vulnerability in Kat's voice was uncharacteristic.

Nodding Caeli replied, "I really think so. I'll feel better when we can let him wake up, but I know we didn't miss anything. He's strong." It was the truth, and they both sighed with relief. Kat took her hand and, looking her in the eye, said fiercely, "Thank you. I mean it."

***

The next several hours flew by in a rush. She treated minor injuries, checked back in on Kat and Drew, and reorganized the infirmary space, which had been decimated by the flurry of activity. She and Dr. Gates worked easily together, and in a quiet moment, when they were reviewing Drew's latest test results, he said to her, "You saved lives today. Please know you have a place in my clinic for as long as you're on this ship."

"This is one of the only familiar things in my life right now." She gestured around at the infirmary space. "It's what I do. It means everything to be welcome here. Thank you."

Just then one of the squadron pilots entered the room. His face was drawn and when he spoke his voice was shaky. "We lost four, Doc. Lieutenant Collins, two of the deck crew, and an engineer."

"Damn," Dr. Gates said between clenched teeth. "All right, bring the bodies up to the morgue."

"Yes, sir," the pilot answered. Caeli could see he was doing his best to hold his emotions in check and that he was as exhausted, both physically and emotionally, as she was.

She looked over at Dr. Gates, "Maybe I could help with that?" He nodded with understanding.

"You're Lieutenant Kline?" She hoped she remembered his name correctly.

"Yes, Matt's my given name, but almost everyone calls me Tree."

She looked at him and tilted her head. He *was* rather solidly built. It seemed an apt nickname, and she couldn't keep the small grin from her face. He smiled too and for a moment they shared a little levity before arriving back at the launch bay and tending to their dead.

# DEREK

## CHAPTER 26

The fighter squadron landed ahead of *Horizon*. The airstrip where they touched down was part of a large military base on Tharsis. They were safe, but Derek was still on edge. Although the firefight had ended quickly, it had been intense, and the adrenaline hadn't quite left his system.

It had been unsatisfying to let the one ship go, but his first and only priority was to protect *Horizon* and assure the diplomatic team's safety. He suspected the mercenary ship had landed somewhere on Tharsis anyway, and that would make interesting work for another day.

He'd been able to see the damage to *Horizon* from his starboard aft position flanking the large ship, and it was daunting. *Horizon* would be grounded on the planet for weeks.

*Well*, he thought, *I'll have time to go looking for that mercenary crew*. His mind was already reviewing the old contacts he had on this planet and thinking through the implications of this bold attempt to take out a high-level diplomatic team on an Alliance vessel. Tharsis was in trouble. He needed to talk to Captain Donovan and start sorting this shit out.

He stood with his pilots at the edge of the airfield in the company of the Tharsian security team. They were all armed and on alert. His thoughts drifted to Caeli. He knew she was okay from the subtle way she had brushed his consciousness earlier. Now that the fight was over, he was worried about the rest of *Horizon*'s crew and the casualties they'd incurred. He was impatient to be back onboard.

\*\*\*

"Again, I'm glad to see you in one piece," Donovan said with feeling in his voice. They had already handed the diplomatic team safely over to the Tharsian military and were debriefing in the captain's quarters.

"We lost four," Donovan continued somberly. "Collins was doing a check inside his ship when the launch bay was hit."

Derek didn't speak for a moment. Two losses in a month; it was an awful blow to his tight-knit unit. Finally he asked, "Who else?"

"Broward, Lewis, and Kent," the captain answered.

He knew who they were. These guys were present at all his launches, they kept his ships in good repair, and they basically handled everything else so he and his pilots could do what they did best. Fly. He exhaled loudly, "It's been a really rough couple of weeks."

Donovan nodded. "Dr. Crys was an asset today. Gates said she was in the launch bay before anyone else could access it and saved lives. I found her in the morgue later taking care of the bodies. She's a good find, Commander." It was high praise coming from the stoic captain, and Derek acknowledged it with a small grin.

"Not sure I deserve her, sir," he admitted with a very uncharacteristic show of insecurity.

Donovan just raised his eyebrows.

Wanting to get to Caeli, and needing very much to share his thoughts on the attack, he changed the subject. "I think I recognized one of the mercenary ships." He had Donovan's full attention. "The pilot's name is Bren Garen. We've used similar connections for arms dealing here on Tharsis, and I've bartered with him for different weapons in the past. He's a true mercenary with almost no conscience. I'm sure he was paid by the Drokarans to take out the diplomatic team. Maybe the other attacking ship was insurance." Derek's speech was stream of consciousness now.

He stood up and began to pace the room, but Donovan knew enough to let him work through his thoughts without interruption.

"He must have landed on Tharsis. His ship was too damaged to make it to another system. Can we get Allied ground intelligence to start looking for him?"

There was a small complement of Alliance intelligence officers and locally paid Alliance informants on Tharsis.

"Make the request," Donovan ordered with a nod.

Derek continued, "This attack was bold. We knew the Drokarans were looking at Tharsis, but this action strongly suggests they've committed to taking the planet. I'm willing to bet they already have operatives on the ground. We need to review all the intelligence data that our guys here have gathered, and I think I need to make contact with Garen."

He was still pacing. "I can put the word out that I'm interested in whatever new stealth tech he's got, and that I'm interested in brokering a deal for it. Maybe we can actually figure out who developed it, but that would just be my in for making contact. I can find out who hired him and see what else I can learn about the Drokaran plan."

He made eye contact with Captain Donovan again, his mind finally slowing down. Donovan shook his head and grinned. "This is really why you're part of my crew. Contact our people here. They shouldn't have any trouble finding Garen if he's on the planet, and then you can work with them to start rebuilding your cover. We're going to be here for a while anyway. We might as well try to stop a war." This was as close to humor as Donovan got.

"Now," Donovan finished, standing up, "get yourself into the shower, go see your team, get some sleep, and spend some time with the lovely doctor, and not necessarily in that order. We'll brief again first thing in the morning."

"Thank you, sir." Derek was already on his feet.

*** 

He really did need a shower. His flight suit felt like it was plastered against his body with dried sweat, but he headed directly to the infirmary anyway. He knew Caeli was okay, but he needed to see for himself. And maybe she would consider taking the necessary shower with him? Inspired, he quickened his pace.

The clinic was quiet and in relatively good order, and he could only imagine what it had been like earlier. He nodded at Dr. Gates, who motioned over his shoulder. "She's back there with Kat and Drew."

"Thanks, Doc." He kept walking and then paused at the entryway to the dimly lit room. She was standing by Drew's bed, looking at the monitor above his head. Kat was in the bed next to Drew, and beside Kat was Lieutenant Williams. They were all sleeping peacefully. Caeli turned toward him, sensing his presence in the room.

"Derek," she breathed his name, and he could hear relief in her voice. Then she was in his arms and he felt her rapid heartbeat against his own chest. She touched her mind to his, sharing her memory of the day, the fear, the carnage, the loss, and then the satisfaction of being able to help. He could also feel her desire to be as close as possible, and it was as intense as his own. Brushing a few curls away from her face, he kissed her.

"Ahem," a voice from one of the beds interrupted. He looked over to see Kat grinning at them.

"Hey boss," she said drowsily. "You look like shit."

"Better than you," he answered back, smiling at her.

He let Caeli slip out of his arms, and they both walked closer to Kat's bed.

"How are you feeling?" he asked with genuine concern.

"Like I got blasted into next week by some asshole," she remarked cheerfully. "Oh wait, I did."

They all laughed, and then she answered more seriously, "I'll be okay. Everything's already patched up. Just need a day or two for the bones to heal all the way."

"And Drew and Williams?" He turned to Caeli.

"We've got Drew in an induced coma while his brain is healing. I'm hoping to wake him up tomorrow and then we'll know for sure, but every indication says he should heal completely," Caeli answered, and Derek noticed that she looked at Kat as she said this.

Continuing, she motioned to Williams, "His internal injuries are fully repaired, and like Kat, his broken bones just need a little time to mend. He lost a lot of blood, so we're still rebuilding his volume, but he'll be fine too."

"You've all had a rough day," he acknowledged.

"I'm sure yours wasn't much better. Who was it? Do you know?" Kat inquired, jumping right back into the game. He and Kat were a lot alike.

He nodded, "Bren Garen." Kat raised her eyebrows with recognition, and he added, "I'm betting the Drokarans paid him. We don't know about the other crew because there wasn't anything left of their ship, but Garen is almost definitely on Tharsis," he said, sure the note of satisfaction in his voice didn't escape Kat.

"You're going after him?" she asked, although it was clear she already knew the answer.

"Donovan's given the okay," he affirmed.

"What's the plan?" Kat's eyes were lighting up. "And I want in. I've worked this planet. I know this place as well as you do . . ."

Before she could go any further, and he knew she was going to bite into this with a vengeance, he stopped her, saying, "I want you in, but first you need to get better." He walked over and kissed her forehead, stunning her into silence. "So shut up and go to sleep."

"Yes, sir," she said, with only a little sarcasm.

"I'm really glad you're okay," he said earnestly and then added, "Drew and Williams too."

Kat swallowed and nodded. "First Tommy and now Collins," she whispered, her voice breaking. "This sucks."

He squeezed her hand, "Yeah, it does."

They stood together silently for a few moments and then Caeli spoke, "Kat, I'm going to give you something to help you sleep."

Kat looked over at her gratefully. "Thanks. I can't seem to

shut my brain off," she admitted.

"I know," Caeli said and drew up the syringe.

\*\*\*

They went to the shower in his quarters. It was bigger, a privilege that came with his rank. He pushed her up against the wall as hot water poured over them, and he thoroughly enjoyed licking the rivulets that dripped off her neck and down her shoulders. She shivered and lifted her face up to kiss him. There was desperation in her eyes, and her kiss was urgent. He understood. They both needed to feel alive.

But he pulled away. Tonight he wanted to give her something more than raw physicality. He wanted to replace the ugliness of the day with something beautiful, and he realized that he wanted this as much for himself as for her. First, he washed her hair, lathering the wet curls on top of her head, and then he held her under the water to rinse. He poured liquid soap onto a cloth and washed every inch of her body. "You are so beautiful," he said out loud, even though he knew she could hear the thought.

She smiled. "My turn," she said taking the cloth out of his hands and adding more soap. He closed his eyes.

They dried each other, the heat between them rising. Pulling the blankets off the bunk, he laid her down, covering her body with his. He kissed her neck and her shoulders then began to run his tongue down her chest toward her stomach. He lingered there for a moment and then shifted lower. She gasped and tangled her fingers in his hair, arching her back in response. He breathed in her smell—so clean, soapy, female, *so Caeli*. Groaning, he moved back on top of her.

Later, when he lifted his head up to kiss her, he noticed the tears streaming down her face. He pulled the blankets up and rolled her into his arms. He understood her tears. Today they had nearly lost each other, and it wouldn't be the last time.

"I love you," he said. It was all he had to offer.

# CHAPTER 27

Waking up every morning with a woman in his arms was an experience Derek hadn't had in years, and he was both surprised and pleased by how much he enjoyed it. Rising early was a habit he and Caeli shared, but this morning neither wanted to move. Partly it was exhaustion from the previous day's events, and partly it was a need to be with each other. He held her close for a few long moments and did not let himself think about what *could* have happened to her.

"I'd like to stay here for a few more hours," he sighed. "Hell, a few more days would be good."

"Definitely days," she yawned and then pulled the blankets up over her head. "I miss the beach."

"That was a nice time." He grinned broadly at the memory.

She laughed and he was struck again by how resilient she was. Yesterday she was patching together members of his crew and cleaning bodies in the morgue, yet today she seemed unburdened. He knew how deeply she was affected by the death and destruction, but she woke up ready to face another day. Well, almost ready. She still hadn't emerged from under the blankets.

"Okay, we can't avoid it any longer. Let's get going." He sat on the edge of the bed and pulled on his pants.

She was lying on her side, watching him dress. "What are

your plans today? I heard what you said to Kat about Bren Garen. You think he's here?"

"I know how much damage his ship sustained, and he couldn't have made it out of this system. I'm checking in with Donovan and our intelligence guys this morning, but I really need to meet with the Alliance agents on the planet. I need to see their data." He tucked his uniform shirt into his pants and stood up.

"Tharsis is in more trouble than we originally thought, and Kat and I have connections here from a few years ago. The Drokarans are ready to make a move—I can feel it—and we have to stay ahead of them. Garen's involved, and even if all he can do is point me to the Drokaran who's paying him, that'll be a start."

The more he talked about the situation, the more anxious he was to get to work. He knew she was sensitive to his mood shift. In fact, he was probably projecting his anxiety directly into her mind right now.

She was moving now too, pulling on her jumpsuit and running a brush through her hair. "You're leaving the ship today?" she asked.

"Probably in the next few days," he confirmed as he walked into the bathroom. "I have to arrange a few things first."

"I've never been on another planet." She followed him in to wash her face.

He stopped what he was doing. "I'll make sure you get to leave the ship," he promised, and she smiled eagerly.

"I'll come find you in the clinic later today," he said as he finished his morning routine, gave her a quick kiss goodbye, and walked out the door.

\*\*\*

His meeting with Captain Donovan was brief. He outlined his plan to connect with the intelligence team on *Horizon* first and then to make contact with the Alliance operatives on Tharsis. If possible, he wanted to be looking at their data live, today. Donovan agreed and asked for periodic updates.

There would come a point where his activities on Tharsis would become independent of *Horizon*'s, but until they knew what they were up against, he would gather information and bring it back for analysis.

His first stop was the tech deck. He had to admit he was envious of all the complicated gadgets the science team and intelligence analysts got to work with. Right now, he was interested in tracking Garen's ship. There was a vast array of sensors on *Horizon*, and he knew that someone in the room would be able to make sense of all the data.

"Hey Reece," he called to one of the officers who he thought was particularly sharp.

"Commander, how's it going?" Reece looked up from his screen.

"Not too bad, considering," he answered and sat down next to Reece. "I need to track the ship that got away."

"I figured you'd be looking for it," Reece began to manipulate his touch screen, "so I started to pull together all the infrared spectrum data, the ion trail, the heat signature data . . ."

"Uh, Reece," Derek interrupted, with as much patience as he could muster. "Can you just tell me where it landed?"

Reece nodded. "Sure, Commander," and he was quiet for a moment, working. Then he looked up and explained, "*Horizon* orbited the planet once before landing. I can try to match up the sensor data from right after the firefight with anything we recorded while we were in orbit."

Reece slid his chair over, and a three-dimensional image of Tharsis appeared hovering over a horizontal tablet next to his screen. He continued manipulating his own screen, and finally satisfied, pointed to a white path making its way through the simulated planet's atmosphere. He tapped his screen, the holographic planet rotated, and they were able to follow a ship's trail. "There you go. Southern continent, northwest region," Reece pointed again. "It's definitely here."

"Nice, Lieutenant." He stood up. "Thank you."

Next he found the communications officer on duty. She was young and had joined *Horizon* at the start of this tour, but she was smart and the daughter of diplomats, so she understood the subtleties of intelligence work as well as anyone he'd ever met. "Riley, what's up?" he greeted her cheerfully.

She turned to him and smiled, "What can I do for you, Commander?"

"I need a secure communication link with one of our operatives in Darien," he told her, referring to the region on the planet's southern continent closest to where the mercenary ship had landed.

"Okay, I'll get to work on that. Reach you by com?" she asked.

"Yes please," he said over his shoulder as he left the deck.

Connecting with the operatives on Tharsis could take some time, anywhere from an hour to a few days. He hoped it would be sooner rather than later. It completely depended on which agents, what they were involved with, how quickly Riley's message got to them, and then how quickly they could disappear and acquire a secure communication line. In the meantime, he headed for the launch bay to check out the damage there and assess the progress on repairs.

It was worse than he imagined, and he exhaled loudly when he entered. Nearly every smaller ship *Horizon* carried, from the fighters to the shuttles, had sustained some damage, and the deck space itself needed major repairs. Even with the flurry of activity and the added ground team from Tharsis, it was going to take some time.

He walked over to Collins's fighter, the one he knew his friend had been killed in yesterday. He hoped Collins never knew what hit him. His mind wandered back to his crash on Almagest and the brief but awful moment of terror and pain when his ship hit the ground. If Caeli hadn't found him, he would never have regained consciousness, and that memory would have been his last. It was a sobering thought, and he ran his hand over the cold metal of Collins's ship.

*** 

Three weeks for repairs. This was the estimate the chief engineer gave him before he left the launch bay and headed to the mess hall to grab something to eat. The smaller ships would be moved onto the military base where there was more room to work, and crews from Tharsis and *Horizon* would be working around the clock.

He ate quickly, not really paying attention to the food on his plate. His mind was racing again, moving from the damage assessment, to finding Garen, to retrieving the information he needed as efficiently as possible. As he thought about this, an idea that had been hovering in the back of his mind began to assert itself, and he got up to find Kat.

"You look much better today," he commented, finding her dressed and sitting in a chair next to Drew in the clinic.

She grinned at him and lifted her arm to show him how well it was healed. "I had a good doctor or two," she acknowledged.

Derek looked over at Drew, who looked back at him, weary but alert. He breathed a sigh of relief. "Nice to have you back," he said.

"Thanks. My head hurts like hell, but it's better than the alternative," Drew said with equal feeling.

"I hear that," Derek answered. "I need to borrow Kat for a few minutes. Catch you later." Kat followed him out of the clinic.

"Is Caeli here?" He looked around for her as they left Drew's room.

"She was earlier, but I think she went to go do some personal work on the rec deck," Kat answered.

"Okay good. I need to run something by you, and I need your honest feedback." And then he added almost under his breath, "As if I won't get it anyway."

"It's why you love me," she grinned.

He nodded in agreement. "True. You're a pain in the ass, but . . ."

She smacked him in the arm, playfully but hard.

"Isn't there a rule that you can't strike a superior officer?" he joked.

She just rolled her eyes at him so he found them a place to sit in an empty office space and started talking, "I've asked Riley to set up a secure communication link with the operatives in Darien. I know for sure Garen's here, and I want to see if he's back in the market for anything. I'm sure he needs equipment to get his ship repaired, and he'll be working the local contacts for that. Hopefully we can track him that way. I also want to know if the Darien guys have any sense of the Drokaran objective here."

Kat nodded and then added, "Well, they wanted the diplomatic team out of the way. But if they follow their past pattern, they'll have more than one plan in the works. Drokaran operatives must be in play on the ground already. We need to know if the locals have any clue."

"Once we have more information, I'll assemble our team and get out there," he continued. "Obviously you're in. We can work out the rest a little later."

He paused, and she caught his hesitancy. "What's bothering you?"

"I want Caeli with us." He thought it best to put the idea right out there.

He expected an explosive response from Kat and was surprised when instead she only asked in a matter-of-fact tone, "Why?"

"You know that she has certain gifts or skills or whatever." He waved his arm through the air with slight frustration. "I don't really know what else to call them."

Kat just nodded again, "I got a little taste of it in the launch bay."

He looked at her pointedly and said, "Healing isn't the only thing she can do. With one touch, she could have every piece of information we need out of Garen's head, or anyone else's for that matter."

"Shit," Kat whispered, and he knew right away she understood his dilemma. "She won't want to do this."

"No," he confirmed. "The rules in her society forbid it, and hell, you can understand why. But time is critical, and Garen is a tough bastard. He won't give up anything he doesn't want to, at least not for a while," he added meaningfully.

"Shit, Derek," Kat said.

"Yeah," he sighed and ran his hand through his hair. They

both sat for a moment, and then he asked her, "Well, first things first; are you willing to work with Caeli on the ground?"

Kat nodded, "A few days ago I would have said no way, but I saw her keep her head on straight and do her job while things were blowing up around her. I don't think she'd be a liability in controlled circumstances."

"I know what she was doing on her own planet with their resistance movement, and I'm pretty confident she could manage a limited mission with us," he agreed. "My plan would be to bring Garen to her anyway, somewhere safe."

"Will she do it?" Kat asked.

"I don't know," he swallowed. "My real question is, should I even be asking her?"

Kat took a moment to respond. "Hundreds, maybe thousands of lives could be at stake. A whole planet is at risk. I think you have to ask her."

He always appreciated Kat's clarity, even if things weren't as black-and-white for him. He knew what he'd be asking of Caeli. He knew how she'd felt when she forced her way into Connor's mind. He also knew that she'd done it because the thought of sacrificing an innocent was more repulsive than violating her own ethical standards. He fully understood the position he would be putting her in, and he felt like shit for doing it.

# CHAPTER 28

Derek was on his way to see Donovan when Riley reached him to say she'd made contact and scheduled his communication, so he headed for the tech deck instead of the bridge. Better that he had as much information as possible before he began to assemble his team anyway.

He followed Riley into one of the workrooms and with a few finger taps she had a live image up on the small screen.

"The feed is quantum encrypted, so it's secure," Riley assured him. "You have the room, sir." And as she left, the door slid closed behind her.

He recognized the man on the screen from his past work on Tharsis. Andreas was native to the planet and was an Alliance operative only in the loosest sense. He was actually a criminal, and his business interests generally fell far outside the mainstream laws of his society. But he recognized that there were bigger threats to his home world, and that the Alliance provided a defensive wall between Tharsis and those threats.

It was a delicately balanced relationship, but when Andreas was convinced a situation warranted his involvement, the information and connections he provided were invaluable. Of all the potential contacts Derek had in this region of the planet, Andreas was the best choice for what was needed. He'd have to remember to thank Riley later.

"Markham, it's been a while," Andreas greeted him.

"Almost two years, I think," he answered. "How's business?"

"Booming," Andreas grinned. "But I understand we have a problem?"

"I think there are Drokarans on the ground planning terrorist activities," he said bluntly. He noticed Andreas did not look surprised, so he continued, "I'm sure you know about the attack on the diplomatic team?"

Andreas nodded, "I'm glad it was unsuccessful."

"It was Bren Garen," he stated. Andreas *was* surprised by this piece of information.

"I know he's been on the planet for over a month," Andreas shared. "He's been interested in high-yield explosives. Not my area, so I haven't had much to do with him. You think he's working with the Drokarans?"

"I'm almost positive. They failed to take out the diplomatic team, but if the Drokarans are interested in totally destabilizing Tharsis, like they did on Mira and Delphis, then that won't be their only play. They must have agents on the ground here already, and my only potential link to them is Garen."

"So you need to find him?" Andreas asked. "And you want my help to do it?"

"Are you willing?"

"If that fuck is working with the Drokarans, I have no use for him," Andreas growled, his voice quiet but deadly.

However convoluted Andreas's code of ethics was, he *did* have one, and working with the Drokarans clearly violated it. "What do you need from me?" he asked.

"I want to bring in my own team, so I need a secure place

for them to work, and then I need housing, preferably in the same area. An apartment that looks like we've lived in it for a few weeks would be good." Derek's mind moved quickly, creating the plan as he spoke. "I need local currency and a lot of it. You know I'll get it back to you, plus your fee for service." Andreas nodded so he kept going, "Can you put it out there that I've been on Tharsis for a couple of weeks now, and I've heard Garen has some kind of new stealth tech that I'm interested in acquiring?"

"Does he?" Andreas asked, interested.

"Yes, actually," Derek admitted, "and maybe I'll get a hold of it too, but that isn't my primary objective."

"Understood. I can have everything ready by tomorrow."

"Excellent. I'm going to send my technical team in first because some of my ground team will need another day or two to recover from injuries. Can your people escort them to the safe house and provide security?"

"Of course." Andreas seemed almost insulted by the question.

Derek laughed and then added more seriously, "I don't know what else we might need as we go. Weapons, tactical support— it could be anything, depending on what the Drokarans have planned." He paused for a moment then continued, "And there may be a point where I'll have to involve the Tharsian government. You know I'll protect your interests if that becomes necessary," he promised. If the Tharsian government became involved officially, Andreas and his people would have to disappear back into the underworld.

"I wouldn't be here now if I didn't trust your word or your intentions," Andreas answered, raising his eyebrows for emphasis. "I'll send instructions to the attractive young woman who contacted me. Riley, I believe?" Andreas grinned charmingly. "I'll let her know where my people will meet your team. Once they're set up, I'll communicate directly with them until you arrive."

"Sounds like a plan. I'll see you soon." And they ended the communication.

***

For the second time that day Derek was seated across from Captain Donovan, this time updating him on his conversation with Andreas. "I'm concerned about Garen's interest in high-yield explosives," he explained.

The captain shook his head, "Andreas has no idea who Garen's been dealing with?"

"He wasn't really paying close attention. But he will be now. I want to send the technical team in tomorrow. I'm thinking about Riley, Reece, and Jacobs. Riley is pretty inexperienced, but she's got great instincts." He was again remembering how she could have put him in touch with some of the more "official" Alliance agents, those known to the government on Tharsis, but she had clearly researched his past mission history and chose the contact she thought would be most effective. "Reece talks too much, but he's a genius, and Jacobs has the experience."

Donovan agreed, then asked, "And your ground team?"

"I'll give them another day, but I want Kat and Drew. You know Kat and I have worked this planet before, and with talk of explosives, Drew seems the logical choice." Drew had been on Mira during the worst of the fighting there, and although the planet had ultimately been lost to the Drokarans, Drew's expertise had disabled some nasty devices.

Derek paused, and then with a hint of apprehension in his voice said, "I want to bring Caeli."

Donovan sat back in his chair, waiting for more of an explanation.

"She can get the information we need from Garen quickly and easily. Kat and I can do it, certainly with Andreas's help, but it won't be quick and it won't be pretty." He waited for the captain's response.

"I'm sure you've already thought about what my objections will be, but I'll say them anyway," Donovan looked at him directly. "She's a civilian. You're involved with her. We will be putting her at tremendous risk."

"And if I hadn't seen the destruction on Mira, I wouldn't even consider it," Derek said quietly. "Tharsis will end up the same way, and the Alliance won't send a fleet without more proof than we've got right now."

They both sat still for a moment. He knew he was treading dangerously close to the line drawn in his own conscience. He'd had to make difficult ethical calls before, but this was different, for all the reasons Captain Donovan stated and more.

He knew Caeli was going to say yes. How different was this than Marcus holding a gun to Connor's head? The end result would be saving lives, hopefully, but was that enough? He was counting on Donovan to pull him back if he'd already crossed the line.

"Ask her," Donovan said stonily. "I don't like it, but she could save us valuable time."

Derek knew he looked conflicted as he stood up to leave.

"Commander," Donovan stopped him before he walked out.

"Sir?" he turned back.

"Keep her safe," the captain ordered.

"Yes, sir." He hoped with all his being that he could.

***

He was avoiding her. He knew Caeli was at the clinic, so he headed for the tech deck to prep Riley, Reece, and Jacobs for their mission. Riley especially was keen to be a part of things, and he knew she'd spend the rest of the day, and probably the night, researching and gathering data. He was counting on it.

When he finally ran out of things to do with this team, he sighed and headed for the clinic to start prepping with Kat and Drew, and to have the conversation he was dreading with Caeli. He found Kat in nearly the same spot she'd been in that morning. Drew was sitting up, looking much more alert and attacking the food on the plate in front of him. Kat was sampling things off his tray, and they were involved in what appeared to be a lighthearted conversation.

"Hey," he said. "Sorry to interrupt dinner."

"Pull up a chair. Drew's got more food than he can manage," Kat offered.

Drew looked like he was managing it all fine, so Derek just pulled up a chair next to them. "You're looking much better," he commented.

"Feeling much better, thanks," Drew answered between mouthfuls.

"Are you up on what's happening?" he asked.

Drew nodded. "Yeah. What's the plan?"

"Well, how's your head?"

"Nearly as good as new," Drew grinned. "I can't remember *her* name," he quipped gesturing at Kat, who gave him a scowl, "but other than that . . . another day or so and I'll be out."

"Excellent. We have some intel that Garen's been acquiring high-yield explosives, so I'm going to need you on the ground."

At once Drew's expression became serious. "He's selling to the Drokarans?"

"That's my guess. Garen is well-connected on Tharsis, and if the Drokarans are here and want to stay out of sight, he'd be the perfect middle man." Both Kat and Drew nodded their agreement. "He'll deal in anything profitable—weapons, explosives, tech. We need to get to him," Derek finished.

"This can't become Mira all over again," Drew said quietly, and they knew that behind his even tone a very raw wound still existed.

"It won't," Derek said, with more confidence than he actually felt. "The tech team leaves tomorrow, and we're going to head out the following day." He turned to Kat. "Riley found Andreas, and he's in."

"Smart girl," Kat said, with a rare show of approval. "I'm glad he'll have our backs."

He stood up to leave. "Donovan's given the whole thing a go." Throwing Kat a meaningful look he said, "You can fill Drew in on the rest."

She nodded and tilted her head at him.

"I'm going to find her now," he said, answering Kat's unspoken question.

***

Caeli was in an empty office, manipulating a three-dimensional image of a brain on a holographic screen. She looked up and smiled when he entered. "Hi. I'll be finished in a minute."

"Take your time," he said sitting down in the chair across from her. As he watched her work, he was reminded of the many moments he'd watched her on Almagest tending to one task after another and caring for him. She was beautiful. When he first opened his eyes after the crash, her face was the first thing he saw. He remembered her hand on his chest and the feeling of peace it brought amidst his confusion and pain. He'd convinced her to come with him and be a part of his world, thinking she would be safer, and now he was putting her at risk.

"What's wrong?" she looked up, concerned.

"Am I thinking too loudly?" he teased gently.

She didn't answer but moved out from behind the desk and knelt at his feet. Leaning in, she kissed him and said, "Tell me."

He swallowed hard but looked straight into her eyes and said, "I'm going to ask you to do something. You will not like it, and I think you may not like me for asking," he paused and closed his eyes. "But it's important."

She was still in front of him. "What is it?"

"I need information from Garen. I want you to get it," he said directly. The details didn't matter. The weight of what he was asking did.

"If I say no, people will die, won't they?" He could tell from her tone that she knew the answer.

"I will try to get the information another way, I promise you, but every instinct tells me we don't have much time." He searched her face for any trace of emotion. "I'm sorry," he whispered.

They sat quietly for a long moment, and then she said, "I think maybe this is the best awful choice out of only awful choices." He recognized his own words and gratefully pulled her into his arms.

# CHAPTER 29

With Andreas as their ground support and contact, they wouldn't have to take nearly as much equipment with them. They'd have easy access to weapons, transportation, tech, and more eyes on the ground in more places than they could otherwise arrange.

Caeli had been outfitted by Kat in civilian clothes and was seated on Derek's bunk, watching him pack his personal items. They hadn't spoken much about the actual mission. For the first time since they'd met, he felt slightly uncomfortable with her.

He *thought* he knew how she was feeling, but he wasn't really sure and he didn't want to ask. Truthfully, he didn't want to know. It would probably just make him feel worse than he already did, and he *had* to keep his head in the game. If she sensed his discomfort, and he was pretty sure she did, she wasn't offering anything in response.

"Ready?" he asked.

She nodded and picked up her pack.

"Let's go find Kat and Drew," he said, just to fill the silence.

Kat and Drew were waiting on the lower deck at the ship's ground exit. Captain Donovan was there as well.

"Be careful," Donovan said to the group.

There was a round of "thank you, sir" and then the door slid open.

*Horizon* had been maneuvered into a dry dock in a large hangar on the military base, so when they left the ship, it was only to step into a space filled with engineers and Tharsian military personnel. Derek led them toward the far end of the building and through a security checkpoint, and then they were outside.

Caeli stopped and blinked up at the sky. The Tharsian sun cast a slightly reddish glow, and while the sky was blue, it was a pale color with pinkish hues blending into the horizon. He couldn't help but smile at the wonder on her face, and he was filled with gratitude that he was able to share this moment with her. She stood perfectly still, staring upward, until finally she turned to him and shook her head.

"I have no words for this," she whispered.

He remembered his first off-world experience and grinned at her. As a boy, he'd anticipated that trip for weeks and was excited when it was finally time to go. But his experience paled in comparison to this moment. He had always known there were other worlds, that they were accessible to him, and that he would eventually visit some of them. For Caeli's entire life, her world was it. Even though she and her people knew there were others, they had no real imagination for what that could mean.

He took her hand, and they continued walking. Andreas had sent ground transportation to meet them outside the Tharsian base, and two men Derek vaguely recognized stood casually beside a vehicle, waiting. He greeted them with a nod and they silently slid a door open, gesturing at his small group to get inside.

Caeli was still wide-eyed, staring out the window as the landscape sped by. The capital city was visible in the distance, but they stopped at a building just on the outskirts, in a crowded, lively neighborhood. The driver turned and said, "He's waiting for you inside."

Derek nodded and got out first. Drew, Kat, and Caeli followed as he approached the entryway. The structure was old and ornate but in good repair, and the large doorway opened into a grand foyer. Andreas welcomed them inside.

"Kat, you lovely thing, it's been far too long," he said with typical flourish but genuine feeling nonetheless.

Kat smiled at him and then stepped into his open arms for an embrace. "It has been a long time," she agreed.

He greeted Derek next with equal enthusiasm and then looked over at Drew and Caeli expectantly.

"Let me introduce you to the other members of my team," Derek offered. "This is Drew Chase. He's an expert in explosives. I hope we don't need him, but . . ." He raised his eyebrows and his voice trailed off.

Andreas cringed, "I fear you will, though. I have some more detail about Garen's recent inquiries and purchases." He waved his hands. "I'll fill you in once you're settled here and we can interface with your team downstairs."

Derek sighed and nodded. "I'm not surprised."

When he introduced Caeli as Dr. Crys, he caught the look of interest on Andreas's face but didn't elaborate further. Gracious and mannerly, Andreas simply welcomed her with a charming bow.

"Let me show you to your apartment," he said to the group, and then privately to Derek, "I own this building. The security is tight, and no one will bother you."

Derek knew Andreas had a significant amount of property. He probably owned this building and most of the neighboring ones as well. From his experience with Andreas in the past, he knew the older man enjoyed power and wealth, but mostly he liked being in charge. It was Andreas's opinion that the average person was just not as competent and capable as he was. Certainly the government on Tharsis didn't measure up. And in truth, Andreas wasn't wrong on all counts.

The Tharsian government had struggled with deep-rooted corruption for generations, and the planet had not progressed. In many ways it had actually regressed, and people like Andreas could either be considered opportunistic criminals or visionary saviors, depending on the point of view.

Derek's opinion was that he was a bit of both. Because the infrastructure on the planet was barely functional and the leadership ineffectual, the people's needs were not being met. A network of enterprise grew to fill the gap and ambitious, intelligent people like Andreas built small empires. In his region, Andreas provided protection, security, and productive work for the people he looked after and, in turn, had their loyalty. That some of his wealth and power came from less-than-legal ventures didn't matter in the least.

Andreas led them down a quiet hallway and stopped in front of a door to program a code into a security pad. The door to the apartment slid open, and with a gallant bow he gestured them all inside. The space was beautiful and well furnished. A large kitchen and dining area opened into a living room with plush, inviting sofas; a bar; and a large, ornate fireplace at the far end of the room.

"Take a few moments to settle yourselves, and I will meet you on the lower level. I'll have food brought in for your whole team shortly," Andreas said as he left the room.

The bedrooms and washrooms were off the main living area, and Derek led Caeli into a large, luxurious space with an imposing bed centered against the back wall. He couldn't help his ridiculous grin. He looked over at Caeli, who was biting her lower lip in an effort not to laugh.

"Well, that's . . . roomy," she said, and they both laughed.

He put their bags down in a corner and shut the door. Turning, he tentatively reached for her hand. "Are you okay?" he asked and then softly, "Are *we* okay?"

Her expression turned serious. "I know you need me to do this." She paused, and it seemed as if she were trying to gather her thoughts. "I can't do anything for my own world right now, and I'm really glad that I might be able to help these people. It's just distressing that the way I'll be able to help is by doing something I've been taught my whole life is wrong. But the more I think about it in this context, the less I'm sure it *is* wrong."

She stepped out of his arms and sat on the edge of the bed. "I don't really know what to think, actually. I used to be so clear about right and wrong, good and bad. I was always certain I knew who I was and how I would respond to things." She looked up at him and her expression was confused. "But that changed the day Novalis was destroyed. Things have happened, and are happening, that I couldn't have imagined a year ago, and now I don't know what I should do." She shrugged and sighed.

Derek sat down next to her and brushed a piece of blonde hair out of her face. "We do the best we can where we're at and hope our intentions and our essential character comes out when it needs to." He gestured toward the door. "I have to trust the integrity of the people I work with, and I have to believe the purpose of my work is ultimately for the greater good. Then I make the best choice I can," he paused for a moment, "and I live with it."

She held his gaze and nodded. He stood, and she followed him when he walked back out the door.

\*\*\*

The team was assembled in the basement of the building where Andreas ran his clandestine activities. It was well hidden, well guarded, and equipped with secure communication lines, surveillance technology, a large weapons cache, and underground access to other neighboring buildings. The *Horizon* team had brought their own tech with them, and they were already plugged into the planet's network.

True to his word, and in keeping with the hospitable nature of the Tharsians, Andreas had provided an impressive spread of food. Spicy fish, piles of colorful vegetables, loaves of fresh bread, and pitchers of ice water now covered one of their worktables. Despite the seriousness of their task, Derek's mouth watered and his stomach growled noisily.

Derek watched Caeli's face as she sampled the cuisine. Their eyes met across the table, and she smiled with pleasure. He grinned back at her, remembering their last meal on Almagest fondly. The team concentrated on eating for several silent minutes until finally Riley spoke up between mouthfuls.

"For the first time in centuries, this planet has a legitimate president with the potential to effect change," she began, and everyone shifted their attention to her. "She has managed to navigate the complex criminal network without pissing anyone off and also without compromising her principles."

Andreas didn't react to the mention of the "complex criminal network," but nodded his head slightly in agreement with her assessment.

Riley continued, "Her first major projects are modernizing the planet-wide shuttle system and upgrading the water distribution and irrigation systems. She requested the Alliance diplomatic team to come and work with her because she wants to bring community leaders from the different factions to the table. She needs their support for her plan." Riley stopped for a breath.

Derek asked her, "Was she aware of any Drokaran threat?"

"Well, based on the communications I intercepted between her head of security and Tharsian intelligence, she understands the implications of the attack on the diplomatic team," Riley answered. "Captain Donovan updated her directly from *Horizon* with our suspicions and she certainly wasn't surprised, but she didn't realize the outside threat was so imminent. She's been more worried about her own people rioting."

Derek nodded, and Riley continued, "She knows we're here and she's asked to be informed of our progress."

"I'll make all reports to her personally," Derek informed the team. "We have no idea if her inner circle is compromised. We need to protect ourselves and our intel."

Everyone nodded.

"So what do we know about Bren Garen's whereabouts and activities?" Derek asked Andreas.

"He's actually been in Darien for six months. He planned the attack on the diplomatic team from here, but I don't have much information on his earlier activities," Andreas began. "Since you contacted me, I've had my people keeping track of him. He's been acquiring labor and parts for repairing his ship, and he's just purchased a significant amount of thermal charges and explosive material. He didn't have it in his possession for long, and the hand off was quick. My people have no idea who he sold it to."

"Andreas, can you give all that information to Drew for analysis?" Derek looked over at Andreas, who nodded.

He turned to Drew and added, "We need to know what we're looking for and the possible scale of damage. Andreas, have you been able to let Garen know I want to meet with him?"

"Yes. We've put it out there that you've been in Darien laying low for a while, but you heard he has something new, and you're interested in a possible deal."

"Good. Can you set up a meeting?"

"Already done," Andreas said, smiling. "Tomorrow morning near the docks at the port. He has his ship under repair in one of the large holding containers. I'm leaving Pietr and Alex here with you." He gestured at the two men who had met them outside the military base. "They will transport you and your team anywhere you want to go and will provide whatever you might need. Just say the word."

Derek stood. "Thank you, my friend." He held out his hand, and Andreas shook it firmly. "I hope we can stop whatever is about to happen here. I know we have a much better chance because of you." There was a chorus of goodbyes and thanks from the team, and then Andreas was gone.

Derek ran his hands through his hair and sat back down, his mind racing. He took a deep breath and said, "All right, let's get to work. Drew, start reviewing the data on the bomb materials Garen purchased. Caeli and Kat, work with Riley to see if you can figure out potential targets—markets, malls, schools, transportation centers, any large scale gatherings or activities planned for the next few weeks. You get the idea."

"Jacobs, I want all of the president's communications monitored. I want to know where she is at all times and where she plans to be. Also see if anyone from her inner circle is making suspicious or unauthorized communications. We may need the Tharsian military at some point, and we have to know if there's any kind of threat from inside. Reece, I want a detailed log of Garen's movements since you've been tracking him."

He turned to Pietr and Alex. "I need to be ready to go tomorrow morning for that meeting, and I'll need a different weapon. Something small and quiet would be good." His Alliance-issued sidearm was too obvious and bulky to conceal.

It was Pietr who responded, "I'll be driving you tomorrow, and Alex will stay here." He moved to the back of the room and touched his thumb to a square sensor pad on the wall. A nearly invisible drawer smoothly slid open to reveal an impressive array of weapons. "Take your pick," Pietr offered.

Derek raised his eyebrows and grinned at the display of hardware. He chose one as the rest of his team dispersed and got to work.

# CHAPTER 30

The day flew by. Another meal appeared, as extravagant as the first, and the team continued to work late into the evening. Urgency and frustration kept them moving forward. They had enough evidence to be convinced that terrorist activity was imminent, but no real indication of where it might happen or when it would take place.

He knew the team was exhausted. He'd pushed them to their limit, and they had to get some rest before his meeting. It was well after midnight when he called it a night, and everyone gratefully stumbled to their beds.

"We may just have to *sleep* in this tonight," he joked wearily, gesturing to Caeli at the oversized bed.

She snorted and began to undress. There was nothing seductive about her movements at all, but it didn't matter. The sight of her naked, even for just a moment, gave him a burst of renewed energy.

She turned around grinning, "Seriously?"

"It's your fault," he admonished, pulling her down next to him.

"My fault?" she retorted with mock indignation.

"Yes, this is what happens when you take your clothes off in front of me."

He kissed her before she could respond. Running his hand

over her stomach and down her hip, he appreciated the subtle changes in her body since their rescue. When they met she was fit but slender, almost too slight. Now, although she complained about the food on his ship, she was gaining weight and looked curvier. He loved it. By the time they fell asleep, they'd worn each other out completely.

*** 

Derek woke up early, clear-headed and anxious to start the day. Caeli was still soundly asleep. He left the room, closing the bedroom door quietly behind him. Kat and Drew were already moving around the apartment.

"Good morning, sunshine," Kat greeted him.

"Did you sleep well?" he asked innocently and caught Drew's embarrassed grin.

"As well as you, I'm sure," she answered brightly, and then, "What's the plan?"

"You guys keep on analyzing the data. With any luck, I'll have Garen back here by lunch time." He only hoped it would be that simple.

Pietr was waiting for him on the basement floor, and they left the building. The day was bright and clear, as were most days in this region of Tharsis. Darien had been built centuries ago in a desert. Careful manipulation of the planet's weather patterns allowed the population to expand into challenging, almost uninhabitable regions. Now, controlling the water supplies and irrigation systems was a contentious, sometimes violent activity.

Derek found it promising that the new president identified the need to handle this as a top priority. He wondered how she planned to work with the local criminal organizations that currently controlled the resources. He'd have to ask Andreas. But that was a question for another day and one that would be meaningless anyway if they didn't figure out how to stop the impending attack.

He slid into the vehicle next to Pietr. As they made their way out of the town and toward the coastline, he reviewed the cover story he had created for himself. While his team was busy analyzing data the day before, he had been catching up on the current situation in Darien and integrating events and people into his fabricated life. Riots, criminal activities, political dramas, anything that had happened in the last few months that he could casually reference in conversation.

As they neared their destination, he felt confident in his ability to slip into character. It was one he'd created years earlier for an assignment on this planet and was not so far off from his real personality. He knew he had an edge, and he was completely comfortable in the shadow world he had to navigate when on assignment. Ultimately, the thing that separated him from men like Garen was the fact that he believed in something bigger than himself. But otherwise, well, there *were* certain similarities.

They arrived at the port of Darien and stopped in front of a factory building. "I'll be within sight of the docks if you need me," Pietr said.

"Thanks. I shouldn't be long," Derek answered, opening the door and stepping out into the bright sunshine.

Darien's coastline was a working port. There were spectacular beaches in other regions of the planet, but this area was good only as a seaport. The salty air was crisp, tangy, and familiar, and Derek breathed it in with appreciation and some nostalgia.

Garen's hangar could easily shelter a damaged ship, and

the constant, frenetic activity of the area would certainly camouflage suspicious behavior. It was a perfect place to stay hidden in plain sight.

Derek approached the entrance of the nondescript concrete building and knocked on the door. Almost immediately it opened and Garen himself was grinning broadly on the other side.

"Derek Markham! I heard you were on this side of the galaxy." Garen shook his hand vigorously.

"It's been a while," Derek smiled widely back. The last time he'd seen Garen, Derek had been posing as an arms dealer, and his cover had never been blown. "Good to see you. How're things?"

Garen stepped outside. "Business is booming. Always a lot of opportunity here on Tharsis." He gave Derek a knowing look.

Derek nodded back in agreement. "Yeah, that's why I'm here. It's time for me to find some new employment."

"What are you looking at?" Garen leaned casually up against the building.

"I'm not sure yet. I've been here a couple of months just scoping things out. This place has definitely changed since last time I was here. I'm trying to figure out if I want to stay." He shrugged. "Things could either be really good or really bad, depending on how it shakes out with this new government."

Garen nodded in agreement but didn't offer anything, so Derek continued, "I was working out of Elista for a while and then took some time off." The planet's beautiful name was misguiding. Its underworld made Tharsis look tame.

"Dangerous place to be," Garen commented, raising his eyebrows, impressed.

"But the payoff was outstanding," Derek shrugged, grinning. Then he added, "I do want to stay alive to enjoy it though, so it's time for a change."

"I hear that," Garen agreed, waiting.

Derek took the hint and moved straight to business. "Thanks for meeting. I understand you have some new tech, and I might be interested in a purchase." He waited, and Garen gave a small nod.

"Seems like a worthwhile acquisition in our line of work, if I have my information correct." Derek paused again and then added, "and *if* it's effective."

"Oh, it's effective, all right." Garen's voice became more animated. "I have an exclusive deal with the designer." Garen named a high price for the piece of equipment and Derek raised his eyebrows.

"I definitely need a demo," he countered.

"Yeah, well, that's a bit of a problem right now." Garen motioned Derek inside the hangar where a small crew and a few locals, most likely engineers and ship's mechanics, were working on the craft.

Derek recognized the ship immediately. As he walked around it, he whistled with mock empathy. But remembering Collins's broken ship in *Horizon*'s launch bay, and the deaths that Garen had helped to cause, he was secretly pleased knowing that *he'd* been responsible for this damage. "Damn, how'd you even land this thing?" he asked.

"Not easily," Garen answered, shaking his head.

"What happened?" Derek inquired casually.

"Occupational hazard," was Garen's evasive response. He moved closer to the ship and pointed toward the flight deck. "So I can show you how the tech integrates into the ship's systems, but I can't get it online. It'll probably be another week."

Derek stood thinking. "I'll give you a week for the demo. If I'm interested, how long before I can get it delivered after that?"

"I'm in the middle of another job right now, so not for a couple more weeks," Garen shrugged apologetically. "After I demo it, I'll take a deposit and then full payment on delivery."

Derek nodded, secretly frustrated. He was hoping to lure Garen back to the vehicle with the prospect of a deposit, but Derek would never turn over money for a product sight unseen, so that plan was out. Even though he wanted to, Derek couldn't just put a gun to Garen's head and walk him out of the hangar in broad daylight. He needed to get back to the team to come up with an alternative plan.

"Okay, I'll be around. You know how to reach me when you're ready." They shook hands, and Derek left to find Pietr.

\*\*\*

"He didn't share much about his current activities, and there was no way to get him back out without seriously compromising my cover or getting killed by his crew," Derek explained, mostly to Kat. "He'll contact me again, but that will be too late."

The team was assembled around the table on the basement level of their headquarters. "How else can we get him to us?" Kat asked, tapping her fingers on the table. "Where's he been going, Reece?"

"Well, since we've been watching, he's acquired supplies for his repairs, hired local engineers, and spent a lot of time at his ship. We've tracked him purchasing the explosives and we know where he handed them off to the Drokaran agent, but we have no information on the agent or where he went." Reece took a breath and continued, "He spends almost every night at a bar on the city strip and seems to require very little sleep."

"We could 'coincidentally' run into him," Kat suggested.

"Think you could get him to leave with you?" Derek asked her.

Kat considered that for a minute and then shook her head. "I have no cover in place right now, so I have no reason to approach him, and you know I've played it very cold and professional with him in the past. I don't think he'd buy it if I suddenly expressed an interest in him *that* way. It'd be way out of character for me," she answered. Derek agreed.

Kat looked over at Caeli thoughtfully and then turned back to Derek.

"No," Derek said, instantly following Kat's train of thought.

"He's never seen her before. She's beautiful. We'd have eyes on her the whole time." Kat was making sense and he knew it, but it made him deeply uncomfortable.

"He's a pig," Derek said in a low, disgusted voice.

"Well, yes," Kat agreed, "and that's why it will probably work."

He looked over at Caeli. Her eyes widened as she realized what Kat was suggesting.

"Derek, she's on this mission with us, and failure is *not* an option," Kat continued, cutting off his continued protest. "We have to find a way to get Garen back here quietly and without attracting attention. Do you have a better idea?"

He shook his head, frustrated. "No, I'm out of ideas," he admitted.

"Derek, I want to help," Caeli said, meeting his gaze.

"Give us a minute," he ordered the group. Everyone except Caeli got up and wandered to their workstations.

"I don't want you to," he said emphatically.

"I think I have to," she answered, her expression blank. "I've been looking at all the information too, and I know we need to get him here. Time is running out."

He ran his hand through his hair and searched her face.

"I can't stand the thought of Garen anywhere near you."

"But you'll be there too," she countered.

He still wasn't convinced.

She leaned in and her expression became animated. "If there is something I can do to help these people, and I don't do it . . ." She shook her head. "I can't live with that. And Derek, neither can you."

Finally, he closed his eyes and nodded.

After a moment she asked, "How do we do this?"

"I have an idea," he said with more confidence.

"What if he's not interested?" she asked honestly, and he gave a short laugh.

"I promise you, that won't be the case."

"Well, I do have experience dragging strange men off to my lair," she teased. "The last one was unconscious, though. This could pose more of a challenge."

He smiled at her and shook his head, then called the team back to the table. "Okay, let's do it."

# CAELI

## CHAPTER 31

Caeli and Kat had the whole afternoon together to prepare for the "surprise" meeting. The nightlife on Tharsis wouldn't be in full swing until long after dark, so Derek sent them off to purchase clothes and otherwise get ready for the evening. Despite the gravity of the coming mission, it was easy to pretend she was just a visitor. Caeli was eager to be out exploring the town, and Kat was an excellent guide.

"We have to stop in the market for lunch. You can't imagine how good the food is," Kat said.

The market was busy, and children ran laughing through the streets. Stalls held brightly colored pottery, handcrafted baskets, jewelry, woven cloth, and fresh produce. Vendors bartered their wares, arguing animatedly with customers. Bakers removed steaming bread from ovens.

Caeli's senses were overwhelmed. "There's so much color here, so much energy," she observed, trying to put into words something she felt about these people.

"I know what you mean," Kat agreed. "The Tharsians are passionate and warm. And as fucked-up as they've been politically and socially in the last few years, they're a people you easily fall in love with."

Caeli nodded in agreement. They stopped at a stall where a young woman was stirring a large pot over an open-air fire. Her thick, dark hair was pulled away from her face and tied with colorful ribbons. She was speaking cheerfully in the local dialect to several younger boys around her.

"What can I get for you?" she asked when she noticed them standing at the stall.

Kat ordered two bowls of the steaming soup and they were served in small, carved-out loaves of fresh bread. "Oh, I've missed this," Kat grinned, closing her eyes and inhaling the scent of the spices.

The young woman laughed. "My grandmother's recipe," she offered. "It's always popular."

They found seats at one of the tables set up at the perimeter of the marketplace. They ate in silence for a while, soaking up the sights and sounds and lost in their own thoughts.

Eventually, Kat sat back on her bench and brushed crumbs of bread off her lap. "I know an excellent little clothing shop where we should be able to find you something for tonight, and then we'll do hair and make-up, and we'll be ready for anything," Kat said with a cheerful tone, but she looked cautiously at Caeli.

Caeli nodded looking down at her hands in her lap.

"Are you nervous?" Kat asked and Caeli nodded again.

"This is a bit out of character for me," she acknowledged.

"I know it is," Kat agreed. "A technique I use, and Derek too, is to keep as much of my own personality as I can. I know I'm direct and in-your-face sometimes, so I use that as part of my cover," Kat offered. "Don't try to be aggressive. That's not who you are, and it will feel forced. Stay a little tentative and shy, but add sensual to that. You'll have Garen eating out of your hand."

Caeli smiled. "Thanks, Kat." Her smile faded a little and she added, "I know how important this is."

"I am sorry you have to be part of it," Kat said. "You didn't sign on for this."

"No, but I can't ignore the situation in front of me. My people did that. They chose not to see, not to act, and it cost us everything." Caeli's voice lowered to a whisper, "These aren't my people, but they don't deserve what's about to happen to them any more than we did. I have to do whatever I can, just like you do."

Kat nodded wordlessly in agreement. They sat for a few more minutes in thoughtful silence and then left the market area, walking a few blocks to the clothing store. Kat was efficient and purposeful as she perused racks of material. The clothing, reflective of the Tharsian people, was exotic looking, richly textured, and colorful.

Kat was frowning, though, as she looked back and forth between Caeli and the various fabrics on the shelves and hangers. When the shopkeeper subtly approached them and asked if they needed any help, Kat nodded emphatically.

"What is the occasion?" the woman inquired.

"Ladies night out on the town," Kat smiled.

The woman nodded, looking Caeli up and down. "I think most of this is too brightly colored for her. She'll be lost. Come this way. I have something in mind."

When the woman had finished dressing her, Caeli looked into the mirror and could barely contain her discomfort. "There's so little of it . . ."

Kat cut her off. "It's perfect!" she exclaimed brightly. "We'll take it all, the shoes as well."

Although Caeli had never worn anything quite like it before, she had to admit that the clothing was well suited to her fair coloring and body type. It was just far more revealing than anything she would be comfortable wearing in her normal life. *But then, what exactly is normal life anymore?* she mused to herself, touching the beautiful, silky material as the woman carefully folded and wrapped it in delicate tissue paper.

Their next stop was a salon. When asked what look they were hoping to achieve, Kat replied "expensive." The stylist didn't raise an eyebrow.

Every stray piece of hair on her body was waxed off; her fingernails and toenails filed and polished to perfection; her hair washed, dried, trimmed and styled; and her body massaged with luxurious lotions. When they finally returned to the apartment, Caeli barely recognized herself.

Derek was not there, but it was already dark and Kat suggested they be ready to leave shortly. Caeli dressed carefully and then surveyed the results in the large bedroom mirror. Her short skirt was white with gold threads woven into the material. It fit low and tight around her hips, displaying her belly. The matching top clung to her revealingly and was held up by the thinnest of gold straps. The shopkeeper had given her a demonstration on how to drape a gauzy, transparent shrug over it all, and this helped her feel only slightly less exposed.

Her hair flowed to the middle of her back, and whatever product the stylist used made the lighter blonde streaks shimmer and the curls hold their shape. Her skin, pale from a lack of sun over the last few weeks, also subtly glittered in the artificial light of the bedroom. Artfully applied make-up brought out the blue of her eyes and darkened her lips slightly. The effect made her look and feel quite exotic and, she had to admit, like the character she would be playing. Taking a deep breath, she walked out into the living room.

Kat, Drew, and Derek were talking animatedly in the kitchen. Kat was stunning in all black, and Derek and Drew appeared nothing like the professional soldiers they were. She had a moment to look at Derek before he noticed her. His dark hair was still cut short, but he had several days' worth of scruffy growth on his face and his demeanor had shifted slightly since their arrival on Tharsis. He had a darker edge, and strangely that suited him.

As soon as he realized she was there, the room fell silent. Derek's eyes widened in surprise, and Kat grinned with amusement at the look on his face. Caeli blushed under the intensity of his gaze.

"I think that'll work," Derek said in a low voice, and Drew and Kat laughed in agreement.

"You think?" Kat quipped.

Derek ignored her. He walked over to Caeli and spoke so softly that only she could hear, "Wear this for me again sometime." She swallowed hard and nodded, blushing even more deeply.

"Ready?" he asked the group, but he was still looking at Caeli.

"As I'll ever be," she answered, trying to keep her breathing under control.

"You've got this," Kat encouraged, "and we've got your back."

"I know," Caeli answered, and of this fact she was confident. It was her own ability that worried her.

***

The plan was for Drew and Kat to arrive at the bar ahead of time and only to provide backup if something went wrong; otherwise, they'd stay mostly out of sight. They left the apartment first, and once they were gone Derek went over a few last minute instructions with Pietr, then they rode in silence into the city.

Caeli noticed the changing landscape with interest. On the outskirts of town, where they had been staying, the buildings had a particular style and character and there was a community feeling in the neighborhood. Cobbled, narrow streets ran between houses and the open-air market provided a thriving town center. Vibrant colors from potted plants on doorsteps and from blooming kitchen gardens peppered the landscape.

But in the city, tall, shining buildings were interspersed with crumbling ruins, bright lights illuminated heavily populated strips bursting with activity, and yet she could see people living in alleyways under makeshift shelters.

"It's like they can't quite move themselves forward," Derek broke the silence. Caeli nodded at the accuracy of his description. "But they're a people you want to see make it," he added.

Caeli looked at Derek. "This has to work."

"Yeah, it does," he agreed as the vehicle pulled to a stop in front of a crowded bar.

Pietr opened the door and helped Caeli out first. The place was familiar to Derek. He'd been here before. But the loud music, dim pulsating light, and crush of humanity threatened to overwhelm Caeli, and she unconsciously took a step backward. Derek held her arm and guided her toward a table near the back corner of the room.

"He's not here yet. Sit for a minute," he suggested. Even with the crowd of people, they had a clear view of the entrance. "You really look incredible." His eyes were on the door, but his words were for her.

He ordered them drinks and although he barely touched his,

he encouraged her to take a few sips, hopeful it would help her to relax. The strong, sweet liquid burned her throat and gave her a warm tingling feeling all over. She smiled at him. He grinned back and stood up, "Dance with me."

His left hand was at her lower back, pulling her in toward him. "Garen just walked in the door." He looked down at her swaying to the beat of the music and whispered, "We have to play him all the way to the apartment. He's dangerous, and he'll be armed. This can't turn into a firefight."

The whisper became a kiss at her neck, and she automatically opened her mind to him in response. He closed his eyes. "Please don't," he pleaded in a low voice. "I won't be able to do this, if . . ." and his words trailed off.

She nodded almost imperceptibly and withdrew the connection. In a moment his face was composed again and he looked at her with cold, raw desire. There was no trace of intimacy in his eyes, just lust, as his hand trailed possessively over her body. She knew it wasn't all an act. She could feel his rapid heartbeat and his hardness pressed up against her.

Out of the corner of her eye, she could see that Garen had noticed them and was sauntering across the floor. "He's coming." She sent the words into Derek's mind.

He leaned in and kissed her aggressively, shoving his tongue into her mouth. At the same time, his hand began massaging her ass under the short skirt. A deep, amused voice resonated next to them, "Are you going to fuck her on the dance floor?"

Derek unhurriedly withdrew from the kiss and took a slow step back, turning toward Garen. Grinning dangerously he answered, "I might."

They shook hands in greeting, and Derek offered to buy him a drink. He didn't introduce Caeli and, in fact, didn't even speak to her. He just offhandedly gestured for her to follow them.

Caeli stood behind Derek at the bar while he and Garen spoke casually about meaningless things. She could tell by Garen's body language and drifting gaze that he was interested in her, but just as Derek was doing, he ignored her. After a few moments Derek glanced at her. "Drink?" he asked.

She shook her head no. Garen finally looked directly at her and a leer slowly spread across his face. "Where did you get her?" he asked Derek, his eyes traveling from her legs to her face.

"Elista," Derek responded, taking a drink and leaning up against the bar.

"Expensive?" Garen asked.

"Very," Derek answered, and then added, "But worth it." He ran a finger down her cheek and over her bare shoulder where the shrug had fallen away.

Caeli gazed up at Derek with as much sensuality as she could manufacture and then turned back to Garen. She formed an image in her mind and, as subtly as she could, projected it into Garen's consciousness, hoping he would think the idea entirely his own. She kept her face carefully neutral and noticed his breathing speed up slightly, and his eyes sweep up and down her body again.

"Willing to loan her out?" he smirked at Derek.

Derek raised his eyebrows. "For a price." He took another drink and waited for Garen's response.

"How much?" Garen's eyes still lingered on Caeli.

Derek named a price. "And at my place," he added. He said it with levity in his voice, but the implication was clear. He was willing to share, but he didn't trust Garen *that* much.

In one quick motion, Garen tossed back his drink and said, "Done. Let's go."

Derek paid the bar bill while Garen walked ahead of them. Turning to Caeli he mouthed silently, "Nice."

# CHAPTER 32

Pietr was waiting for them outside. The drive to the apartment passed quickly, and Caeli felt surprisingly calm. She wondered if she owed this to her drink back at the bar, but she was grateful regardless. Derek and Garen continued their casual conversation until the vehicle stopped in front of the building.

"I'll be downstairs if you need me," Pietr offered, his double meaning clear to Caeli. Derek acknowledged him with a nod.

"Nice place," Garen commented as they walked through the decorative foyer and onto the lift.

"I'm enjoying it," Derek answered.

When they reached the apartment, he entered the security code and opened the door. Motion sensors detected their presence and softly illuminated the room. He nuzzled Caeli's cheek and whispered, "Do it quickly."

Caeli led Garen toward the sofa. As she turned toward him, he caught her off guard and shoved her backward onto the cushions. One hand circled her throat, applying just enough pressure to take her breath away, and the other moved under her skirt roughly between her legs. She could feel the energy rippling off him, hitting her in waves and making her dizzy. The corners of his mouth turned up in a salacious grin.

Fighting her rising panic and the urge to resist him, she emptied her mind. Just as she had done to the soldier in the holding cell on Almagest, she constricted the blood vessels traveling to Garen's brain and cut off the flow. His eyes widened briefly in surprise and then he collapsed on top of her.

As she struggled to push Garen's heavy body off hers, Derek was there, grabbing the back of his shirt and throwing him to the ground.

Caeli sat up, wrapped her arms around herself, and began to shake. Derek moved to check Garen's pulse. Vaguely Caeli noticed Kat and Drew out of the corner of her eye. "He'll be fine in a minute," she said, her voice a choked whisper.

Derek nodded at Kat and Drew, who wordlessly dragged Garen's unconscious body onto the other end of the couch and restrained him. Then he knelt in front of Caeli, making no move to touch her. "Are you okay?"

She nodded, but her body was trembling violently, and her voice was barely audible. "I just need a minute." She looked into his eyes and knew that he saw her panic and that he understood how hard she was fighting for control.

His gaze was steady and his voice confident. "Just one breath at a time," he encouraged, now tentatively reaching out to touch her.

The physical connection was an offer to make an empathic one, and she gratefully surrendered her own frenetic mind to his. He filled her thoughts with his memory of their day at the lake. He had felt light, easy, content, and *safe* there. In moments their breathing was in unison, slow and even, and gradually she was composed enough to disentangle their minds.

She became aware again of the sounds in the room, of Kat and Drew on the other side of the couch, of Garen regaining consciousness, and of the work she still needed to do. Derek sat back on his heels and waited for her.

In a moment she stood up, straightened her twisted clothing and moved to the other side of the sofa, close enough to Garen that she could put her hand on his knee. He was wedged into the corner of the couch with his arms bound behind his back. Drew was behind him, holding him upright by the shoulder as he blinked himself back to consciousness. Kat was off to the side with a weapon in her hand, tense.

Derek reached behind his back and withdrew his small weapon. Then he squatted in front of Garen so that they were eye to eye.

When Garen's gaze cleared, he looked darkly at Derek. "What the fuck, Markham?"

"I have a few questions for you," Derek said, his voice professional, cold, and expressionless.

Garen raised his eyebrows and smirked, "Well, I guess we'll be here a while."

"I don't think so." Derek looked at Caeli.

At the bar she had touched Garen's consciousness subtly and almost imperceptibly, but now he was aware of her presence in his mind. She sensed his confusion and discomfort and felt him rebel against the foreign intrusion. But she held her ground, digging her fingernails into his knees. He winced and glared at her.

Derek stood up and began to speak. "The Drokarans ordered you to take out the diplomatic team?"

Garen raised his eyebrows. Caeli could feel more confusion, and his rising anger. "Why do you care?" he asked.

Derek ignored him and looked at Caeli. "Yes," she answered.

"Who's buying the explosives from you?" Derek continued.

His questions would guide her toward the information she needed in Garen's head.

Garen's expression turned deadly, and he remained silent.

"A Drokaran. He uses a name, but it's not real," Caeli answered. "I have a clear image of him." She turned to Derek. "I could pick him out in a crowd."

"Good." Derek ran his free hand through his hair. "What's the target?"

"He doesn't know," she answered, but then found what seemed to be a relevant thought. "He was warned to stay away from Meridian Square during the president's weekly address." This was one of the public gatherings she, Kat, and Riley had identified as a potential target.

"Who else is involved?" Derek took a step closer to Garen.

Garen narrowed his eyes and leaned in toward Caeli, "You want to be in my head? Here's something for you to think about." In her mind he was on top of her again, forcing his way inside her. The feeling was so violent and real that she gasped and nearly broke the connection. "This is what you're missing," he jeered, and Drew roughly jerked him backward.

Derek glanced at her with concern, but she swallowed and nodded at him.

"Who else is involved," Derek repeated forcefully.

Caeli pushed her way deeply into Garen's mind and found a name and a face. "Taran Sher." She looked again at Derek to see if this was meaningful to him.

"He's a local. What's his role?" Derek demanded. She could feel his anxiety rising, but his voice remained steady and devoid of emotion.

"The Drokarans are dealing with him too. A different agent. Garen doesn't know why. He thinks it's for high-powered assault weapons, but he's not sure," she finished.

Derek gave a slight nod. "One more thing." He squatted so once again he was at eye level with Garen. "Who developed the stealth tech?"

Garen glared at him, but answered, "The Baishan."

Derek didn't look surprised and stood back up.

"You're Alliance, aren't you?" Garen said accusingly. Caeli could feel the dawning realization sweep over him.

Derek didn't answer him. "Step away, Caeli," he ordered. Stiffly she got up from the couch.

"Kat, get her out of here," he nodded in Kat's direction.

But Caeli shook off Kat's arm and backed a few steps away. "Derek, what are you doing?"

"Fuck you, Markham," Garen said, his voice a challenge. Derek shot him three times in the chest.

# DEREK

## CHAPTER 33

"Kat, get downstairs and make contact with Andreas. We need eyes on Taran Sher yesterday," he barked.

"Drew, have Pietr and Alex clean this up," he gestured at Garen's slumping form. And then, "I'll meet you downstairs in five."

Kat and Drew hurried out of the room.

He turned to Caeli, who was still standing motionless a few feet from the couch and staring at Garen's body. He had no idea what to say to her. She glanced over at him, her expression blank.

"I'm going to change my clothes," she said without moving at all.

"Okay," he answered, waiting.

There was a soft knock at the door. "It's probably Alex and Pietr," he said to her.

Finally, she walked toward the bedroom while he went to let them in. Little explanation was needed.

"Got what you needed?" Pietr asked casually, nodding his head toward Garen.

"Yeah," Derek confirmed.

He very much wanted to get to work downstairs, but he went to the bedroom door first, tapped softly, and let himself in. She was undressing, and in a very un-Caeli like fashion, dropping her clothes haphazardly all over the floor. Her movements were stiff and her expression pained. He had learned to recognize when she was trying to keep control, and for the second time in a day, he knew this was one of those moments.

Abruptly she turned to him and said, "If you weren't there . . ." She paused and her words trailed off. Then she continued more boldly, "I would have killed him myself if I had to." Finally she stopped moving and looked at him, her eyes glassy, "But . . ."

"But we had him, and you think I could have done something other than kill him," he finished for her.

"Maybe. I don't know," she said and began searching through drawers.

"He was *never* walking out of here," Derek said, not meaning to sound callous but pretty sure he did anyway. "Caeli, the rules in the field are different. Garen was a threat to this mission and too much is at stake." He sat at the edge of the bed and exhaled loudly. "If I handed him over to Andreas, he'd be dead anyway. And truthfully, turning him over to the Tharsian government or even the Alliance at this point would be a huge risk. If he got away, my team would be compromised. I can't take that chance. I *won't* take that chance."

She stopped moving and sat next to him on the bed. "I saw inside his head. I know what he's done, and I know what he's capable of." She paused. "And it still feels wrong."

"It's one of those choices I have to live with." He touched a piece of her hair. It was still loose and shimmering. Mostly *he* had to live with it, but he knew that on some level now she did too.

\*\*\*

He left her to finish dressing and went to join his team. As soon as he entered the room, Riley spoke. "Commander, I have a secure link with Andreas. Do you have instructions for him?"

"Yeah, thanks, Riley. Hook me up." He sat at a workstation and picked up a tiny ear bud. He called Kat over to join him.

"I need eyes on Taran Sher." He quickly got to the point, knowing Andreas would pick up on the urgency in his voice.

"Right away," Andreas answered. "Once I have him, what do you want me to do with him?"

"Don't engage him at all," Derek instructed. "Hopefully he'll be setting up a meet with a Drokaran agent. We don't know the identity of this man, but he'll most likely be purchasing some kind of weapon. This is who we want. I'm going to have Kat run point on this and interface with your guys. Leave Taran in play if you can, and grab the Drokaran out of his sight," he finished.

"Understood," Andreas said. "Send Kat with Alex. He'll know where to bring her, and we'll set her up with whatever she needs."

They ended the communication, and he looked over at Kat. "You got this?"

"Absolutely," she answered.

"I know I don't need to say it, but this has to be done as quietly as possible," he said to Kat, who nodded. "If he has a chance to communicate with the other agents, they'll disappear and regroup and we'll be screwed."

"I got it," she answered. "I'm going to get ready. Is Caeli still upstairs?"

Derek nodded, avoiding her gaze.

"Derek," Kat said sharply. He knew she was too astute to let this go by. He sighed and looked at her.

"Is she okay?" Kat asked more gently.

"I don't know," he answered. "It fucked her head up that I killed Garen. And I never should have let him touch her." He shook his head and closed his eyes briefly.

"She handled him," Kat said, touching his arm.

He just nodded.

"Something happened to her, didn't it?" Kat asked.

"Yeah," he acknowledged.

"She's strong," Kat said.

"I know," he answered. "This isn't what I had in mind when I brought her with us. Shit, Kat, she just watched me blow a hole in an unarmed man."

"Derek, she's already been inside your head. She knows who you are, all of you, and she loves you. No accounting for taste. But seriously, she'll put this in context. There were no good options. You did what needed doing." He hoped that was true.

Just as Kat was turning to leave, Caeli entered the room. Her hair was pulled back into a tight braid, the makeup was washed off her face, and she was wearing comfortable civilian clothes. He noticed that she'd lost most of the haunted expression she'd had when he left her in the bedroom, but she didn't make eye contact with him.

"Hey," Kat called to her as she walked by. "Nice work today."

Caeli gave her a small smile. "Thanks," she said.

Kat nodded at them both. "Catch you in a few."

Derek stood and faced Caeli. His eyes held a question. "I'm fine," she said quietly, but he knew she wasn't.

# CAELI

## CHAPTER 34

"Why don't you wait for Kat?" Derek suggested, and Caeli nodded. "I need to start prepping for this op, and I promised the president an update before things start moving too quickly."

He was rambling uncomfortably, but Caeli couldn't bring herself to engage him in conversation. She numbly went back into the apartment and sat at the table. Kat looked surprised when she came out of the bedroom and found Caeli staring vacantly into space.

"Hey, you okay?"

When Caeli didn't answer, Kat pulled out a chair and sat opposite her.

"Please don't let me keep you. I know you have work to do."

Kat waved her hand through the air dismissively. "It could take hours to find Sher. Talk to me," she demanded. "Some of us can't read minds."

Caeli gave Kat a small grin. She opened her mouth to say something, but then stopped and shook her head.

"Things are really fucked up," Kat said.

Caeli nodded weakly.

Kat leaned forward. "He has to make the hard calls."

Caeli looked searchingly at Kat and then nodded. "I know."

"It costs him something every time," Kat added.

Caeli looked down and nodded again. "You've know each other a long time," she said softly.

"Ten years," Kat confirmed, grinning. "He was a young, smart-assed pilot when I met him. We were teamed up pretty regularly doing security work." Then her expression turned serious. "Things got a lot more dangerous when the Drokarans decided to make us their enemy."

Caeli listened intently. She knew so little about Derek's life compared to what he knew about hers.

"We had to adapt. The mission of the Alliance shifted from mostly exploration and diplomacy to providing a multi-world military defense," Kat explained. "Derek went from a cocky, sometimes insubordinate kid to a leader in a very short amount of time. He got thrown into the fray and chose to stay and fight."

Kat paused and sat back in her chair. "I sometimes wonder who we would all be in a different kind of world."

Caeli looked up at her and swallowed hard. "I was that person. Now I'm not anymore."

"None of us are," Kat said, staring down at the table.

\*\*\*

Derek and Drew came back to the apartment talking about explosive devices and discussing yield and scope of damage. When Derek saw Caeli, he stopped and his expression changed. Her heart raced with his apprehension. Kat quietly stood and led Drew out of the room.

"How was the president?" Caeli asked, tentatively.

"Worried."

She nodded and looked away.

He sat down across from her. "Please talk to me," he begged.

She swallowed back the lump in her throat and wrapped her arms around herself. The memory of Garen's touch still made her want to retch. "I wanted him dead. I wanted to kill him," she admitted. "And then he *was* dead."

Her mind played over the image of three neat, silent holes appearing on Garen's chest and his body slumping forward. The sob that she'd been trying to hold back finally escaped. "You killed him." She took a shuddering breath, tears now streaming down her face. "And I'm horrified and relieved at the same time. I don't know what to do with this."

"I'm sorry," Derek began, but Caeli cut him off, unable to check the flow of her words.

"For the second time, I've violated someone's mind. I've done something unconscionable. But if I didn't, I couldn't live with the consequences." She looked up at him. "I know it's the same for you."

Derek's face was expressionless, but Caeli could feel his emotions churning. He got up from his seat and knelt in front of her. "I wanted to keep you safe. And every decision I've made so far has done just the opposite," he said, closing his eyes.

"Safe is an illusion," she answered, wiping her cheeks with the back of her hand.

"Caeli, I *am* sorry," he said, and she could feel the weight of his regret settle into her own body.

# DEREK

## CHAPTER 35

"Okay," Derek said to Reece, "there's someone we need to find. What are our surveillance options?" He was leaning over Reece's shoulder at his workstation.

Reece shook his head. "There's not a lot we can tap into on this planet. They don't have much, so we'll have to deploy our own drones. I've got about ten on site. How large an area are we looking to cover?"

"We have to think strategically. We know something is going down at Meridian Square, and if I'm the guy planning a move, I'm scoping the area," Derek explained. "Deploy drones to cover that park." Reece nodded and began typing onto his keypad. "I also want some at the dock area. Shit is always happening down there," Derek continued. "Then distribute the rest in the market and the downtown strip. It's a shot in the dark, but if we can get eyes on this guy, we'll have a huge advantage. We think he's the one who will be planting explosives."

"Got it." Reece continued typing. "I'm inputting the locations and powering the drones up now." After a few minutes he said, "Now I just need a face to put in the recognition program." He looked at Derek expectantly.

"We're going to give you a picture." Derek looked over at Caeli.

"Great," Reece nodded. "You want to download it into the file?" he asked.

"Um, no." Derek hesitated for a second. "We're going to download it into your head, and then you're going to use the facial reconstruction program to generate the image."

Reece's eyes widened. Caeli squatted down next to him and, attempting to keep a straight face, said, "This won't hurt a bit."

Reece nearly tipped over in his chair, and Derek laughed out loud. "Seriously though," he explained, "Caeli has an empathic ability, and this is the most efficient way to give you the information."

Reece looked back and forth between Derek and Caeli and finally just swallowed and said, "Okay. Sure."

Caeli gently touched his shoulder and sent the image of the Drokaran agent she'd gotten out of Garen's head directly into Reece's. Once again his eyes widened. "Damn! That's awesome!" he blurted out and immediately corrected himself. "Sorry, sir."

"Don't worry about it, Reece," Derek said indulgently. "Just find him."

"Yes, sir," Reece turned and began working furiously.

"And Reece . . ." Derek got his attention again. "This," he gestured at Caeli, "is classified."

"Of course, sir." Reece vigorously nodded his head.

Caeli was biting her lip to keep from smiling. "That was a little bit fun," she whispered in Derek's ear.

"It was," he grinned back at her.

\*\*\*

A few hours later, Andreas sent word that he'd located Taran Sher. Kat was ready to leave with Alex and interface with

Andreas's men. She'd need to be available at a moment's notice to move in and grab the Drokaran.

"I hope we aren't too late," Derek worried out loud. "If Sher's already handed off the weapon . . ." He didn't finish. While they were much farther ahead in understanding the Drokaran plot, they still didn't know enough to prevent the impending disaster. The tension in the room was rising.

"Get Kat wired," he ordered Reece. "We need to have a two-way com. And put a tracker on her just in case."

Kat raised her eyebrows but didn't object. Reece nodded and took a small device shaped like a tiny gun out of a case. He approached Kat—rather nervously, Derek thought—and asked her to lift her hair up from the back of her neck. She smirked and pulled the mass of dark hair out of the way. "It's just a tiny pinch." Reece looked pained.

"I've had one before, thanks." Kat rolled her eyes. She didn't flinch when Reece put the device to her neck and pressed the release mechanism to implant a small, subcutaneous tracker at the base of her skull.

Reece sat back down and tapped away at his tablet. Almost immediately, a blinking flash appeared on the three-dimensional screen at his workstation. "We've got a nice, clear signal." He turned to Derek.

"Get the com online," Derek barked, and Reece scurried to work again. He handed Kat a small, metallic square that was barely the size of a fingernail.

"The best spot will be below the temple, just in front of your ear," Reece advised.

Kat took the chip and touched it to the spot Reece suggested. It stuck in place and immediately changed colors to match her skin tone. "Okay, let's give it a test." Reece reached for a small receiver on his table and plugged a thin wire into the back of it.

"Test, test," Kat said softly. They could clearly hear her voice coming through the speaker on the table.

"Commander, your com." Reece handed Derek the ear bud he'd used to speak with Andreas earlier.

"Okay, good. Can we have visual?" Derek asked.

Reece thought a moment. "If we reroute one of the drones, absolutely." Reece began to type enthusiastically again. "I'll program it to stay in visual range of Kat's signal. It has a wide angle camera, and I'll keep it high enough to get a clear view of any action on the ground."

"Excellent," Derek said and then turned to Kat, "You'd better go and start prepping with Andreas's team. Stay safe, Kat," he added as she and Alex headed out the door.

She grinned and nodded, "Yes, sir."

Drew walked her out and Derek could hear him quietly say, "Be careful."

Kat's expression softened when she looked at Drew. Derek smiled to himself. *This is certainly a different side of Kat*, he thought.

"I need to go outside and release the drones," Reece's voice snapped him back to attention. Reece opened a box to show the ten small drones resting in their cushioned casings.

Caeli came over to look at them. "They're so small," she said as she peered into the case curiously.

Reece nodded, pleased to have someone interested in his area of expertise. "They're only a little bit bigger than the transmitter Kat's wearing, but they have a camera in addition to the audio transmitter and receiver embedded in their bodies. Watch this," he said, carefully placing a drone in the palm of his hand. He tapped the side and a small propeller emerged from the body, began to spin, and lifted the tiny drone off his hand.

"That's awesome," she whispered to Reece, who turned a very bright shade of crimson.

"Pietr will take you up to the roof." Derek's voice was behind them.

Reece hurriedly put the drone back in its case and shut the lid with a snap. "All set," he said and rushed to join Pietr at the door.

When he returned a few moments later, he carried a portable device to the large table at the other end of the room and began tapping keys again. Ten holographic pictures appeared hovering above the table, all projecting aerial views from the drones' cameras in real time. "Clear signals all around," Reece reported. "I can maneuver them remotely if we want a different view or if we need to reposition them."

"Good work, Reece. We need to split up our surveillance. Riley, Drew, Jacobs, and Caeli, I want you monitoring the majority of the drones. They're searching for the Drokaran who was working with Garen. The recognition program will alert you if it finds a potential match, but this guy could have his face covered or whatever. You need to be looking for suspicious behavior, especially around Meridian Square," Derek ordered. "Reece, you and I are going to have eyes on Kat once she's in the field. We may have to do this in shifts, but we'll start off together and relieve each other as needed."

Everyone settled in and began to watch the city.

***

Andreas's men had been tracking Taran Sher since late in the afternoon, and Kat's detail picked him up by early evening. She was in a vehicle with Alex and the two other men who'd been assigned to her by Andreas. She'd been making regular, smart-assed comments into Derek's com for hours now. "We're stopping at a small club. The nasty bastard just felt up some poor, unsuspecting girl at the door. I'd like to blow his nuts off."

Derek just shook his head, grinning to himself.

"I need to go inside," she said out loud, both to him and to the men in the car. "Who's coming, boys?"

The little drone hovering outside the vehicle sent him the live video feed of Kat getting out of the car with Alex. She had taken off her outer jacket and was wearing a low-cut black tank top, tight pants, and high black boots. He watched her fluff out her hair then turn toward the vehicle to subtly check her weapon and place it in the small handbag she was carrying.

"Kat, we're going to lose visual when you're inside, but I'll let you know if anyone interesting comes your way," he advised.

"Copy that," she answered. "Andreas's guys are all wired too, so they'll give us a heads up if they see anything."

He watched as she began to stagger and grab hold of Alex's arm. She giggled flirtatiously into his ear as they moved toward the entrance. Alex paid the fee, and in a few minutes Kat's voice came back over the com, "We're in and I have a visual on Sher."

Derek listened as she chatted animatedly with Alex, ordered drinks at the bar, and found them a seat. "Ugh, he's harassing the wait staff," she sniped into the com, and then without missing a beat, continued her pretend drunken banter with Alex.

Several people came and went, mostly couples and small groups of young men and women, but about an hour later a single man entered the building. Derek didn't get a look at his face, but there was something about the purposeful way he carried himself that caught Derek's attention.

"Kat, head's up," he said into the com.

"I see him," she answered a few moments later. "He's heading straight for Sher," she reported. Then, "They're going up the back stairs. I'm positioned between the two exits, so when he comes down we'll see which way he goes. Alex, get someone outside the second exit," she ordered, and Derek could hear Alex's voice speaking into his own com to the team outside.

"Keep talking, Kat," he prodded. He really hated not being able to see her. But he did see one of Andreas's men get out of the vehicle and make his way around the side of the building to the other exit. He leaned casually up against the adjacent building with his eyes on the door.

"They haven't come down yet," she said.

It was a tense few minutes on Derek's side of the operation. While he knew Kat was the best person for this job, he didn't like sitting around watching a video. He tapped his fingers anxiously on the table and listened to Kat quietly tell Alex her plan.

About fifteen minutes later she began to have a mock argument with Alex. Derek could hear her slurring her words and raising her voice just above that of the general crowd. "He's heading out the front exit," she said into the com.

"You're a stupid ass," she yelled at Alex and then burst out the front exit several steps ahead of the Drokaran. As soon as she was out the door, she reached into her purse and pulled out her weapon. When the Drokaran agent stepped out, she was at his side. "Hello handsome. Don't move a muscle."

Derek watched as the Drokaran froze in his tracks. Alex was by his other side within seconds. The vehicle powered up and the door slid open. "Get in," Kat said in a deadly voice.

\*\*\*

"They're on their way back," Derek announced to the room. "Jacobs, stay on surveillance." He turned to Drew and said, "She's good." Drew nodded and kept his eyes on the streaming video.

Caeli was sleeping on one side of a small couch in the corner of the room, and Riley was on the other side. Derek gently shook them both awake and they sat up, bleary-eyed.

"What's going on?" Riley asked.

"Kat has one of the Drokaran agents, and they're close," Derek explained.

Riley stood abruptly. "What do you need me to do?" she asked.

"Get fresh eyes on Meridian Park. I need Caeli and Drew with me," he said briskly.

Riley yawned and then sat down next to Drew. Caeli leaned forward and put her face in her hands. After a moment, she looked up at Derek and sighed deeply, "Okay."

He knelt in front of her and took her hands in his. "I'm sorry." He seemed to be repeating those words a lot lately, but there was nothing else he could say. He saw the dark circles under her eyes, felt the tension in her body, and understood the dread she felt at what still had to be done.

"Don't," she said. "We'll get through it."

He leaned in and touched his forehead to hers.

About a quarter hour later, Kat let them know she was on her way up.

"Drew." Derek pulled his weapon out and Drew did the same. "Let's get him secured in the back room."

Alex entered first, followed by the Drokaran, with Kat at his back. They had his arms restrained and all their weapons drawn. Alex put a bag he was carrying onto the table.

"That's what he got from Sher," Kat gestured at the bag. "It's high-powered, laser-guided, silent, and deadly. He's probably looking to take out a single target. I can guess who that might be," she finished, moving the Drokaran further into the room.

"Back here." Derek led them into the small room off the main area. "Drew, Kat, Caeli, in. Everyone else, clear the space," he ordered. "Alex, keep your guys right outside."

There were several metal chairs in the room and Derek motioned for the Drokaran to sit on one. He did so, his demeanor eerily calm. "Drew, four point restraints. Kat, keep your aim at his head." Derek's voice and movements were controlled and his face expressionless.

The Alliance had never had a Drokaran in their custody. In fact, they'd had no official contact with this race in centuries. Derek pulled a chair up directly in front of the man and sat facing him. He was large, well over six feet tall, and although lean, he was powerfully built. His face was chiseled, and he had sandy brown hair and light blue eyes.

"What's your name?" Derek asked, mostly out of simple curiosity.

The Drokaran stared straight ahead, his face unchanging.

Derek glanced at Caeli and then at Drew and Kat. Caeli knelt slightly to the right of the man and put her hand on his knee.

Derek watched the Drokaran's face while Caeli made the connection. A slight flicker of interest, and maybe discomfort, appeared and was gone before Derek was sure he'd seen it at all. Caeli tilted her head to the side and furrowed her eyebrows.

"His name is Daksha Karan," she said in a strained voice. The Drokaran turned to stare coldly into her eyes. Derek saw her shudder and then take a breath. "Ask a question," she said, her gaze unmoving.

"Who is your target?"

Karan didn't speak or move. Caeli answered, "The president."

"When and where?" Derek continued, not wasting words.

"Meridian Square, at her public address, tomorrow." It was still Caeli's voice responding.

"Who is the other agent and what's his objective?" Derek demanded.

"He's an explosives expert, and he is wiring a section of Meridian Park." Derek exchanged a meaningful glance with Drew.

"How do you contact one another?"

"They won't have any more contact now until after the mission is completed."

"How does this play out?" Derek continued.

"Karan fires the shot to take out the president and then a few more into the crowd to cause a panic. The other operative waits for the shots to be fired and the crowd to stampede. The most direct exit route out of the square is through the park, under the bridge. The explosives will be planted there, and he'll be waiting to remotely detonate them." She paused a moment and then finished, "Once the damage is done and the continent erupts into chaos, they'll contact their command."

"And they'll send an invasion party to restore order," Derek finished, barely hiding the contempt from his voice now. "If we hadn't been paying such close attention, they'd have gotten their claws into this planet before the Alliance could deploy a defense. Again." He stood up so abruptly that he nearly knocked the chair over.

"Why all the destruction, though? The Alliance can't be everywhere. Why not just invade the planet?" he asked, not really expecting an answer.

But Caeli's voice continued, "Because they want to minimize any kind of immediate, coordinated resistance from the targeted planet. It's a tactical decision. It costs them little in assets and saves their resources later."

"Fucking cold bastards," Drew said bitterly.

Derek nodded and then said to Caeli, "We may not have a chance like this again, so anything you think is relevant, anything at all, you take it out of his head," he ordered. "We'll debrief later."

She gave a small nod, and then she and Karan sat staring at each other for several moments. Finally she leaned back on her heels and dropped her hand to her side. Derek could tell she was exhausted. Somehow this interrogation had drained her energy far more than the last one.

Derek went to the door and called Alex into the room. "I'm going to have to turn him over to the Tharsians and then to the Alliance," he explained to Alex. "Keep *all* your guys on him until I can arrange it."

Alex called his team into the room to relieve Kat and Drew while Derek lifted Caeli off the ground. She swayed into him, and he helped her onto the couch. "Rest," he said to her. She was already asleep.

# CHAPTER 36

"When is the president's address?" Derek was pacing the small room.

"In six hours," Riley answered.

"We have to let her know what's happening, and I have to get this Drokaran out of here and into official custody." He stopped next to Jacobs. "You've been monitoring the president's people. Is there anyone on the inside we need to worry about if we hand him off?"

Jacobs shook his head, "I don't think so. There's nothing out of the ordinary happening, and there have been no unauthorized communications or meetings, at least none that I've seen."

"Hopefully the other Drokaran doesn't know we have this guy," Derek gestured to the back room, where Karan was detained. "But we still have to be careful. They could be monitoring her communications just like we are."

He stood still, thinking for a moment. "We have to find those explosives and disarm them. There's nothing to stop him from detonating them even if the shooter fails. The president doesn't have enough of a record or enough support yet to manage a crisis of this magnitude."

Drew nodded. "I agree." He continued, "I think the explosives are already in place. What he's using requires significant setup time. We've been watching the area, and there's been zero activity. They have to be there already."

"Shit. Drew, we've got to get you out there. Interface with Pietr for whatever equipment you need." Derek continued his pacing. "Riley, keep watching the park. Maybe he'll come around for one last pass to check on his work and we can track him back to his hideout."

He turned to Jacobs. "I need the president to authorize Alliance military in her airspace. If this whole thing goes to shit, the Drokarans are coming. Get me a secure communication link with her, and she needs to be alone."

"Yes, sir." Jacobs turned and began working diligently.

Within ten minutes Jacobs had a holographic image of the president projected on the tabletop. "Even if things aren't totally secure on her end, I'm running a quantum scramble. If someone's looking, they can tell she's making a communication, but no one will be able to intercept or decode it," Jacobs assured Derek.

"Commander," the president's face was serious. "You have a report for me?"

"Ma'am, sorry to disturb you at this hour."

She gave him a tight smile. "I'm quite sure it's warranted."

"We've captured a Drokaran agent who was planning to assassinate you at the public address later this morning." He cringed. There was no nice way to deliver that piece of information.

"I see." She raised her eyebrows but otherwise didn't flinch.

"Another agent is at large," he continued. "We have reason to believe he's planning to detonate several high-yield explosive devices during the address."

At this, she paled. "I don't think I can cancel the engagement. It's nearly dawn, and I won't get the word out in time. People will be assembling in the square soon," she said, with a horrified look on her face. But she quickly pulled herself together to ask, "What do you recommend?"

He exhaled. "We believe the explosives are already in place. If this agent thinks we're onto him, he could blow them ahead of schedule. My recommendation is to let my team try to disable them."

He paused to let the idea sink in before adding, "Regardless of that outcome, ma'am, please authorize the Inter-Allied Forces to enter your airspace. The Drokarans are planning an invasion. You *need* the Alliance here."

"Agreed," she said pragmatically. "I'll contact Captain Donovan and make an official request." She pushed a falling strand of hair back from her face and closed her eyes briefly. The weight of responsibility was plain to see, and Derek felt a wave of empathy.

"We'll get through this," he said, with a note of confidence in his voice that he didn't actually feel.

The president nodded appreciatively. "What do you need from me?" she asked.

"First, I have to transfer the Drokaran agent into your custody. I'd request that you turn him over to the Alliance at your earliest convenience." Much more than Tharsian security was at stake. While she might like to bring this man to justice on her planet, the Alliance would make better use of him.

"Of course," she agreed. "What else?"

"If we're able to locate the Drokaran agent still at large, I'd like to have access to a Tharsian military team to help bring him in. They have to act under my command, and we have to stay out of the way until my team disarms the explosives," Derek insisted.

"Understood," she answered. "I'll handpick a group. They'll be standing by if you need them."

"Thank you, ma'am," he concluded. "I'll have the Drokaran transported to a location of your choice. Please have your security detail send coordinates."

"Will do," she nodded. "Good luck, Commander." The president's image dissolved in front of him.

He put his head down on the table and stayed there for a minute. He was about to send one of his team members, one of his *friends*, into some deadly shit. If the mission failed, not only would Drew be killed, but so would hundreds of other innocent people. And to make this day even better, a Drokaran invasion fleet was probably looming in close proximity. Fuck, fuck, *fuck*.

Riley's voice pulled him back to the present. "Commander, Lieutenant Chase, take a look at this!" She was leaping out of her chair.

Derek and Drew were behind her quickly, staring over her shoulder at one of the video feeds. They watched as a lone man lingered beneath the bridge in the sparsely populated park. He paused casually at several locations, and then exited the square. The recognition software didn't identify him because he never faced the drone directly, but everyone around the table knew they were looking at the Drokaran agent.

"Reece!" Derek shouted. "Get that drone to follow him."

Reece manipulated his touch screen and the little drone pursued the Drokaran to the edge of the park. The man entered an apartment building, and this was as far as the surveillance camera could go.

"Reece, I need the total layout for that building, every exit, every window, every staircase. And then find out how many occupants live there and where. Send all the drones to that location. I want a three hundred sixty degree visual," he demanded.

"On it sir," Reece answered.

"I've got a place to start now," Drew grinned pointing at the video feed from the park bridge where the Drokaran had paused to check on his handiwork. "This will cut down on time."

"Drew, that building he entered has a clear view of the bridge. He's watching," Derek cursed.

"I've got to do this now," Drew said, his grin fading as he stared at the video. "Can we create some kind of diversion outside?"

"We'll have to try. Kat . . ." Derek began, and then Caeli's voice interrupted from the couch.

"I can hide Drew," she said, and everyone turned toward her.

The room was still as Derek stared at her in silence.

"We're running out of time," she said. "It's dawn. People will be filling up that park in just a little while. Unless you think you can find him in that building and take him out now?"

He knew he couldn't. Even if he could manage to assemble the team, spec out the building, and find the Drokaran's exact location in the next hour, the chances that the bombs would be detonated before the military team could take him out were too high.

He and Caeli looked at each other for a long moment, and then he turned to Jacobs and said, "Link us all up on a two-way com."

Everyone began to move again. Jacobs received coordinates from the president for Karan's delivery. As Alex and his team escorted the man out of the building, Derek briefly wondered what strange, disturbing information Caeli might have picked out of the Drokaran's mind. He hoped they would all be alive to hear about it later.

# CAELI

## CHAPTER 37

Her head still ached fiercely and she was exhausted, but when she and Drew left the building and walked out into the cool predawn air, she was calm. She knew Derek was not faring so well. He was successfully hiding his anxiety from the rest of the team, but she knew he was struggling. He wasn't used to worrying about anyone else in this way. There was nothing she could do but walk out the door.

Pietr was transporting them the short distance to the park, and they rode in silence. When they stepped out onto a grassy walkway near the park entrance, Pietr shook Drew's hand and, with a rare show of concern, told him to be careful. He gave Caeli an approving nod, got back into the vehicle, and left them to their work.

Street vendors were beginning to set up their booths as the sky turned a brighter shade of pink and the city began to wake up. They picked up their pace. It was a short distance to the park from where Pietr had dropped them, and as they walked Drew asked, "What exactly are you going to do?"

"Well," she began, "I'm going to create an image in my mind of the two of us as shadows, and then I'm going to project it out as far as I can. Anyone in the area won't see us."

"That's an impressive trick," Drew glanced over at her. "Have you ever done it before?"

"Yes," she replied vaguely.

Drew didn't press her to explain, and she was grateful.

"So what exactly are *you* going to do?" she asked with real curiosity.

"I know the kind of devices this guy's using, and I'm going to do my best to disarm them," he answered. "There will be a receiver that I need to disable first thing, so he can't detonate the bomb remotely, and then I'll disconnect the trigger from the bomb." He looked over at her again and added somberly, "There are three separate devices. We don't have a lot of time."

She nodded. When they got closer to the bridge, Drew said, "Time to engage your com. And time to make us disappear," he added with a grin.

As they approached the bridge, she began to project the shadow image into the surrounding area. Drew stopped at one of the bridge abutments and pulled a small, handheld device from his bag. He tapped a few keys, and a green light began flashing. He began circling the abutment and stopped when the green light turned red.

"It's here." He pointed to a cement bench built into the abutment. Placing the bag on the ground, he got down on his knees and then peered underneath. "This one will take down the whole bridge, and the blast radius will carry all the way to the market area," he remarked conversationally.

Caeli didn't answer. She just focused on her mental projecting and reminded herself to breathe, while beads of sweat trickled between her shoulder blades.

He laid down flat on his back and shimmied himself under the bench, dragging the small bag with him. Neither of them wore any kind of protective gear. It would just hinder Drew's movements, and if the bombs blew, they'd never know it had happened.

"Okay, I'm disconnecting the receiver now," he reported, and she could hear his voice coming from under the bench and in her communication device at the same time. There was silence from the other end of the com. And then a few tense moments later, "The mechanism is disarmed."

She exhaled and could hear a collective sigh of relief through the com. "Nice work Drew," Derek's voice was in her ear.

"One down, two to go," Drew answered serenely, picking himself up off the ground and swinging the bag over his shoulder.

"How are you so calm?" Kat shouted into the com. "I'm pissing myself, and I'm not even there!"

Drew chuckled and Caeli grinned. "It will either work or it won't," he said matter-of-factly, shrugging at Caeli.

"We're heading toward the next site now." Drew's voice was more serious as they approached the opposite side of the bridge, closer to the apartment building where the Drokaran agent was hiding out. There was an open common space that was already filling with vendors and people arriving early to find a good spot for the president's address. Drew was holding the sensor device again and walking slowly toward a public washroom in the center of the greenway.

"In here," Drew motioned, and they entered the small deserted building. The device was tucked against the wall behind a container. This time Caeli could see him work. His hands were steady and his face relaxed, though she suspected there was much more going on inside his head than he was expressing. She'd repaired part of Drew's brain with her empathic ability and had brushed up against the essence of his personality. She'd only made a brief connection, but it was enough to give her a measure of him. She knew that as calm as he appeared on the outside, he felt things deeply on the inside.

His movements were quick, efficient, and confident, and within a few moments he announced, "Two down." They both stood and left the building. It was near sunrise and their sense of urgency increased. Drew picked up his pace, and she hurried to follow him.

"I'm retracing his steps," Drew said to her. "He gave me some clues when we were watching the video feed, places where he paused."

"Drew?" she started to speak.

He stopped and looked at her with a worried expression on his face. "We're running out of room." He confirmed her own thoughts. They were too close to the Drokaran's hideout, and they hadn't found the third device.

"What's the matter, Drew?" Derek's voice came over the com.

"I've followed his path from the edge of the park all the way to the apartment complex, and we've only found two devices. I *know* there's a third. No way does he acquire it and not use it," Drew answered.

"I agree," Derek acknowledged. "We have an hour. Recommendations?" he asked.

Drew rubbed his eyes with the back of his hand, the first gesture of stress that Caeli had seen from him. "They could be at the platform, where the president is speaking. It would make quite an impression to blow the whole stage," he thought aloud, "but that would be redundant if she's supposed to already be dead, and besides that, they're trying to get the crowd to exit in this direction."

He looked thoughtfully at the apartment. "Derek, what are the specs on this building?"

"Shit," Derek cursed, already following Drew's thoughts. "I'm looking at them right now. There are five floors, twenty apartments on each floor, and the basement floor contains all the systems. It's residential." He waited for Drew to answer.

"I think we need to get in there," Drew said.

"Shit," Derek said again. "You think the basement?" he asked.

"It's where I'd put them," Drew affirmed. "He's remote detonating, so he can blow the first two, get out of the building, and then take it down."

"That would destroy any evidence," Derek added. "If the Drokarans left anything behind they don't want us to find, this would be a way to get rid of it."

"It sounds like their style," Drew agreed.

"Okay, I'm going to route you to the back entrance," Derek said. "My team is ready to breach the building, but we'll stay out of the way until you disarm this last one." He paused. "If it's there."

"My gut says it is." Drew was already walking around the building. Caeli scurried to keep up.

"When you get inside, there will be a door to the far left. That opens to the basement staircase," Derek instructed.

They came to the back doorway and found a security panel that needed a code to be unlocked. "I don't suppose you can convince that thing to open with your mind, could you?" Drew joked.

"That would be useful," she answered, "but sorry, no."

"We've got it on this end," Derek interrupted, and they could hear him give orders to Jacobs. Within seconds the panel flashed and the door slid open.

"Thanks," Drew said. Then, "It would be good if he's not monitoring the building too carefully."

"On the upside, he doesn't know we're on to him," Derek remarked lightly.

"Let's hope," Drew mumbled under his breath.

They made their way through the hall and walked carefully down the basement stairs. Drew stopped for a moment to pull a small handheld light from his bag. With the light in one hand and the sensor in the other, he began to wander around the dark space.

"Can I help?" Caeli asked. She had already released the shadow image from her mind in the emptiness of the basement and very much wanted to do something useful.

"Just make sure no one's coming," he suggested. She moved back to the staircase and sat wearily on the bottom step, listening.

Drew's movements became very methodical as he searched from one end of the large room to the other. Finally, after a quarter hour had passed, he announced, "Found it."

"It's about time," Kat teased over the com, but Caeli could hear the genuine relief in her voice.

"I'm going to have my team ready to move," Derek announced. "Let me know the second you have that thing disarmed."

"Will do," Drew said, already at work.

After several tense, silent moments, he spoke into the com again, "It's done."

"Excellent work, Drew," Derek commented. "And I know that's an understatement." They could hear him giving orders to his team, and then he said to them, "Do *not* move from that basement. We're ready to engage, and I need to know where you are."

"Roger that," Drew answered, moving all his equipment back to the staircase next to Caeli. He reached into the bag one last time, pulled out a gun, and then sat next to her on the steps. "Now *we* have to wait," he said to her with a deep sigh.

# DEREK

## CHAPTER 38

His group was assembled. Once he officially involved the Tharsian government in the operation, true to his word, he needed to disentangle himself from Andreas. Although Alex and his men had transferred Karan to the president's security team, Derek wasn't willing to compromise Andreas's safe house or any of his assets by bringing the president's team there. This required moving his tech team to a staging area at the nearby military base.

He and Kat were also wired with a secondary com system that linked them with the Tharsians, and he had divided the group into three teams; the first would cover the exterior perimeter of the apartment complex, the second would enter the front side of the building, and the third would enter through the back. Based on information Riley had obtained about the residents in the building, there were potentially two apartments that the Drokaran agent could be using. Only one faced the park. As soon as he received the all clear from Drew, he gave the go-ahead to move out.

He ordered their vehicles to loop behind the building, hoping to avoid notice for as long as possible. Once the team of soldiers surrounded the apartment, he knew they'd lose the element of surprise, but he had to have the building covered. The Drokaran's escape was not an option.

The drive was short and the com quiet as everyone mentally prepared themselves for the mission. When the vehicle stopped, Derek snapped back to the present and gave Kat a quick nod.

"See you on the other side," she said, leading her team toward the front of the building.

His unit entered the building through the back, fanning out to cover all the stairwells and lifts. He and two other Tharsians went up the nearest staircase heading to the third-floor apartment.

"Sir, we have the building surrounded," the perimeter team leader announced over the com.

"Copy that," Derek answered and then looked back at the two men following him. "This means he knows we're here." Both men nodded and they continued moving up the stairs.

When they reached the third floor, they made their way to the apartment unit, staying low and tight to the wall. Kat's team came up the stairway at the far end of the hall and merged with his group. When they reached the doorway, he and Kat crouched on either side. When everyone was in position he spoke into his com, "Jacobs, open the door."

As soon as the door slid open, weapons fire erupted into the hallway, blasting through the doorframe and straight through the adjacent walls. They covered their heads as pieces of wall collapsed on top of them. Derek yelled into his com, "Stay down!"

"What the fuck!" Kat shouted as parts of the building fell around them.

Derek risked a glance into the room, then stuck his weapon around the corner and blindly fired. Kat did the same. They stopped for a moment to listen and silence greeted them. He nodded at Kat, who peeked around the corner cautiously.

"This room's clear, but he must have gone into the bedroom," she reported.

He thought for a moment and then said softly into the com, "If we enter here, he'll pick us off before we can get across the room. Kat, take a small team to the adjacent apartment, clear it, and let's blow a hole in the common wall between this bedroom and that one." He pointed at the apartment down the hall.

Kat gestured at three men behind her, and they followed her down the hall.

Derek watched as a nervous family was evacuated from their home and escorted down the stairs. Other residents were also trying to leave the building. "Get back inside and stay down!" he shouted. "Kat, are you in?" he asked anxiously, knowing that the longer they took, the more time the Drokaran would have to come up with a plan. Derek was confident that the agent would never get out of the building, but he needed to minimize casualties.

"We're setting up," she answered. He knew the kind of charges they were using would disintegrate the wall but wouldn't cause much damage to the surrounding structure. There would be a loud bang and then just a giant hole. As soon as they blew it, the team would have to move quickly to have any kind of advantage.

"Ready," Kat said.

"Do it," Derek ordered.

A strong vibration accompanied the violent noise of the detonating charges. Immediately following the blast he heard weapons fire and painful screams over his com. *Shit, don't let that be Kat*, he thought as he sprinted across the debris-filled living room of the apartment with several Tharsians following him.

Within seconds he was up against the far wall motioning for them all to stay low. Derek looked around the doorway into the bedroom to determine the Drokaran's position. The agent was backed into one corner of the room partially shielded by a large desk. He was opening fire at the hole in the wall. He didn't know Derek was there.

Sliding on his back across the doorway he fired at the Drokaran and watched as a spray of blood splashed across the white wall.

"Hold your fire. He's down," Derek shouted into his com. Within seconds silence filled the space. Getting up off the ground, he cautiously approached the body and kicked the Drokaran's weapon out of the way. The man wasn't moving.

"We're clear," he announced to the group.

Looking toward the gaping wall, he could see two bodies down, sprawled across the opening. Neither was Kat.

"Drew, get Caeli up here. We have injuries," he ordered.

"On our way." Drew's voice was a solace in his ear. His sense of relief and exhaustion was suddenly so profound that he wanted to sit his ass on the ground and not move for at least a couple of days. Instead he called one of the Tharsians from his team to stand guard over the Drokaran, just in case, and then ordered a search of all the surrounding apartments.

"Jacobs, you there?" he asked.

"Yes, sir," another reassuring voice answered.

"Update the president. I believe she's about to give her address." Derek allowed himself a small smile.

"Will do, sir," Jacobs responded.

Caeli and Drew arrived, and then Caeli was on her knees next to the injured Tharsians. He watched as she put a hand on each. She removed one young man's damaged body armor to reveal his bruised, crushed chest cavity. Without blinking, she calmly touched him and began her silent healing. When she was satisfied that he was stabilized, she moved to her next patient.

While she was finishing, he went to see Drew and Kat, who were out of the way sitting up against a wall near the back staircase. Drew's normally impassive expression was replaced with one of concern as he held a wadded piece of cloth up against Kat's bleeding head.

"You okay?" Derek asked, concerned.

"It's just a scratch from all the flying chunks of wall," she snapped, shaking her head with exasperation. "I'm fine."

He grinned at Drew. "Charming as always."

Drew gave a short laugh in response, then grabbed the back of Kat's head, pulled her toward him, and gave her a quick kiss.

Her shocked expression softened a bit and she said, "Yeah, well I was worried about you too."

Derek shook his head at her and went back to check on Caeli.

"Hey," he said, touching her face.

She looked up at him, relief in her expression. "They'll be okay. It was pretty bad, but I repaired the major damage."

"Can you look at one more?" he asked apologetically.

"Of course," she replied.

He helped her up and brought her to the Drokaran. From the way the man had fallen, Derek couldn't see his injuries, only the impressive splatter on the wall and the pool of blood underneath him. Caeli knelt down beside the body and put a hand on his shoulder.

She looked back at him and said, "Derek, half his head is gone. I can't fix that."

He nodded and pulled her to her feet. "We need to get you out of here."

Stumbling forward, she said wearily, "I know a nice cave . . ."

# CHAPTER 39

Eighteen hours later, Derek was still in Darien. He'd sent Kat, Drew, and Caeli back to *Horizon*, but Riley, Jacobs, and Reece were scouring the Drokaran's apartment and gathering any evidence they could. He'd ordered the Drokaran's body transported back to *Horizon* and he'd debriefed with the Tharsian team, generally just to thank them for their competency and good work.

A small but impressive fleet of Alliance cruisers would be arriving in the next several days to assure that the planet was safe from any invasion force, and so far they'd found no evidence of additional terrorist activities on the ground.

He was currently in the president's workroom giving her an abridged version of his team's activities. She was astute enough to know he was leaving out significant details, but she also understood that this was the nature of the game and didn't press him for more.

Hours earlier she had addressed her people, letting them know of the tremendous threat that had barely been averted. He was impressed with her oratory skills. She had framed this event as a way to unite the planet. When it was finally time for him to return to *Horizon*, she gave him and the rest of his team a full military escort.

\*\*\*

In the captain's private quarters, Donovan poured him a liberal amount of rare, expensive ale, generally prohibited during Alliance missions. "To averted disasters." He held up his glass and Derek did the same.

They sat in silence for a moment, and then the captain said, "I spoke with the president after you left her, and she's hopeful this will be the jolt her people need to actually start making some changes. The Alliance diplomatic team is here for a while and the military force is committed for as long as needed. I feel good about that." He rubbed his forehead and continued, "But the Drokaran threat . . ." He stopped, shook his head, and took a long swallow of his drink.

"Could keep us busy for a long time," Derek finished for him.

Donovan nodded grimly. "I hope we can learn something from this agent you captured. The president will be turning him over to the fleet commander when the ship arrives in a few days."

"We questioned him," Derek said flatly, and Donovan raised his eyebrows, interested.

"I assumed as much," he responded.

"Caeli got the information we needed to disrupt their plans," he paused, "and then I asked her to search his mind for anything interesting or relevant, to grab as much as she could. I figured he might never talk." Derek shrugged and then looked at the swirling liquid in his glass. "I have no idea what's in her head, or what it cost her to get it," he added.

Donovan sat back in his chair and looked thoughtful. "Gates hasn't let her out of the infirmary yet." Derek nodded, suddenly feeling anxious to leave.

"I'd like your report before we debrief with the whole team. But go," he ordered with an understanding nod. "We'll talk more tomorrow."

"Thank you, sir." Derek got up and swallowed the rest of his drink. "Don't want to waste it," he commented then put the glass down, closed his eyes, and rubbed his hands over his face.

"You did good work," Donovan said with meaning. "Get some rest."

Derek thanked him and left, heading straight for the infirmary.

*** 

"Hey Doc," he greeted Gates.

"Commander, welcome back," Gates said, smiling. "I don't imagine you're here for your physical?"

Derek grinned wearily. "She's still here?"

Gates face turned more serious. "I've given her a pretty powerful sedative, so she'll be out for a few more hours. Everything was mostly normal on her scans, but there was some unusual activity in her neocortex. I want her to rest and keep her brain quiet for a while."

"Will she be okay?" he asked, a pit forming in his stomach.

"There's absolutely no damage," Gates reassured him, "but I needed that extra activity to subside, and the sedative is working. She was exhausted, anyway. Any empathic activity seems to drain her physically, so this is good for her."

Derek exhaled the breath he didn't realize he was holding and nodded at Gates, grateful. "Something was really different when she connected with the Drokaran," he shared.

"She mentioned that. I'm anxious to do a postmortem on the body we have here. Maybe we'll learn something about these people," Gates said with interest.

"Kat's okay?" Derek asked.

"All patched up," Gates affirmed. "You all had quite an adventure."

"That we did," Derek agreed. Then, "I need to see Caeli."

Gates nodded. "Then *you* need sleep, doctor's orders. Come back in the morning and I'll clear you."

"Thanks," Derek said over his shoulder, already entering the quiet, darkened room.

Caeli looked pale but peaceful. There were two tiny sensors on her temples, and several monitors revealed the activity of her brain, heart, and lungs. He traced his finger down her cheek and leaned over to kiss her. He pulled a chair up and sat for a few minutes, closing his eyes and appreciating the silence.

The events of the last several days were catching up to him, and the adrenaline waves had completely worn off. When he was about to nod off in the chair, he finally left for his own quarters to shower and go to bed.

\*\*\*

He woke up feeling relieved. Caeli was safe, his team was safe, his mission was successful, and *Horizon* would be leaving this planet soon. After getting dressed, he went to find Caeli in the infirmary.

She was awake and looked well rested. When he entered the room, he knew his face held a question

She met his gaze. "It was worth it, I think?"

"I have to believe it was," he answered.

She nodded and finished dressing.

"I'd like to take you to breakfast, ma'am, if you're up to it," he offered.

"I'm starving," she said and finally gave him an easy smile.

"Just a minute," Gates said, coming into the room and interrupting them. "This one," he pointed at Derek, "still needs to be cleared for duty."

"I'd be happy to give you a thorough exam," Caeli said, and Derek nearly tripped on himself, but then he realized she'd said it directly into his mind. Gates looked at him, confused, while Caeli smiled innocently.

He grinned and thought back, "I will be very happy to take you up on that after breakfast."

Gates gave him the all clear after a quick check, just as Derek knew he would, and then he and Caeli left for the mess hall. It was late in the morning, and most of the crew had already come through, so the space was nearly deserted. He was glad, too. He had other things on his mind besides small talk with the crew.

"Distracted?" Caeli asked, with the same innocent smile on her face.

An image appeared in his mind of her wearing the short, white and gold skirt, and he felt his body respond immediately. She looked pleased with herself.

"Not fair." He grabbed her hands and sent his own mental picture back. She raised her eyebrows in mock surprise.

"Finish that," he pointed to some bread on her plate, "and then let's go."

An hour later he was sprawled next to her, sweaty and satisfied. He rolled toward her in the small bunk and at that moment very much missed the expansive, luxurious bed they'd shared at the apartment. Here he needed to be careful not to smack his head on the wall or roll onto the floor.

He ran his hand through her damp hair and thought cheerily that they'd need another shower.

She narrowed her eyes at him and in a rather sexy voice said, "I know what you're thinking."

"I hope so," he teased, and then he stood up, pulled her to her feet, and led her into the bathroom.

***

That afternoon, his entire team was seated around a conference table with Captain Donovan and Dr. Gates.

Donovan spoke first. "I want to start by congratulating you all on a job well done. I've read Commander Markham's report, and every single one of you was integral to the success of this mission. On behalf of the Alliance, thank you for your excellent work."

"Now," Donovan continued, "what kind of material and equipment have we recovered from the scene?" The question was directed toward Reece and Jacobs.

"Well, sir, a lot of it is similar to our own," Jacobs, having more experience, responded. "The weapon we recovered was interesting, though. It's extremely powerful and uses a different energy source than anything I'm familiar with. The guys on Telouros should have a look."

Donovan nodded. "I agree."

"The explosives were locally purchased, so there's nothing to learn there," Jacobs continued. "However, we did find a long-range communication device. Again similar to Alliance issue, but we should turn that over to Telouros as well." The captain nodded again, and Jacobs finished, "I think the most interesting thing was found among his personal items. It's a drug of some sort. We handed it over to Dr. Gates as soon as we arrived back."

Donovan turned his attention to Dr. Gates. "Anything?"

Gates hesitated for a second and then spoke, "I don't have any conclusive evidence yet, but I've started to get an interesting picture." He paused. "My initial examination of the Drokaran's body shows that he has been genetically modified. He also has a degenerative disease that I've never seen. I suspect the drug you found is therapeutic in nature and, if I were to guess, is treatment for this disease. I'd like to continue my research here for now, in addition to handing off my findings to the Alliance."

"Of course, Doctor," Donovan agreed and then stood. Everyone around the table stood as well. "Jacobs, Reece, Riley, you're dismissed. Thank you." The three saluted and left.

When everyone else sat back down, the mood in the room shifted subtly. It became both heavier and more casual at the same time. Whatever details needed to be filled in, now was the time, Derek knew. But before he could speak, Caeli's voice caused all their heads to turn in her direction.

"Captain," she said, "the Drokarans need the people."

Donovan looked at her, puzzled.

"The planets they're invading," she explained. "They need the people alive, well at least some of them." Gates exhaled loudly, and he and Caeli exchanged a meaningful look.

She turned back to Donovan. "As I understand it, the Alliance suspects the reason the Drokarans have become so imperialistic and aggressive is that they need territory and resources, that they've exhausted their own. This is true," she paused for a second and then added, "but there's also something *wrong* with them." She looked back at Gates.

Silence fell around the table. Gates sat back in his chair and after a moment wondered out loud, "Maybe they've nearly engineered themselves to extinction?"

"They could have inadvertently created a weakness in the population," Caeli conjectured. "There's another living Drokaran right here on Tharsis. Provided the two aren't related, we could learn a lot from a sample of his DNA." Gates nodded his agreement.

"He'll be in Alliance custody soon," Donovan said, "and we'll pursue this."

Everyone sat quietly, momentarily absorbed in their own thoughts. Caeli was still, her face etched with concentration and her gaze distant.

"Dr. Crys, I appreciate how difficult it must have been for you to get this information," Donovan acknowledged, breaking the silence. "Is there anything else?"

"The planet that was destroyed by the Drokarans?" she began, glancing at Derek and Kat, who were across the table.

"Arendal," Derek offered somberly.

"It was a mistake." She shook her head, her expression frustrated, "Maybe not a mistake, but the consequences were undesirable. They were conducting an experiment, I think."

"Have they engineered the fucking humanity out of themselves?" Kat uttered in disgust.

"There was something different about Karan's mind, for sure. I don't really know how to describe it. I've shared my consciousness with several different people now, people from different worlds, but I've never experienced anything like this. There *was* something fundamentally different," she reiterated. Shrugging, she made eye contact with Kat. "Maybe there's some truth to what you said."

"Well, we know one thing," Gates interjected, "and that is they're desperate. Their very existence may depend on the success of their missions. And in my mind, that makes them even more dangerous than we ever imagined."

Donovan directed his final comments toward Caeli. "The information you've provided is vitally important to the Alliance. We've been defending ourselves from the Drokarans for nearly a decade, and I don't see an easy end in sight. At least we have something to work with now." His last order was for them to all grab some downtime while *Horizon* finished repairs.

Derek knew just how he wanted to spend his downtime. Would anyone notice if he and Caeli stayed in his quarters for the next few days? Honestly, he didn't really care.

\*\*\*

"I have something for you," he said to her when they had a moment alone.

Derek picked up the portable tablet from his desk, and Caeli peered over his shoulder curiously.

"I had Riley do a little research." He tapped the screen to pull up the file he wanted and then handed the device to Caeli. "She found some links in the Inter-Planetary archives that reference Almagest."

Caeli's eyes widened as she scanned the files.

"Somewhere in there might be your world's original colonization history, and maybe even information about the last war."

She looked up at him, overwhelmed. He leaned in and kissed her hard. "But you can work on this later," he said taking the tablet out of her hands and backing her onto the bed.

She laughed and pulled him down on top of her.

"I love you," he said, burying his face in her hair. "I can't imagine my world without you in it."

Pulling her tighter into his arms, he poured all his fear, all his hope, all the depth of his feeling into that one embrace.

"We'll find a way," she promised.

***

On the day the Alliance fleet arrived, the captain sent him a communication. It contained only two words. "He escaped." Derek was on the bridge within moments.

"How is that possible?" Derek's voice betrayed his anxiety.

Donovan answered, "The Tharsian security team was preparing to turn him over to Alliance command, and they were attacked in transit. The president is beside herself. It seems as if he's disappeared into thin air."

# EPILOGUE

Alizar Sorin tapped his fingers lightly on his thigh. The strange signal was still active. It hadn't even come in over his regular communications device, but instead through an old receiver he'd salvaged from another job. According to his database, there was nothing interesting about the planetary system where the signal originated, just a few uninhabitable gas giants orbiting a single star.

His crew was bored. Very soon this would become problematic. They'd had a successful couple of jobs and then caused some significant damage with their earnings, but he knew they'd been idle for too long. He needed to find them something to do, and soon. Almost impulsively, Sorin changed course. Who knew, maybe there'd be something at the other end of that signal?

When they arrived in the system a day later, they found that a lovely, blue and white, *habitable* planet also circled the star. "And where have you been hiding?" he muttered to himself as he tracked the signal to its source and made preparations to land his ship.

# ACKNOWLEDGMENTS

It takes a tremendous amount of effort to bring a book to life, and there are so many people to thank, but three rise to the top of this list. Grateful thanks to Laura Zats of Wise Ink Creative Publishing, who surrounded me with a team of talented professionals and kept me moving toward the finish line. Kudos to Amanda Rutter, editor extraordinaire, whose attention to detail and thoughtful suggestions on plot and character were always just what the story needed. And last but not least, Steven Meyer-Rassow, who created the cover art and interior design for Horizon. I'm still in awe of his masterful work.

Many people read this manuscript at various stages of its life, but some took the time to give me valuable, detailed feedback. Special thanks to Ron Delaney, Jr., Ben Singer, Trissa Luzzi, Uli Brahmst, and my Wickford Highlands Book Club gals. Your input absolutely made this book better!

Without the love and support of my family and friends, I wouldn't have had the courage to put my writing into the world. Amy Hawes, fellow writer and best friend since childhood, your encouragement kept me going when I wanted to toss out the whole project. And finally, to my husband, Ray, my kids Nick, Noah, RJ, and Kyra, and my mom, dad, and sister Amanda, you are my biggest fans and I love you.

Tabitha Lord lives in Rhode Island with her husband, four children, dog, and cat. *Horizon* is her first novel.

Visit her online at **www.tabithalordauthor.com**